"Find her!"

Annja caught the reins of one horse in her hand and with her knife sawed at the cord that kept the herd tied to the spot. When the ground tie parted, she grabbed the pommel and heaved herself into the saddle.

A light pinned her in the darkness. Instinct pulled her eyes toward the beam, but she caught herself and looked away as she put her heels to the horse's sides and yelled, "Hiii-yaaahhh!"

"Mustafa! The woman is among the horses!"

"Do not let her get away!" Mustafa pointed his pistol and shot. A bullet ripped through the air over her head. "Get the horses!"

Lying low in the saddle, Annja kicked her horse again and fought to stay in the middle of the sudden crush of bodies headed away from the campsite. She ran with the herd, pausing once to glance over her shoulder at the campsite.

Muzzle flashes flared against the darkness. Two of the horses stumbled and dropped, but a few seconds later the rifles fell silent.

Annja stayed low over the horse's neck, feeling the animal's muscles bunch and flex, and made a promise to herself.

No matter what, she would return in time to save the others.

Titles in this series:

ROGUE ANGEL

Alex Archer

THE THIRD CALIPH

A GOLD EAGLE BOOK FROM

WORLDWIDE®

TORONTO • NEW YORK • LONDON
AMSTERDAM • PARIS • SYDNEY • HAMBURG
STOCKHOLM • ATHENS • TOKYO • MILAN
MADRID • WARSAW • BUDAPEST • AUCKLAND

Recycling programs
for this product may
not exist in your area.

First edition January 2013

ISBN-13: 978-0-373-62160-6

THE THIRD CALIPH

Special thanks and acknowledgment to
Mel Odom for his contribution to this work.

Printed in U.S.A.

The LEGEND

...THE ENGLISH COMMANDER TOOK JOAN'S SWORD AND RAISED IT HIGH.

The broadsword, plain and unadorned,
gleamed in the firelight. He put the tip against
the ground and his foot at the center of the blade.
The broadsword shattered, fragments falling
into the mud. The crowd surged forward,
peasant and soldier, and snatched the shards
from the trampled mud. The commander tossed
the hilt deep into the crowd.
Smoke almost obscured Joan, but she continued
praying till the end, until finally the flames climbed
her body and she sagged against the restraints.

Joan of Arc died that fateful day in France,
but her legend and sword are reborn....

PROLOGUE

Basra, Iraq
656 CE

Shifting quickly, Hamid avoided his opponent's curved sword. The blade tugged at his burka only for a moment before slicing through it. His sandals punched through the top crust of sun-baked soil as he moved and dodged, and turned his footing treacherous as he aimed a swing at the swordsman's head.

The man was older than Hamid's twenty years, and he'd been in many more fights. But the older man wasn't invincible judging by the scars on his face and hands. A rime of dust coated his fierce black beard. He was stronger and thicker set, and Hamid knew he could not allow the man to get an upper hand. He had to depend on his speed and skill, and pray that God was truly on his side.

"Defiler." The warrior swung again and this time Hamid blocked with his sword. The impact vibrated through his arm. The metal rasped as Hamid quickly gave ground. "Treacherous cur, I will spill your blood upon the ground for the glory of God."

Hamid stepped back again and shook his sword arm. All around them, the battle raged. In the distance he still saw the howdah mounted on the camel's back where Aisha bint Abu Bakr directed her troops. She was the third widow of the Prophet Muhammad, and believed by many to be the prophet's favorite wife.

Many also believed that her claim to the true teachings of Muhammad, and thus of God, were more legitimate than Ali ibn Abd Munaf, who had been the cousin and son-in-law to Muhammad. Hamid supported the lady Aisha's claim because his father told him Ali would lead the Muslim people from the rightful path of God.

The swordsman swung again and Hamid managed to block once more. Steel rang and the curved sword vibrated in Hamid's hand. He gave ground yet again, forcing his opponent to pursue him. The bigger man sank even farther in the sand. Hamid waited for his opportunity.

He had lost track of how many men he'd seen killed over the past few days, and how many he himself had killed. When he had joined the supporters of Aisha bint Abu Bakr, he had only come to leave behind the village and the work. It had been a chance to see more of the world. He had not given thought to dying for the opportunity.

"Surrender your sword and I will let you live." The older man drew in a breath.

Hamid shook his head. "I cannot turn from God's work." He knew that was what his father would say, and he had no other words to offer. Never before had Muslims risen up to strike down Muslims on a battlefield.

"You are a fool. This is not God's work." The swordsman facing Hamid swung again and again, and the clang of metal on metal rang within Hamid's skull. "You could live your life in the glory of the one true God. Instead, you strive to waste it in the name of that harlot."

The disrespect firmed Hamid's resolve. Muhammad's widow should not be spoken of in such a cavalier manner. She had been the prophet's favorite wife. None contested that.

This time when his opponent strode forward, Hamid

dashed the blade to one side, stepped in quickly and turned to his right. He grabbed the man's extended right wrist with his left hand and trapped the warrior there off balance. Then he whirled suddenly and sliced his opponent's throat open.

Blood spilled over the front of the man's clothing as he stumbled back. He clasped a hand to his throat and stared at Hamid in disbelief before lifting his sword and rushing Hamid. Caught unawares, paralyzed by the sight of the man dying before him, Hamid couldn't get out of the way in time. The man's bulk bore him to the ground and knocked the air from his lungs.

Frantic, Hamid grabbed the man's sword arm, barely able to restrain the man who was trying to saw the sword into Hamid's face. The blade nicked Hamid's cheek before the man's strength fled. Rolling to one side, Hamid knocked the corpse from him, then climbed wearily to his feet to search for another foe. He knew there would be one because the widow Aisha's forces were outnumbered.

Horns blared over the plain. Recognizing the signal to withdraw forces, Hamid gratefully stumbled back, sucking in air. He glanced at the corpse stretched on the ground and at the sand greedily absorbing the spilled blood. His sword now felt like a boulder at the end of his arm.

A warrior mounted on a black stallion raced along the line of warriors, and his counterpart did the same in front of the armed men that fought for Ali.

"Stand away! Stand away! The battle is over!"

One of the older warriors next to Hamid dropped to his knees in prayer. Another man stepped forward and raised his voice to ask, "But who has won?"

As he looked across the battlefield littered with the dead, unable to know who was friend and who was foe, Hamid wished to know the answer to that question, as well. And with all the bodies, could there truly be a winner?

The rider reined in his horse. His thick face was bleak. Blood trickled from his nose and his eyes were bloodshot. More blood matted his black-and-gray beard. "A bargain has been struck."

"What bargain?"

"The lady Aisha has asked that you—her faithful warriors—stand down."

"Why?"

"So that your lives might be spared. She would honor you by letting you live." The messenger looked along the troops. "Ali has us outnumbered. The lady knows that we will not win this day." The horse snorted and pawed at the ground. "She asks that you live so that the prophet's true teachings will be remembered and be taught to your children and your children's children."

The announcement drained Hamid of his remaining strength. He slumped to his knees, supporting himself with his sword.

"Then who will avenge Uthman ibn Affan?" The older warrior beat his breast in agony. "Two of my sons have died during this battle. I will not have their blood shed in vain. They remained true to the teachings of Muhammad, and to the true caliphs. To stop now is to dishonor them."

Uthman ibn Affan's murder at the hands of assassins had caused the civil war that now consumed them. Dying as he had without a true heir, the caliphate succession was a contentious mess. Everything was done in the name of God, but there were several who claimed to represent God's will.

The messenger rode his horse over to the distraught father and spoke quietly in a tone that carried so they could all hear. "To stop now means you may sire more sons, my friend. Raise those sons up under the grace of God and know that this struggle is not ended here. No true Muslim will allow this sacrilege to stand."

Screaming with unbridled rage and loss, the warrior threw himself down and rent his hair and clothing, crying out for vengeance on his enemies.

Through tears, Hamid stared at the man he'd last slain in the name of God and honor. If only the horn had sounded earlier, the death would not be on his hands. So many would not now be dead.

In his heart, though, he knew those numbers would only have been saved today. Tomorrow and tomorrow and tomorrow, they would continue to die by one another's hands. As the messenger had said, this struggle was not over.

He closed his eyes and remembered the six hundred Muslims Aisha had ordered beheaded in Basra. The blood had spilled across the cobblestones, and the executors had cheered their victory. The only cheers now were from Ali's warriors on the other side of the battlefield.

Looking at those men, Hamid knew he could never again accept them as brothers. Ali had warped their belief, had seized the caliphate for himself, and he would guide those who followed him away from the true path of God. The best they could hope for was to walk in the shadow of God, not the light.

This battle might be over, but the struggle within the believers would never die. Hamid bowed his head and prayed that mercy might be granted in time. He feared that generations would war among themselves, and Muslims would again kill Muslims.

1

The ground beneath Annja Creed's feet shivered, giving her a slight warning. The only warning she got. She threw herself against the nearest earthen wall and pressed her face against the hard-packed sand while raising her right arm over her head to shield herself. With her left hand, she fumbled for her neckerchief and succeeded in bringing it up to cover her nose and mouth as the tunnel caved in and dust rose in a whirlwind. She closed her eyes and fought to remain calm.

Falling earth pummeled her and drove her to her knees, pounding the air from her lungs. She kept her eyes closed. Getting buried alive under tons of sand was one of the most horrible deaths she could imagine.

"Look out!" The man's warning barely penetrated the thunder of the tumbling earth, and it came far too late to do any good. Everyone who had been down in the *khettara* when it collapsed was now at risk of suffocating.

The sand covered Annja and everything went dark. Panic set in then as she automatically fought to push herself up. She couldn't budge the sand and in her fear she imagined that it was still falling, burying her even more. The sound of falling earth echoed in her head, but she told herself it was just the beating of her heart.

Calm down. You lose your head, and you're dead. And there are other people in here that may need your help. Not many of them could have escaped the cave-in.

She struggled to take a breath. It felt as if an elephant was standing on her back. Realizing that she couldn't just push up from all the dirt, she concentrated on shifting her right arm.

Professor David Smythe had been in the tunnel with her. He'd left her exhuming the pottery shards while he'd gone for the brushes. Theresa Templeton, the grad assistant from Harvard, had been there, as well. Cory Burcell, the BBC cameraman, had been filming. Three of the *muqannis*, the Moroccan irrigation diggers…

Annja thrust her arm up, hoping she hadn't gotten twisted around during the collapse. She used her open hand open like a knife blade to slowly slide through the shifting dirt. Lifting her arm let more sand slide in under her chin and her next breath was even more difficult to take.

Finally, her hand broke free of the sand. Knowing that freedom was less than two feet away galvanized her. She contorted her body and heaved her way out of a premature burial.

She broke through to her waist and blinked sand out of her eyes as she stared down the dark tunnel. She pulled the neckerchief down and filled her lungs with air. The dust made her cough.

"David! Theresa! Cory! Anybody!"

"Annja?"

A male voice. To her left. Annja peered through the gloom and barely made out Professor Smythe standing against the far wall twenty feet away. The lean archaeologist, caked in sand from head to toe, looked pale in the darkness. His thin blond hair was wet with sweat and stuck to his scalp.

"I thought we'd lost you," he said in relief, looking much

younger than he was—late thirties, she remembered. Experienced enough to be of some use getting out of this.

Annja brushed off her legs. "Not yet. Have you got a spare flashlight?" She'd lost hers during the cave-in.

Smythe rummaged in a backpack near the wall and came up with a Mini Maglite. He started to cross to her, then stopped, obviously realizing there were people still under the dirt. "Here." He pitched the flashlight to her underhand.

It was almost invisible in the darkness but Annja managed to catch it. "Who are we missing?"

Smythe ran his light over two men standing beside him. One of them was Cory Burcell, the BBC cameraman. In his early twenties, lean and black, his once-khaki shorts and Batman T-shirt were covered in dirt. Cory was used to laid-back assignments, not roughing it in Morocco. The other man was one of the *muqannis,* in his fifties and experienced at irrigation construction. He was already digging through the sand by hand like a human mole.

"Theresa's missing. Two of the *muqannis.*" Smythe reached for a trenching tool.

"No. No shovel," the *muqanni* barked. "Hand. Use hand only. Work from edge. Quickly. *Quickly.*"

Smythe put the trenching tool down and started digging. "Do you know where they were? Where they were standing?"

Annja turned on her flashlight and saw that during the confusion she'd moved, but she hadn't been more than three feet away from this position before the cave-in. Theresa had been helping her with the pottery shards, getting firsthand experience with the process of pulling the pieces from the earth.

Theresa was young, and though she'd been on digs before for the BBC, this was the first time she'd been in danger. She'd probably gone down where she'd been kneeling.

Annja felt guilty that she hadn't thought to reach out for the young woman.

She worked swiftly, heaving sand and loose rocks over to the tunnel's side. With the flashlight on, she saw that the ceiling had given way, dropping what looked like at least three feet of earth onto them.

At present, they were thirty feet underground, so that left plenty of earth above them to either provide support—or to collapse. That wasn't a pleasant thought, so she concentrated on finding Theresa as she dug a shallow trench across the area where she thought the woman had gone down.

Less than a minute later, movement shifted one side of the trench. Annja focused her energies on that spot, seizing handful after handful of earth. The sand and rock felt coarse against her skin and she was thankful for the years of calluses she'd built up through martial arts and her archaeological work.

Annja uncovered Theresa's back, then managed to run her hands down either side of the woman's body and grab hold around her middle. Pulling steadily, Annja lifted Theresa out. Gasping, the young woman came free of her impromptu tomb.

"Are you all right?" Annja shined her flashlight over the woman. She checked her pulse, which seemed strong—if a little wild.

Theresa nodded and coughed. She tried to talk but couldn't.

Trusting that the intern was going to be all right, Annja turned back to the pile of sand and tried to remember where the two irrigation workers had stood. One of them had been the older man's son, a boy of fifteen or sixteen. Souad. He loved Japanese *manga,* she remembered. His father had been training him to be a *muqanni* because there was always work for a man who could build irrigation tunnels for the farmlands. Without those tunnels, drought would force people to move or starve. The excavations were dangerous, though.

Clearly.

Fear stole over Annja as she dug, driving her hands into the dirt. She didn't want to uncover the boy's lifeless body.

Souad's father, Nadim, pulled the other *muqanni* out of the dirt, then dove back in. This time he couldn't keep his fear at bay. He cried out his son's name over and over again and his voice reverberated along the *khettara*.

A moment later, Annja's hand struck flesh. She shifted closer and ran her hands into the pile until she made certain she had hold of the teen. Hauling him up by herself proved impossible. She looked up at the others.

"Here. He's here."

Nadim scrambled over to her. The other *muqanni* was only a half step behind. Annja felt along the boy's body, figuring out how he lay beneath the dirt.

"This way." She indicated with her hand and they fell to.

Annja didn't like how limp Souad was as they uncovered him. Panic would have made him struggle.

Unless he'd been knocked unconscious.

Judging from his position, he'd borne the brunt of the collapse.

A moment later, they managed to pull the teen out into his father's embrace.

He wasn't breathing.

"Give him to me." Annja took him from Nadim's trembling arms. She laid Souad on the ground on his back. Dirt caked his face, but when she opened his mouth, there was no blockage. More dirt crusted his nostrils. She wiped that clean, then leaned in and put her mouth on the boy's mouth, breathing air into his lungs.

His chest rose and fell as she breathed into him again and again. Then she knelt beside him and started chest compressions, counting off in her head. "C'mon! You're young! You're strong! You can do this!"

Still seeing no response, Annja leaned down and breathed

into his mouth again, filling his lungs with more air. This time Souad coughed and choked, and blinked his dark eyes open in panic that quickly dissolved to surprise.

Annja placed her fingers on the side of the boy's neck. His pulse beat strong and steady beneath her fingertips. His breathing rasped and came rapidly, but he was doing it on his own now. "How do you feel?"

Souad grinned up at her. "I am in love."

Annja smiled back at the teen, then gave way as his father bulled in and crushed Souad to his breast. Tiredly, she sat back against the *khettara* wall and stared at the father and son as they embraced.

"Well, that was bloody close." Smythe sat beside Annja and knocked dirt off his shirt.

"It was." Annja gazed around at the *khettara*. "This puts us behind schedule."

Smythe sighed and leaned his head back. "Ready to call it quits?"

"Are you kidding?" Since she'd left the New Orleans orphanage where she'd been raised, she'd never felt any more at home than on a dig site or prowling through a musty library or museum. Morocco had all of those. She'd spent the past few days in heaven. A little cave-in hadn't put her off.

Smythe took off his hat and banged it against his knee. He grinned ruefully. "Me, too. But we'd be better off getting above. The kid needs fresh air, and it wouldn't hurt us, either." He stood and offered Annja his hand.

She took it and let him help her to her feet even though she could have managed easily on her own. She was five feet ten inches tall, an inch or so shorter than Smythe, and more athletically built. She pulled her chestnut hair off her neck and enjoyed an all-too-brief breeze that entered the chamber from above.

Ten feet away, a rope hung from the nearest mouth of the

subterranean ditch. The *muqannis* first located an underground water supply by digging wells in the foothills of the Atlas Mountains. Once the water table was determined, they sank a vertical shaft down to it, then began the process of digging toward the farmland at a lower level. New shafts were dug every sixty to one hundred feet, depending on what was needed and how easy the soil was to work. Fresh air and potential rescue avenues always figured into the time needed to construct the waterway.

Men stationed around the well mouth above called down in concern. Midafternoon sunlight slanted into the chamber.

Annja couldn't keep up with the rapid-fire dialect, but she picked up enough of it to know the men on the surface had felt the quivering earth and known immediately what it meant. Several of them knelt at the side of the well and peered down.

Souad walked under his own power now, but he lacked his usual surefooted grace. He smiled at her shyly as he stood woozily under the well mouth. Nadim carefully tied a padded rope under his son's arms, then called to the men to lift him.

Directing her flashlight beam to the end of the irrigation tunnel that led back to the underground water source, Annja saw the dark water lapping at their makeshift dam. The water was already two feet deep. With the setback they'd incurred, the dam was going to have to be higher to hold back the water. The farmers at the other end of the *khettara* wouldn't be happy.

And the crops suffering from the drought would have to go a few days longer without water. That would be the biggest problem and the one most complained about.

The men at the top of the well swiftly hauled Souad out. Then the rope loop was thrown back down. Nadim picked it up and handed it to Annja, who wriggled into it.

One of the men called, "Are you ready?"

"Yes." She held on tight and resisted the impulse to kick

her feet against the side of the shaft as they pulled her up. Any impact might trigger another cave-in. The sides would have to be shored up before they could return to the dig.

On her way up, though, she stared into the hollow left by the falling earth. The concavity ran for a dozen feet or more and had been at least six feet thick. She couldn't even guess at the raw tonnage that had dropped on them. She shone her flashlight into the concavity out of curiosity.

Above, the workers set themselves to hauling again. "Wait." She'd seen something.

"Annja?" Smythe peered up at her. "Is something wrong?"

Without answering, she shifted in the rope loop until she hung upside down by her feet. She caught hold of the concavity gently and pulled herself toward it. In her other hand, she held the flashlight steady. The yellow beam revealed long bones embedded in the chamber's new roof. "I found something."

"What?" Smythe shifted below her, tracking her movement cautiously, striving not to get under the treacherous section.

Annja played the flashlight along the ulna and radius to the humerus, knowing immediately she was looking at a human arm that had been reduced to bone. Above the humerus, she spotted the dark eyeholes of the skull that lay sideways, as though the skeleton had turned its head to glare at her.

"A body."

2

"Careful. *Careful*," Smythe said anxiously as he stood below Annja.

Rigged in climbing gear now, Annja hung upside down in the concavity the *khettara's* collapse had revealed. The harness secured her to a rope that ran between two fixed points in the chamber that Nadim had judged stable. The points didn't allow her easy access to the skeleton, but she could reach it from her position on the rope with difficulty.

Smythe had wanted to accompany her but Nadim hadn't wanted to risk putting any more weight on the line.

In addition to the flashlights Annja and Smythe held, Nadim and his companions had affixed lanterns in the tunnel. The bright light from Cory Burcell's camcorder was almost blinding. Souad stood beside his father, who knelt a short distance away with a trench tool clasped in one hand. The other *muqannis* stood behind them.

Annja placed the toes of her hiking boots against the concavity's rough surface and placed her left hand against the roof to brace herself. With a stiff brush in her right hand, she knocked away loose dirt from the skeleton. Gradually, the long bones of the lower arm came more prominently into view as streams of dirt and dust fell gently to the chamber floor.

"How close is the skeleton to the lower surface?" Smythe

took another step to the right and angled his flashlight along the arm as it was revealed.

"Two or three inches." Annja kept brushing. The body had been buried beneath eight feet of earth. "I'm surprised it didn't fall with the rest of the roof."

"Yes, but doubtless the body buried there helped cause the collapse of the roof."

Annja shoved the brush into the space above the skull. The stink of death had long since vanished. "That was definitely the case."

"Cool." That came from Souad, in English, and was immediately followed by an admonishment from his father in their native tongue. Annja smiled to herself, totally understanding the boy's fascination with the buried skeleton. Stories about archaeologists had been some of Annja's favorites back in the orphanage, and she'd loved the Discovery Channel specials involving Egyptian tombs. Those mysteries had seemed imminently more soluble than those surrounding her own birth parents.

Theresa hadn't regained enough confidence in the roof's stability to stand under the weakened section, but she took a step closer. "Do you know if it was a skeleton that was buried?"

Annja returned to her efforts with the brush. "No. There was definitely flesh on it when it was put here. See the hollow that formed around the body? It took a while for beetles and other carrion feeders to strip the corpse down to bone. That loss of flesh is what left the spaces around the bones."

"Well, that's gross." Theresa looked mortified, then sighed and shook her head. "Sorry. I'll edit that out of the final cut."

"By that time the earth over it had hardened and taken on the shape it's held all this time." A small shower of debris trickled from around the skull as Annja revealed more of the features. Slowly, the back of the skull started to come into view, and she knew immediately that something was wrong with it.

She took the brush away, sliding it into the tool pouch she wore, and took out her flashlight again. Switching it on, she pointed the beam at the skull.

The bright light revealed broken shards of the back half of the skull. The pieces now lay in a heap under the skull, but she was certain that the bones had been held together by flesh when the person had been laid to rest.

"What is it?" Smythe shifted below and strained to see what she was seeing.

"The back of the skull is caved in."

"Doesn't sound like natural causes."

"Doesn't look that way, either."

"A victim of brigands?"

Annja played the flashlight around and spotted a gleam in the debris of the skull. "Brigands wouldn't have buried the body."

However long the skeleton had been in the ground, Annja was certain things hadn't changed much in Morocco. The country's mountains still harbored a thriving community of thieves and murderers.

"Quite." Smythe grinned ruefully and wiped his stubbled cheeks. "My bad. So either this was the result of an accident, or whoever put this poor person into the ground didn't want anyone else to know. Otherwise, they might have packed the body back to whatever village the person came from. Unless someone stumbled across the remains and simply planted them where they found them." He shook his head. "So many questions."

"We should be able to get at some of the answers soon." Annja continued brushing at the skull.

A tremor shivered through the earth again. Annja grabbed hold of the support rope with her left hand and braced herself as best as she could. She held her breath as a small cloud of dust and debris swirled over her.

The skeletal arm came free of its moorings and dangled loosely. The sudden flash of dark metal that spilled among the debris caught her attention. Without thinking, she dropped the brush and flicked her hand out to catch four of the tumbling coins. Twice that many hit the ground.

"Annja?" Smythe played his flashlight over her.

"I'm all right." She pulled out her flashlight, resting her weight from the support rope, and studied her find.

Despite their dark tarnish, she could read enough of the language to know it was Arabic. There were also a few annulets, small circles that made up the coin's design. They all looked the same.

Closing her hand over the coins, Annja studied the skeleton. "This body's been here a long time. Maybe as long as those pottery shards we've been digging up."

HOURS OF CAUTIOUS WORK later, Annja had exhumed the skeleton piece by piece. None of the connective tissue remained. There were two hundred and six bones in an adult body, and she was convinced she'd gotten all of them, though she had lost count. The skeleton lay on the ground on a blanket a short distance from the open mouth of the *khettara.*

As Annja had freed the bones and placed them in a bucket Nadim had rigged to raise and lower, Smythe had been lifted to the surface and began reconstruction of the skeleton. The process was labor-intensive and Annja's body ached.

Smythe knelt on one knee beside the skeleton and looked at Cody Burcell as he rolled video. Theresa knelt next to him.

"Honestly, I'd thought the cave-in was going to be the death of us," Smythe said matter-of-factly in his clipped British accent, but Annja saw his passion and excitement. He was every bit as drawn to historical mysteries as Annja was.

"Then, while we were scrambling for our lives, Annja Creed, my collaborator on this dig, chanced upon a most remarkable discovery."

Annja stood to one side and sipped an energy drink to replace her electrolytes. She watched the recording with only slight interest. Professor David Smythe was good in front of a camera, and this was his show. Annja knew that she'd be called upon for input, as well.

Notoriety wasn't her endgame, not when it came to archaeology, anyway. That was something that had just happened along the way. She wanted the knowledge, the ability to go where others hadn't in years. *Chasing History's Monsters,* the television show she cohosted, had helped create a fan base that was growing larger all the time. Of course, the fact that her costar, Kristie Chatham, often finagled ways to lose her top drew lots of attention. Annja had never appeared topless and never would. But the fan base loved her segments as much as Kristie's because she usually brought a lot to the historical aspect of the various "monsters" the show explored. Annja won over the watchers through the wonderment of history. Curiosity was a human trait that would never go away.

"Can you tell us what we're looking at, Professor Smythe?" Theresa sounded very much like the college student she had been probably not so long ago.

"Certainly." Smythe smiled. He touched the bones on the blanket. "I have determined that from the thick brow ridge and external occipital protuberance, the rear section of the skull, the narrow pelvis, the wide rib cage, as well as the size and density of the arms and legs, that this is the body of a male." He tapped the skeleton's chest. "This is the xyphoid process, this small bit of bone at the bottom of the sternum. The xyphoid process here is fused to the sternum, indicating that this person was probably in his early thirties or older at the time of his death."

"Do you have any idea about the man's identity?"

Reaching into his shirt pocket, Smythe laid out the coins Annja had caught, as well as seven others that had been found at the bottom of the well where they'd fallen. "He was possibly Arabic, maybe from what is now known as Saudi Arabia. These coins are quite fascinating."

Theresa waved to Cody. "Bring the camera in for a closer look, please."

Cody stepped forward. The camcorder's bright light stood out in the darkening haze of the gathering evening. To the west, over the Atlas Mountains, the sky had turned deep purple with bright stars.

"What can you tell us about the coins?"

Smythe pointed to one of the dark ones. They had successfully cleaned the tarnish from half the coins. "Arabic. Dirhams, actually. Silver coins, which is why they're so discolored—silver tarnishes quite easily. It even oxidizes in salt water, which is why salvaged treasure usually nets gold coins but not silver ones. The Arabic dinars were stamped in gold, but dirhams were silver. The tarnishing is a result of contact with hydrogen sulfide, a natural byproduct of simply handling them. Human skin, wool, eggs and onions, and even residual grease from a cut of meat during a meal, could cause this alteration. Simple chemistry, actually."

Smythe moved on to one of the shiny dirhams. "The use of a good silver polish cleaned them right up, you see. And if you look at this writing, you'll understand why I believe this chap might have been from Saudi Arabia."

"You might, Professor, but I haven't a clue." Theresa laughed.

Looking on, Annja admired the younger woman's easy affinity for the camera. She was a natural.

"Upon further examination of these coins, I was able to

translate the language inscribed on them." Smythe picked up one of the coins and held it out.

"Beg your pardon, Professor, but I need just a moment." Theresa turned to Cory. "We'll put an extreme close-up here."

The cameraman nodded. "I'll have to do that with one of the other lenses."

"Of course." Refocused on Smythe, Theresa smiled. "Sorry. Production necessitates a few interruptions."

"Nonsense. Just let me know what you need from me. I'm in your hands."

"Thank you. Now…back to that intriguing coin. Start with the translation, if you will."

"Most Arabic coins of this period—the time of the Umayyad caliphate, the second of the four major governments that ruled the Muslim world—have the same legend stamped on them. 'In the name of God, this dirham was struck in'—what is essentially Damascus these days—'in the year 79 AH.' Basically 698 CE by our conventional calendars."

Theresa's eyebrows rose. "So these coins are over thirteen hundred years old?"

"Correct." Smythe smiled with childlike enthusiasm. "As I said, quite the find. Also of note, 79 AH was the *first* year these particular coins were struck. Abd al-Malik ibn Marwan, the fifth Umayyad caliph, chose to make changes in the coinage at that time. So these are really special."

"The British Museum is going to be quite taken with you, Professor."

"I certainly hope so. They funded quite a lot of this particular foray, you see, and most of that on faith in me. I'm happy to provide a return on that investment."

"What had you expected to find on this dig?"

Smythe put the coins back on the blanket beside the skeleton. "I wasn't exactly certain. i've been intensely interested in the period of the caliphates in Muslim history. Particularly immediately following Muhammad's passing and the struggle to agree upon a new leader." He shrugged. "As you know, the Muslims continue to be divided over the true heir of Muhammad's teachings and the path laid out for them by God."

"Do you think the work you're doing will help clear up any of that confusion?"

Annja almost smiled at the naïveté of the question. Theresa was a good journalist, but had no understanding of history and religious strife.

Still, Smythe treated the question with respect, which was probably the best course because some of the television audience would undoubtedly wonder the same thing.

"No. I'm afraid those particular combatants have long since chosen their own courses and declared their battles. What I hope to do here is preserve and bring to light some of the history of the caliphates."

"Why aren't you working a dig in Saudi Arabia?"

"Until a few months ago, I was. Then I chanced upon a lead that brought me here to Morocco."

That clue—a few pages torn from a journal of a moderately successful historian who had completed a translation of an eighth-century treatise—was what had interested Annja, as well. The historian, Farouk Assad, had lived in al-Hejaz, near the Red Sea. Smythe had chanced upon the manuscript during research at the recently established National Museum of Saudi Arabia. In addition to support from the British Museum, Smythe had also secured support from the House of Saud, something that was rarely given to outsiders.

"The Muslim people were great thinkers and travelers." Smythe warmed to the subject now. "In addition to their contributions to math and science and philosophy, they also traveled the world. They set up caravan routes that connected countries and markets." He waved toward the Atlas Mountains. "According to the document I discovered, one of the lesser-known trade routes wound through Morocco to the Atlantic Ocean. And it passed through here."

"This particular location was marked in the papers you found?"

"I believed so." Smythe nodded. "Now, with the discovery of this body and these coins, I'd feel safe in saying that I have proven my case."

When she'd seen Smythe's documentation, Annja had also believed the translation was correct. She'd performed her own check on Smythe's figures, and—at Smythe's invitation—she had joined the dig. She hadn't visited Morocco for any real length of time, and Smythe's proposed excavation had fallen during some downtime from *Chasing History's Monsters*.

Of course, that hadn't kept Doug Morrell, Annja's producer on the show, from trying to drum up additional business. Doug had been the one to point out that Smythe was capitalizing on Annja's popularity to feather his own nest. Annja hadn't argued the point, but she knew that wasn't all there was to the arrangement. Smythe was a good archaeologist and Annja had gotten to be friends with him through email and a couple of small projects that had led to this.

"Can you tell us what you've found?" Theresa asked Smythe.

The archaeologist grinned. "You mean other than this skeleton and these coins?"

"Please."

"When Miss Creed and I began this dig, we contacted some of the locals who worked around here, seeking any knowledge they might have about the area and the history. You'd be surprised how many people don't really know the background of their locale. We were fortunate because these men—the *khettara* builders we employed for the dig—knew some legends about the trade route, and they had discovered some of the potsherds and other artifacts left by the previous travelers a thousand years ago or more. They had already been turning those artifacts over to the museums here in Morocco."

Seated nearby at a flickering campfire, Nadim translated Smythe's words for those who didn't speak English. Several of the men smiled and nodded. Pots hung over several cook fires and Annja's belly growled in anticipation of a hot meal. With the coming of the night, the temperature plummeted and she looked forward to her tent and sleeping bag.

A flicker of movement caught Annja's attention and she focused on the ridgeline of the hill not far away. Even as she made out a man's head and shoulders in the darkness, two more joined him.

Annja started to step back, but froze as hooves beat against the ground and a rider on a white horse exploded out of the shadows behind her. Three other riders followed him. They rode into the campsite as other men in long flowing burnooses rose from nearby hiding places.

The leader guided his horse into the camp, scattering the locals and aiming for Smythe, Theresa and Cody. He reined in his horse quickly, causing the big animal to rear, then pointed a Russian-made pistol at Smythe. "Do not make any sudden moves."

3

Confronted by the robed men on horseback with untold others moving in from the darkness, Annja stood her ground. She thought of reaching for her sword, knowing it would only take a moment to free the weapon from the mysterious place it resided, the otherwhere, as she thought of it. Adrenaline surged through her and she recognized that call to action from so many other confrontations.

For the moment, though, she left the sword where it was. She didn't like the idea of being robbed or losing their find, but that was better than causing anyone's death.

Souad stared at the man in amazement. The teen stood beside his father, who had quickly dropped to his knees. Annja heard Souad's awestruck voice even over the horses' restless hooves against the earth.

"Mustafa."

The mounted man turned his attention to Souad and spoke in Berber. Annja spoke just enough of the language to pick up the gist. "You know me, boy?"

Nadim caught his son by the arm and yanked Souad down to his knees. Souad's frightened eyes never left Mustafa's.

The mounted man grinned at the boy, and in the flickering campfire light, he looked evil. Mustafa wore a forked black beard. Exposure to the sun and the elements had turned his skin nut-brown. A ragged scar that looked like an upside-down *V* puckered his left cheek and added a squint to the eye above.

"Yes, you know me." Mustafa laughed, but his pistol never left Smythe. "I could take you away from this life, from all this digging in the ground like a worm, and make a proper bandit of you."

Souad ducked his head and Nadim threw a protective arm around his son. His other hand dropped to the knife at his belt, but he didn't draw the weapon.

The white horse shifted and turned in a half circle. Mustafa twisted in the saddle and kept the pistol trained on Smythe. His dark eyes swept over Annja, as well.

"You are a pretty one," Mustafa said in broken English.

Annja made no reply.

Turning his attention back to Smythe, Mustafa glared at the BBC crew. Theresa had closed ranks with Smythe, and Cody had stopped filming and looked around uneasily.

"I had heard you were here." Mustafa said it almost like an accusation.

"We have the proper permissions," Smythe said in a neutral tone.

"You do not have permission from me."

Smythe didn't reply.

Mustafa guided his horse toward the skeleton on the blanket. Firelight flickered dully over the ivory. "Whose bones are these?"

Smythe shook his head. "I don't know."

Peering more closely at the blanket, Mustafa called to one of his men, pointed and spoke rapidly. The man, younger and smaller, dismounted and trotted over to the blanket while keeping his grip on the bolt-action Russian rifle he carried.

The bandit knelt beside the blanket and picked up the silver coins. He held them up to Mustafa, talking excitedly.

The bandit leader pointed his chin toward the coins in his man's hand. "Where are the rest?"

Smythe shook his head. "We haven't found any more."

"Where did you find these?"

"In the well."

Mustafa's expression hardened. "Then there are more. You have not found them all." He stood up in his stirrups and called out in his native tongue.

Four of his men quickly separated from the others and walked over to the *khettara* opening, which was high and banked to look like the entrance to an anthill. The bandits picked up a collection of oil lanterns from the tools sitting next to the opening and began lighting them.

"You can't just go down there." Smythe took a half step forward, then froze as Mustafa aimed his pistol with more deliberation.

"Do not think you can tell me what to do."

Smythe held his hands up higher. "It's not safe."

"You do not want us to find the fortune hidden there." Mustafa spat. "That is how it is with you foreign dogs. You come into our country, pilfer our heritage, take our treasures and leave."

"That's not true. Everything we find here is going to Moroccan museums. We're only here to seek greater understanding of history."

"The Koran tells us all we need to know of history." Mustafa waved the pistol at the skeleton. "Those old bones have their own story, and it is nothing we need to know now." He turned to his men. "Find my treasure."

Helplessly, Annja watched. She and Smythe had agreed to hold off further exploration of their find till morning when the light would be better. Nadim had promised mirrors that would bring natural light down into the well so they wouldn't have to use lanterns. They would have been fresh in the morning.

Now potentially everything down there was about to be lost. The losses wouldn't just be the material things the Bedouin raiders took, but also the placement of those things. Archaeologists could tell almost as much from the *placement* of artifacts as from the artifacts themselves. She clenched her fists, knowing there was nothing she could do to preserve the integrity of the dig. Mind you, the cave-in had possibly made determining placement impossible, anyway.

At the *khettara* opening, the bandits grabbed the ropes that had been left there and cautiously scrambled over the side. They wore their weapons—rifles and curved swords—strapped over their backs. In short order, they disappeared into the yawning mouth and dropped into the earth.

Mustafa leaned forward in his saddle and surveyed Theresa. "You are a pretty one, as well." He smiled, and the puckered scar on his face turned the expression into a cold leer. "Maybe I will take you with me when I go."

Theresa drew back slightly, and didn't meet the bandit chief's gaze. That reaction had no doubt been learned on the tube, Britain's underground train system. Eye contact made predators more aggressive.

While the rest of his men stood around, Mustafa walked over to one of the cooking pots. He sniffed the contents, then took a bowl from a stack beside the campfire. Snaking the bowl into the pot, he dipped up a portion, blew on it, then drank. Evidently enjoying his repast, he dipped the bowl again.

Several minutes passed before they heard a cry of surprise from the *khettara*. Mustafa threw down his borrowed bowl and trudged over to the opening.

"What have you found?"

One of the bandits climbed up from the well with a small golden chest that had once been bound with iron. Over the years, the metal had oxidized and nearly flaked away, leaving only orange grains worked into the softer metal. The box was about eighteen inches long by four inches high by four inches wide.

Involuntarily, Annja took a step forward. One of the guards standing next to her caught her by the arm. The rough grip stopped her, and she had to refrain from grappling with the man and throwing him to the desert floor. She took a quick breath and let it out.

Smythe also stepped forward, but the Bedouin watching him thrust the butt of his rifle into the archaeologist's stomach. Racked by pain, Smythe dropped to his knees.

"Quickly. Quickly." Mustafa turned the box over in his hands, examining the catches. Then finally he gave up and took out a curved knife. He prized the lid open.

Campfire light gleamed from smooth yellowed-ivory surfaces. Annja strained to see what the Bedouin leader held, and thought she could make out a scroll of some kind. The parchment was wrapped tightly around the ivory bars.

Irritably, Mustafa removed the scroll and cast it aside as he searched the box. He smiled a little as he pulled up a few gold coins.

Annja remained focused on the scroll, trying desperately to fathom the script barely revealed on the section that had unrolled. No matter how hard she tried, though, she couldn't make out any of the writing.

Drawn by her fascination, as well as that of Smythe, Mustafa reached down for the scroll. He squatted and unrolled it. If the Bedouin leader understood any of what was written there, he gave no indication.

He looked over at Smythe and Annja, then pushed the scroll at them. "Can you read this?"

At her guard's urging, Annja leaned toward Mustafa.

Smythe studied the page. "Can I get a torch, please? This is very hard to see."

Mustafa waved to one of the warriors, who immediately tossed him a flashlight. He caught the flashlight and turned it on, shining the beam on the scroll.

The writing was beautiful, swoops and flourishes that showed a steady, artistic hand. Looking at it, Annja decided the writing looked familiar, but couldn't immediately fathom why.

"This is old." Smythe spoke in a low voice, entranced by the scroll before him. "The writing is very hard to make out." He sighed. "If you give me time, I'm certain I can translate it."

"Later, then." Mustafa started to place the scroll back inside the box. He waved his pistol at the dig crew, then barked orders to his men. "Bring them all. They will fetch good prices."

Immediately, the Bedouin raiders grabbed hold of Annja, Theresa and the three archaeology students who had followed Smythe out into the desert.

"Wait. You can't take them." Smythe surged up, still holding his stomach. "These are my students. I'm responsible for their well-being."

The guard with the rifle hammered the buttstock against Smythe's head, catching the professor unaware. Unconscious, Smythe fell face-first. Blood gushed from a wound along his temple.

Annja started to go to him, but the raider next to her tightened his grip on her arm. This time she caught his wrist in her other hand, set herself and yanked him over her hip, throwing him hard. He lost his rifle and she thought briefly of going after it, but she knew she'd never reach it in time.

Instead, she knocked Mustafa backward, causing him to trip. The box hit the ground and opened, spilling the scroll. Hoping to seize a negotiating point, Annja grabbed for it. Before Annja could do anything, Mustafa had the other end of it and it ripped in two. Her heart was in her throat when she saw the damage, but she knew she didn't have time to regret her actions.

She seized one of the nearby climbing ropes equipped with a grappling hook, then turned and ran across the flat, moonlit ground. As she ran, she slid her end of the scroll into her shirt for safekeeping.

"Stop!" Mustafa's hoarse order rang out behind her.

Annja never broke stride. Bullets kicked up the sand around her, then the ringing cracks of the shots split the night. Trusting her unerring sense of direction, she kept on the same heading. From what she had seen of the *khettara* wells, the openings were about sixty yards distant at this point. She counted her strides.

Only a few later, she spotted the rise of the *khettara* wall of the next well ahead of her. Horses' hooves joined the gunshots. She hoped the Bedouin didn't kill anyone at the camp. Taking the women was bad enough and would draw the attention of the local authorities, but a massacre would guarantee retribution.

As she neared the *khettara*, Annja knew the horse would overtake her. She hadn't completely thought out her escape plan, but it was in progress. Lifting her knees, she drove herself forward and shook out the climbing rope she'd seized on her way out of the campsite. The grappling hook had a six-inch span. She told herself that would be plenty, that it would hold, and she hoped that was true.

Another volley of bullets chopped into the bermed rise around the *khettara*. At the top, she spun and planted the grappling hook into the earth, then dropped into the well. The rope slipped through her palms fast enough to heat her hands, but it didn't burn them. She didn't descend into the darkness as much as control her fall. She wrapped a leg through the rope to help slow her plummet. Unfortunately, the extra drag on the line ripped the grappling hook from its precarious mooring.

No longer supported, Annja dropped into the darkness as the suddenly slack rope tumbled down around her. She went limp and hoped the impact didn't knock her senseless.

Her pursuers were coming for her.

4

Annja dropped into the water and mud at the bottom of the *khettara* on her back. The wind left her lungs in a rush, but she remained alert. Instantly, she rolled over and tried to get her bearings, but all she could see was the open mouth of the well above. She got to her feet, soaked, and found the rope by feel.

Hurriedly, she pulled it into a coil and slipped it over her head and left shoulder. Rope was always useful, and she was otherwise empty-handed. She hated being separated from her computer, which was in her backpack at the camp. Taking a couple steps with one hand out before her and the other folded over her chest to protect herself, she oriented herself inside the tunnel, finding both ends but not knowing for certain which led back the way she had come.

Then bright light flashed in the darkness and she recognized the lanterns carried by the Bedouin bandits at the same time they saw her. The illumination spun crazily in the well, throwing shadows across the curved walls and reflecting from the water. She thought there were four of them, but there might have been five. The well kept them close as they closed on her at a dead run. Thankfully, they had swords and knives in their fists and not pistols. In the close quarters, a firearm would have made resistance a lot more dangerous.

Edged weapons she felt she could handle well enough, and her opponents' numbers would work against them.

Knowing she wasn't going to run and leave Smythe and the others to their fates, Annja took the coiled rope from her shoulder in her left hand and held it tightly. She reached for the sword that had once belonged to Joan of Arc with her right hand and pulled it from the mystic otherwhere that she couldn't explain.

Standing in the well canal holding her sword gave her the confidence she needed. She and that blade had shared a lot of danger, a lot of combat, and it had never once failed her. Nothing in her life had ever felt so right as holding that sword.

Their double-edged steel splintering the lantern light, the Bedouin warriors charged her, howling and snapping like dogs. Trying, no doubt, to frighten her. She took a fresh grip on her own unadorned leather hilt. The sword was plain; the crosspiece that formed the guard was a straight line that crossed the blade, and in anyone else's hands—which the sword would never allow—the weapon would have been heavy. She hefted it easily, as though it was a part of her.

The man leading the pack saw the sword too late, and his companions didn't see it at all. He tried to stop, but the other men crowded behind him and drove him forward.

As a general rule, Annja didn't kill if she had a choice. Taking life was a serious business and she didn't like being put in the position of having to do such a thing. But she liked the thought of her friends getting hurt or killed even less.

She whipped the sword at the first man's head. He ducked and thrust his sword up to parry the blow. Annja's sword crashed through the Bedouin warrior's, snapping the curved blade in half and slicing through the top of the man's keffiyeh. The man continued his panicked dive till he was on all fours.

The man immediately following the first tumbled over his fellow, managing a swipe at Annja as he fell. She blocked his blade with her own, stood on her right leg and lifted her left knee into the man's face. His nose broke with an audible crunch and he started screaming. She kicked him once more and laid him out unconscious, draped across the first man.

Two of the lanterns lay on the ground, still providing light. The other two Bedouin held up to reassess the situation. She read their surprise in their eyes. Annja stepped toward them, drawing the swing of a sword from the man on her left that scored the well wall next to her head. A small plume of dust eddied into the light.

With a quick turn of her wrist, Annja set her sword tip against the man's throat. Reversing direction at once, the man tried to backpedal. Annja stayed with him, then menaced the other Bedouin still on his feet, chasing him back to the wall. When the first man tried to get his blade up in front of him, Annja returned her attention to him, driving him back with two quick slashes that filled the tunnel with the ring of steel against steel.

Retreating, keeping her sword at the ready, she flicked the coiled rope over the second man's head, waited till the loops settled over the back of his neck and yanked while he was still trying to get his weapon up. She set herself and torqued her upper body from the hips, driving a fist into the man's face three times in quick succession. The back of his head bounced against the cave wall, then his eyes rolled upward and his knees went slack.

Before the last man standing could get organized, Annja flipped the coil of rope from the unconscious man's head as he toppled. The sword leaped in her hands, driving the swordsman back and back until he slipped in the mud. He tried to scramble to his feet, but froze when Annja placed the point of her sword just under his chin.

"No." She let out a breath, stepped closer and kicked him

in the temple. He screamed, but only briefly before pain took him away.

A shot rang out just as a miniature crater formed in the mud a few feet in front of Annja.

Whirling, hair damp and sandy from her fall, eyes still adjusting to the new angle of the lights, Annja dove to the ground just as another couple bullets split the air where she'd been standing. She released the sword, allowing it to disappear, and caught herself on her palms, rolling and springing to her feet against the wall.

Thirty feet away, a Bedouin hung upside down through the mouth of the well. He held an assault rifle in both hands and swung awkwardly from a rope knotted around his waist. He took aim again.

Annja ripped a knife from one of the unconscious men she'd left sprawled on the ground. Still in motion, listening to the stream of bullets smack into the well shaft behind her, she drew her arm back, then whipped it forward, launching the knife at the man.

The knife gleamed in the torchlight. He might not have even seen it coming. He stopped firing immediately and dropped the rifle, then clutched the knife that had pierced his left thigh. She'd been lucky. She'd been aiming at the man's chest.

Sprinting again, she raced for the fallen rifle, dropped to her knees in a skid and brought the weapon to her shoulder. She hadn't had extensive training in firearms, but she'd learned what she could, first from the ex-SAS soldiers who had taught her on the Hadrian's Wall dig, and then at various gun ranges. Her New York police detective friend, Bart McGilley, had contributed to her store of knowledge through his own tutelage.

The wounded man dangling at the end of the rope screamed

at his comrades to pull him up. He waved his arms helplessly, trying to find some purchase so he could escape.

Annja sighted up through the opening. Three men at the top. In the darkness she could just make them out as they reached for their weapons, letting go the rope that held their comrade.

Screaming, the wounded man landed with a crunch that left him silent and still.

Shifting the rifle from the men to the dirt lip just below them, Annja squeezed the trigger. The bullets stitched into the earth, exploding craters. She didn't want to kill them, because the survivors might take revenge on their prisoners.

That was the thing that bothered Annja most: she was going to have to leave the Bedouin with their prisoners. They'd be somewhere out in the Atlas Mountains while Annja went to get help.

The rifle cycled dry. Annja darted forward through the rain of dust and debris. She stopped by the wounded man just long enough to find an extra magazine for her weapon. Then she was up and moving again, running back toward the campsite through the lantern light.

She picked up her coiled rope and was gone before the men saw which way she headed.

THE PLAN CAME TOGETHER in Annja's head as she fled. Granted, it wasn't much of a plan, but it was all she had. The optimum goal was to get her dig mates safely out of harm's way, and the mysterious gold box and the coins, as well. Slavers worked all throughout Morocco. That danger was always present. She had been warned about that. They all had.

The only hope any of them had was if she could get help. But she had to be able to find Smythe and the others again, and there was only one way she knew of to do that. The only problem was staying alive while she raided the camp.

She ran past the well where they'd discovered the skeleton. A fresh pile of dirt formed a large hill in the canal. She climbed over that, trying not to be seen in the residual light from the campfires, and caught bits and pieces of the conversation among the Bedouin.

"She was there, but now we don't see her."

"Find her!" That was from Mustafa, and from the sound of him, he wasn't far from the mouth of the well overhead.

"We will."

"Get someone down the well. Doubtless she is running scared. Do not allow her to get away."

Running scared? Annja made a face in the darkness as she crawled over the temporary dam that blocked the water flow. Don't bet on it.

At the other end of the canal, men with lanterns descended into the tunnel. Annja stood still in the standing water behind the dam. The water had risen to her chest. Nadim had explained that the reservoir would have to be carefully released so it wouldn't wash away the floor and necessitate further repairs.

The men huddled for a moment, evidently trying to choose a leader, then surged down the tunnel away from her.

Annja blew out a breath through her chattering teeth as she watched them go. Then she turned and continued wading up the tunnel through the water. Finally, another forty yards from the last entrance, she stood under another one.

She slung the rifle over her shoulder and shook out the rope. Whirling the grappling hook experimentally, she tossed it up through the opening and slowly tugged, hoping that it would catch on something without arousing suspicion.

Finally, the rope grew taut. Annja kept the pull steady, then put her weight on it, wishing she knew whether she could trust the hook to hold. A moment later her feet dangled off the ground. Moving steadily, she climbed the rope, straining to be silent as she pulled herself up.

When she reached the top, she paused with one hand hooked over the lip, the rope still wrapped around her leg. Mustafa's voice came from a short distance away, but it wasn't loud enough for her to make out what he was saying.

Horses snuffled and stamped their feet much more closely. That was encouraging. Evidently the Bedouin had chosen to move their mounts to the other side of the camp from the direction Annja had run.

She pulled herself out of the well and over the berm, keeping low as she crawled along the ground. Dirt stuck to her wet clothing and the icy wind bit into her.

Mustafa stood to one side of the campsite so that it was hard to pick him out of the shadows. Annja paused a moment and counted the Bedouin still at the campsite. She spotted six, but there could have been more.

Whatever the actual number, there were too many for her. And even if she managed to subdue them all, there were other Bedouin in the hills and tunnel. The prisoners wouldn't be able to escape before they were gunned down.

The horses stood tied to a ground line twenty feet to her left. Thirty feet in front of her, she spotted the tent where her backpack was, along with her notebook computer and satellite phone.

She also needed the canteen of water in there. Civilization was at least a day's hike away.

Annja crawled forward on her knees and elbows, the rifle in her hands at the ready. The grit and rocks bit into her and she knew some of them were drawing blood. She ignored the pain and concentrated on the Bedouins.

When she reached the tent, she eased up behind it. Smythe, Theresa and Cory all stared in the direction Annja had originally fled. Souad talked in whispers to his father. Nadim shook his head and leaned into the teen.

Annja's heart went out to them, but she knew she had to leave them. If they were going to be safe, she had to go.

She pulled a Swiss Army knife from her pocket, flipped open a blade and cut a slit in the back of the tent. Once the slit was large enough, she pushed her head and shoulders inside.

Her backpack sat against the wall next to her sleeping bag. She grabbed it by one strap, snatched the canteen sitting beside it and pulled them both from the tent without making a sound. She reached into the backpack for two of the battery-powered GPS transponders the dig personnel used to mark finds.

The devices were an inch and a half to a side and only a half-inch thick. The batteries would last one hundred and twenty hours. She had five days to locate Smythe and the others before the unit died. She switched it on and returned to the tent only long enough to slide the GPS tracker into Smythe's computer bag. She kept the other in hand as she returned to the horses.

Holding the backpack and the canteen by their straps, she duckwalked back to the horses. As she neared the animals, they shied and snorted, pulled hard at their reins fastened to a ground tie. She paused only long enough to drop the second GPS locater into a saddlebag. She intended to scatter the horses during her escape, but she felt certain the Bedouin would recover them quickly enough.

"Easy, easy," Annja whispered to another horse, and ran a gentle hand along its neck. She didn't stop moving because she knew if she did and the men saw her, she'd lose a step toward freedom. She caught the reins of one horse and sawed at the ground tie with her knife. When the ground tie parted, in essence freeing all the horses, she caught the pommel and heaved herself aboard.

A light pinned her in the darkness. Instinct pulled her eyes toward the beam, but she caught herself and looked away as she put her heels to the horse's sides and yelled, "Hee-yaaahhh!"

"It is the woman! Mustafa! The woman is among the horses!"

The horses in front of Annja parted as her mount shoved through. She lashed about with the reins, startling the horses into panicked hopping.

"Get the woman! Do not let her get away!" Mustafa pointed his pistol and shot. Bullets ripped through the air over her head. "Get the horses!"

Annja pulled the sword back into her hand, then whacked the flat of the blade against the rumps of the nearest horses as she continued shouting. Mustafa's shots turned the tide, though. Hearing the sharp cracks, the horses galvanized into motion and swept away from the campsite. Their hooves thudded against the hard ground.

Bending low in the saddle, Annja kicked her horse again and rode in the middle of the crush of bodies headed away from the campsite. She ran with the group for a time, pausing only to glance over her shoulder at the campsite.

Muzzle flashes flared against the darkness. Two of the horses stumbled and dropped. A few seconds later the rifles fell silent. Annja stayed low over the horse's neck, feeling the animal's muscles bunch and flex, and promised herself that she would return in time to save the others.

5

Annja spent the night in the saddle, constantly looking over her shoulder for pursuers. Thankfully, she hadn't seen any. She assumed that Mustafa and his men had had a hard time gathering the horses and had decided chasing after her was a luxury they couldn't afford. They had to have time to finish raiding the dig.

Thoughts of the hardships her colleagues might be enduring kept plaguing Annja. She pushed the horse as fast as she dared, and got down and walked periodically to rest the animal.

She kept hoping she would meet someone along the way, but the dig wasn't on any of the caravan trails that fed out of Erfoud, the small city forty miles west. The horse could safely travel twenty to thirty miles a day, maybe more, but the inclement weather worked against that.

Leading the horse now, Annja checked her compass and readjusted her backpack. She was headed north-northwest, hoping to pick up one of the trails.

She put the compass away and scanned the flat horizon. The sun was to her back now, warm at the moment, but she knew it would reach baking temperature by noon. Out of habit she checked her sat phone again. It was as dead now as it had been last night. Theresa had borrowed it the previous day to call in and hadn't put the phone in the charger.

After a few more minutes, still able to safely keep watch in all directions, Annja brought the horse to a halt. She picked the canteen up from the saddle pommel, took a couple gulps, then poured a cup of water into a bowl she made out of a plastic sheet.

The horse drank thirstily as she quietly talked to it. "We're going to be fine. The others are going to be fine." She didn't know who needed to hear that more. She or the horse.

When she'd bailed from camp, the canteen had been full. She'd had to make the quart of water stretch. Under optimum conditions, a human was supposed to drink a gallon of water a day. A horse needed a gallon of water per hundred pounds a day. She figured her mount went at least a thousand pounds, so she needed ten gallons of water for the horse alone.

They didn't have it. By stretching their water, she didn't know if she was staving off dehydration or prolonging the torture.

The horse licked the final drops from the plastic, then snorted and stamped its feet.

"Sorry, pal, but that's all we have for right now." Annja patted the animal reassuringly, then put the plastic and the canteen away. Muscles aching, she pulled herself into the saddle and got under way again.

BY MIDDAY, ANNJA WAS struggling to stay in the saddle. The gentle wind swept up dust devils across the flat landscape, but they were mixing in with the mirages that blurred her focus. She blinked several times to clear her vision, but it didn't help. She needed water, food and rest, and she wasn't certain which was most necessary.

Dust flared in the distance. At first she thought it was just a figment of her imagination, then when the dust moved in a steady stream, she began to hope. It was hard to make out the vehicle through the dust cloud, but she believed it was a four-wheel pickup.

She brought the horse to a stop, then pulled the rifle off her shoulder, pointed it toward the sky and fired. The horse stutter-stepped, but halted when she pulled on the reins. Just too tired to run.

The shot echoed over the flat land. For a moment Annja thought the vehicle's engine had drowned out the noise, then the pickup stopped. The dust that had been trailing behind the vehicle gradually overtook it and sailed on by.

Annja waved before realizing that someone inside the pickup was probably taking aim with a rifle, as well. She tugged off the makeshift keffiyeh and exposed her chestnut hair. That clearly marked her as something other than a bandit, and there was no place for anyone else to hide around her.

Carefully, throat dry, she leaned away from the saddle and dropped the rifle. She held her hands up.

Slowly, the pickup wheeled around and started out across the desert. The dust cloud bloomed again behind it.

"WHO ARE YOU AND WHAT are you doing out here?" The man pointed a sawed-off shotgun at Annja and glanced around suspiciously. He was in his forties, seasoned by the harsh land, his skin dark and weathered. A turban wound around his head and dust coated his beard. His English was good, but the Berber accent was pronounced.

"My name is Annja Creed. I'm trying to get back to Erfoud."

"You're American."

"Yes. I need to speak to the police," Annja said slowly so the man could better understand. "I was with an archaeological team. Last night a group of Bedouin slavers raided the camp. I managed to escape."

"You were lucky." The man still didn't lower the shotgun. "I am Samir."

"It's a pleasure to meet you." At least, Annja hoped it was. From the look of the pickup, Samir was a craftsman of some kind. Several toolboxes sat in the back of the vehicle. Judging from the saws and hammers and carving tools, she thought he was a carpenter.

"Are you injured?"

"No. I'm worried about the horse. We've covered at least twenty-three miles, as best as I could estimate. It hasn't had enough water." Annja eyed the orange five-gallon water container strapped to the side of the pickup. "I can pay you for water."

Samir hesitated, then put the shotgun back under the seat. "Worrying about your horse is a good thing. This desert country can be unforgiving."

"Actually, it's not my horse. I stole it from the Bedouin."

Samir grinned as he got out of the pickup and walked to the back. "Even better that you should be worried about someone else's horse."

"I'm also worried about my friends."

Nodding, Samir unstrapped the water container and set it on the ground. "I understand. We will attend to them, as well. The bandits are even more unforgiving than the desert, and I do not mean to alarm you, but there is no way you will be able to find them in all those mountains."

"I will be able to find them."

"Really?" Samir removed the top from the water can and pulled the horse over to it. The animal stuck its muzzle into the water and started noisily sucking it down.

"Really. I put a device in one of their saddlebags."

Samir patted the horse's neck. "Very clever, but I don't think you understand. The Moroccan police will not be so inclined to go searching for your friends out there." He nod-

ded at the mountains. "Those places are very dangerous."
He frowned. "They will be even less inclined because your
friends are Americans."

"Some of them are British."

The man shrugged. "They are foreigners."

"We employed some locals," she said.

"The Moroccan police would not go into those mountains to find anyone unless they knew they would have the
upper hand. There are too many hostile factions out there.
The Frente Polisario, the Shiites and certain Bedouin tribes."
He looked at her with his deep brown eyes. "You should be
grateful to God you survived."

Annja didn't comment, but she was thinking of the others.
"Can you take me to Erfoud? I can pay you."

"Payment will not be necessary. I would not leave you out
here like this." Samir scratched the horse's mane. "Or this
beautiful animal. That would be a most wicked thing to do.
There is a caravan with animals only a short distance back
toward Erfoud. Let us get the horse there, then we will get
you to the city, yes?"

"Thank you."

THE TRIP BACK ALONG the caravan trail seemed interminable
because they had to go slowly to allow the horse to keep up,
despite the second wind it got from the water. Samir had tied
the reins to the back of the pickup. The pickup ground along
slowly, and the transmission whined in Annja's ears.

Samir also shared the lunch he'd packed. Annja had at
first turned down the offer, but he'd been good-natured and
insistent. She'd graciously accepted one of the *bocadillos* in
his lunch box. The sandwich consisted of a baguette stuffed
with salad and a fried egg and was spiced liberally with pep-
per and mint.

Annja ate with gusto, adding goat cheese and mandarins,

washing it all down with green tea spiced with mint from a large thermos. As she ate, she dug out the piece of the scroll she'd managed to escape with. She spread the parchment out as best as she was able on her knees and took pictures of it with her digital camera.

Samir glanced over at her. "Is that something you found on your hunt?" His voice was muffled through the scarf he wore to keep the dust out of his mouth and nose.

"Yes." Annja put her camera away and regarded the scroll again.

"What is it?"

"I don't know."

Samir glanced at the scroll. "The writing looks Arabic, but it's unfamiliar to me."

"It's Kufic." Annja gently traced the straight lines and angles, then followed the elongated swirls. "The same language the original Koran is written in."

"I did not know that, and I follow Muhammad's teachings."

Annja smiled. "Many Christians in the United States don't realize that the Bible wasn't written in King James English. Their Bible was originally a Greek translation of the Hebrew bible."

"So many things to know."

"I think the primary issue is to believe."

"True, of course." He turned his attention back to the dirt road. "Can you read any of it?"

"A little." Annja scanned the writing again and tried not to give in to frustration. She loved mysteries, as long as they obligingly rolled over and gave up their secrets. She was even more exasperated now because she couldn't give the scroll her full attention.

"What does it say?"

"It seems to be a travelogue. Details of a trip. Something like that."

"Seems fascinating."

Annja could tell by Samir's tone that he really didn't think so, but she didn't hold that against him. Most people didn't care for the things archaeologists found unless curses or interesting stories accompanied them. She seemed to find more than her fair share of those, and she couldn't help thinking again that the sword put her on a collision course with those things.

Annja sipped more green tea from the travel cup Samir had loaned her.

He pointed. "We can leave the horse there."

Annja looked up and saw a small caravan crossing the flat land. Even though she had seen caravans before, she couldn't help but be struck by the primitive nature of the crossing.

Dozens of men and women walked on foot, carrying large bundles and packs on their shoulders. Many of them were going to trade goods at market. Others were moving for better circumstances, Annja knew. Several tourists walked with the caravan. They'd probably be catching buses to take them back to their hotel rooms and air-conditioning shortly.

Some of the travelers rode horses or camels, but many of them rode bicycles. There were even a few motorcycles. Taken all together, the caravan looked as if it had marched through time and sucked in travelers from across the centuries.

"If you want, I can even negotiate you a fair price for the animal."

Annja shook her head. "No. I just want to make sure it finds a good home."

Samir pulled over to the side of the road and got out. Even before the dust settled, he called out to one of the men riding a camel. The other man greeted Samir enthusiastically and guided his lumbering beast over to the pickup.

After a brief conversation, Samir handed the horse's reins

up to the camel rider, accepted a small package of nuts and fruits in return and said goodbye.

The camel rider waved to Annja and called down in English, "I love your show!" He gave her a big thumbs-up.

Despite the situation and her fatigue, Annja couldn't help grinning. She waved back. "Thanks."

Turning, she caught Samir staring at her, and had to briefly explain *Chasing History's Monsters* to him.

"A good day." Samir slid behind the wheel again and cranked the engine over. "You have met a fan."

"Yeah." Annja had to admit, they showed up in the oddest places.

Samir let out the clutch and they got under way at a much faster speed. The rushing air cooled Annja, but it didn't take her mind off her friends and what might be happening to them.

6

With only twenty-four thousand residents, Erfoud had a small police force, which was divided into two sections. The Gendarmerie Royale dealt with traffic problems, and the Commissariat Central took care of criminal problems.

Samir let her out in front of the small building off rue de la Piscine. Moroccan flags flew outside the building, sandwiched between the Protection Civile d'Erfoud and the Maison Tafilalet pour la Culture. Annja thanked Samir again, listened to him refuse any offers of payment and wished him well.

Inside, the building was a little cooler but not much. Despite the size of the city, everyone here was busy. Probably all the foreign traffic through town, tourists as well as archaeologists.

After a brief interview, she was shown to a chair. She looked around the waiting room, spotted an outlet and took the seat next to it under a wall filled with tourist warnings of fraud. It only took a moment to hook into the outlet with her phone and computer chargers. When she checked the bars on her sat phone, she had a strong signal. The satellite phones were supposed to be able to ping a communications satellite from anywhere on the planet, but Annja had learned that wasn't necessarily true.

When the phone came online, she saw that she'd missed

several calls. One was from Bart McGilley, probably just to check in and say hello. Three were from museums she'd promised certificates of authenticity, and eight were from Doug Morrell.

Before she returned any of the calls, she took out her computer and brought up the GPS detective software. She tried to access the Wi-Fi inside the police station but discovered that she needed a password. She took out the portable satellite microdish for the computer and logged in. Only a couple minutes passed before she got two pings—close together—in the Atlas Mountains. Relieved, she breathed easier knowing she could find the dig team.

If they were still alive.

She pushed that thought out of her mind, then got out her portable scanner, brought up the program on her computer and ran the wand over the scroll. She had to stay busy. Only a few minutes later, a high-definition copy of the scroll showed up on the computer screen. She logged on to the archaeology sites she frequented, and uploaded the digital image of the scroll.

In addition to the travel mentioned in the scroll, Annja had also found the name of the author: Abdelilah Karam. She'd gathered from what she could decipher that he was traveling under harsh circumstances.

Her accompanying message was short and direct.

Looking for someone who can help me decipher the scanned document above. Looks like Kufic to me. Any other guesses?

Satisfied with the post, she went through photographs taken by the dig crew and copied them to a folder. The rescue crew would need to know who they were looking for.

Confident she'd done all she could do at the moment, she called Doug Morrell. The time difference between Erfoud and New York City was six hours. Morocco didn't do daylight savings time. With the time currently being 3:40 p.m. locally, that meant in New York it was 9:40 p.m.

Doug picked up on the first ring. "Annja, I've been calling and calling."

"I know. Sorry. I've been out of touch."

"You have a sat phone. You're not supposed to be out of touch."

"The phone was dead." She'd also been busy cataloging the find, but she wasn't going to mention that.

Doug sighed. Despite his tendency toward self-involvement, Annja counted the producer as one of her closest friends. He was young, in his early twenties, and had boyish good looks and a trim figure he got effortlessly because she knew for a fact he didn't exercise.

"Okay, don't worry about it. I'm talking to you now, right?"

"Right." Annja checked the time on her phone. She'd been kept waiting for almost thirty minutes. That was thirty more minutes that Smythe and others had been missing, thirty more minutes of travel time. Or torture.

"I was thinking about this whole Casablanca thing, you know?"

"The dig?"

"Yeah. You're shooting some footage on the old caravan routes, right? Camels. Ships of the desert. That kind of thing?"

"Yes, but we also discovered a find yesterday that looks like it's going to be pretty impressive." Annja couldn't help thinking that she hoped the others were there to disclose the story.

"What did you find?"

"A body that looked like it had been buried for a few hundred years."

"Was it moving?"

Caught off-guard, Annja didn't know what to say to that.

Sometimes Doug's mind worked in mysterious ways. "No, it wasn't moving. They guy had been *dead* for a few hundred years."

"Sometimes that doesn't stop them from moving."

"Doug—"

"Maybe there was a quiver. You shot footage of this, right?"

"Yes."

"Then just go back through your video and see if there's a quiver in there. We could use a quiver. Anything to suggest the guy might still be alive."

"He was dead."

"You know what?" Doug sounded even more excited. "Zombies are dead, too, and they still move. Some of them faster than others."

"Zombies?"

"Yeah. Zombies. People *love* zombies. Nothing's bigger than zombies right now. We're getting pressured to show more zombie love on the show." Doug caught himself. "Not actual zombie *love,* you know, though that would be pretty cool, too. Two zombies making out, their desiccated lips falling off. Pulling on each other so hard that their arms come off. Man, the ratings spike from something like that would be unbelievable."

"Stop!" Annja spoke louder than she'd intended and drew the attention of several people sitting nearby.

"What?"

"Morocco doesn't have zombies."

"Are you sure?"

"I'm sure, Doug."

"Because I think you're wrong about that. They've got mummies, and mummies—in my opinion—are just another form of zombies. Did you know that *The Mummy* starring Brendan Fraser was shot in Morocco?"

"Yes, but it was supposed to be Egypt."

"Evidently the Moroccans believe in zombies or they would never have allowed Brendan Fraser to battle Imhotep in their country."

"I think the money the film industry brought in had a lot to do with that. Anyway, mummies aren't zombies. They don't come back from the dead."

"Annja, there are lots of stories about mummies coming back from the dead. Usually to get the grave robbers that disturbed their tomb." Doug *tched*. "You gotta watch more movies."

"I'm not watching movies about zombies."

"You should be. Everybody else is."

"Not everybody."

"Enough of them are. Didn't I just tell you that the brass wants us to have more zombies?"

"Yes. Not interested."

"Somebody's been sipping bitter-ade." Doug growled in frustration. "Annja, I need a team player here. I need zombies. Dig up one of those mummies that are in Casablanca. Or gimme some of those flesh-eating beetles."

Annja counted to ten. "There. Are. No. Zombies. In. Casablanca." She leaned back in her chair and watched as the satellite pinged the GPS signals of the devices she'd left with the Bedouins. She took a breath. "I'm here on an archaeological dig, not something for the show."

"What kind of attitude is that? You should always be on the lookout for ways to improve the show."

"I am. But I'm not looking for zombies."

"Fine." Doug huffed. He could do that like no one else Annja had ever known. "I've got the zombie angle covered, anyway. One of us needs to be looking. How do you spell Morocco? I keep coming up with those Mexican shaker things."

Annja spelled the name.

"You sure there's not a *k* in there?"

"I'm sure."

Despite the stuff he didn't know, Doug was one of the best authorities on pop culture Annja had ever met. But he also secretly belonged to a vampire coven. He brought a whole new level to the show that the fans appreciated, but one that Annja struggled with.

"I don't know why they didn't use a *k*. I'm surprised your parents used an *o* in your name. Why not just name you Dug?"

"Because my actual name is Douglas, and I was named for my maternal grandfather. I'm searching for zombies in Morocco."

Annja gazed across the room to where the lone secretary manned his desk. She checked the time on the wall and grew more anxious.

A short, somber man in his fifties came out of the back of the building. He wore a lightweight suit that had been carefully ironed and his shoes shone. A pencil mustache framed his upper lip and his hair was slicked back from a receding hairline. He had dark, bluish-purple bags under his eyes.

"Miss Creed." He looked at her expectantly. "This way, please."

Annja packed her computer and satellite dish. "Doug, I have to go."

"Where? I thought you were staying in Morocco."

"I am. I've got a meeting."

"Okay. I'll keep looking for the zombies."

"You do that." Annja broke the connection and pocketed her sat phone. She slung her backpack over her shoulder and walked over to the man.

"I am Inspector Khouri. This way, please." He waved her to one of the back rooms.

7

Riding in the back of the armored luxury sedan, Habib ibn Thabit gazed out over the white buildings clustered along the seacoast and ignored the frantic thumping in the trunk. Evidently his guest's sedative had worn off early. It was no matter, though. Bab el Oued——what was once the fishing district—teemed with noise.

These days, the fishing boats in the harbor shared anchorage with tourist boats and private yachts. Much of the world recognized Algiers as a dangerous place to be, though, so there were very few upstanding citizens on the water. And that made it an even better place to do illegal business.

Thabit's own yacht, *Shabanna*, lay out there waiting for him. So did two cargo ships he was currently doing business with. If he hadn't had a mole in his organization, he would have only needed one vessel.

But that was working out to his advantage. Thabit had learned to be a man who took what God provided and made a feast of it. In fact, he was making a feast today.

In his late thirties, he was a powerful man, and handsome. He didn't have to think that for himself. There were plenty of women who had told him. He'd hired a personal trainer and a groomer who traveled with him. The Americans, the Central Intelligence Agency, had tried to cultivate those people over the years, but Thabit made it a point to never discuss business. He kept an inner circle, and no one ever got into it.

The thumping resumed in the back, and this time there were muffled cries, as well. The man was scared, as he should be. He knew the end that he was about to meet.

Thabit had known exactly when the CIA had turned the man, and he had used that knowledge against the Americans. They wanted him badly, but he always stayed one step ahead of them. No matter how hard they pursued him, and no matter the traps they set, he could not be enticed.

His father had lived the same way, and in the end he had died of old age, not from an assassin's bullet. That was how Thabit would die, too.

The driver controlled the sedan easily, moving swiftly through the traffic. He was older than Thabit, going gray at his temples, but he drove flawlessly.

Thabit pressed the intercom button that linked him to the driver's compartment. "Sanjay, are we still followed?"

"Yes. I have identified five cars. The other men have confirmed this. They are using a rolling tail, swapping out cars every few blocks." Sanjay paused and nodded. "They are very good."

Thabit crossed his knees, straightened the line of his pants and interlaced his fingers. He knew he was secure in the car. Heavily reworked, it was a juggernaut, and he had men waiting to close in.

But he wanted to make a point to his new business contact, not just to the CIA.

"Do not lose them."

"I won't."

Thabit looked at the two other men in the car, also in suits. They were older, marked by war and danger. Both sat with German machine pistols in their laps. Attentive, but relaxed.

"How far are we from the meeting point?" Thabit gazed at the expensive Rolex on his wrist.

"A mile. Perhaps three minutes."

Thabit took his thin sat phone from his jacket. He pressed speed dial and waited.

The call was answered on the other end by a man with a deep voice. Abdul Saidi. "Hello."

"My friend, I look forward to meeting with you in a few minutes. I trust everything is in order?" Thabit was talking about the money.

"Yes. You have my product?"

"I do."

There was a pause. "I was told there were people, possibly Americans or Britons, watching your vessel."

"Do not worry."

"I will worry." His newest business contact sounded angry now. "I will not have you bring trouble to my doorstep."

"There is no trouble I cannot handle." Thabit didn't want to say even that much, but his pride was affronted and he could not restrain himself. "Everything will be well."

"If it is not, you are to blame."

Thabit did restrain himself then; otherwise, there would have been no deal. He could live without the profit, but he had maneuvered his enemies into an untenable position and wanted to rain retribution down upon them.

"I will see you in a few minutes. If everything is not as I say, I will give you your product free of cost."

Thabit closed his phone and put it away. He watched through the windshield as Sanjay drove the car through the next intersection and turned left. The sedan glided down a couple alleys, as out of place there as a greyhound in a wolf pack. The flotsam that lived in the alley shuffled away from the car out of self-preservation.

A moment later, Sanjay pulled the sedan to a stop in front of a three-story warehouse. He honked the horn twice.

The place was decrepit, the stone stained by countless years of hard use and bad weather. Most observers would think it was simply out of business. They wouldn't notice the windows covered in black paint or the closed-circuit cameras hugging the roofline above.

The warehouse doors parted down the middle and slid sideways on well-oiled rollers. A row of lights shone down the center of the building, displaying the emptiness of the warehouse. The place wasn't completely empty, though. Enough crates remained to make a well-placed bulwark where gunners could be stationed.

Both bodyguards in the car shifted their weapons into readiness.

"Sanjay, let us proceed."

The driver lifted his foot from the brake and rolled forward, not stopping till a man carrying an assault rifle stepped out in front of him. Other men lurked in the shadows behind the crates.

Thabit opened the door and stepped out of the car. "Abdul Saidi."

"I am here." A thin man with a wide face and curly hair stepped from the crates on the left. In his forties, he moved with a slight limp. His clothing was plain—a gray shirt and dark green pants that would allow him to vanish into the dock crowd if he had to. He carried an assault rifle in one hand, the barrel pointed up. "I am told you were followed."

Thabit smiled. "CIA."

Several of the men in the warehouse readied their weapons.

"The CIA? You brought them here? What kind of betrayal is this?" Saidi pointed his weapon at Thabit.

Thabit held his hands away from his body. "No betrayal. This has been carefully orchestrated." He gestured to the warehouse entrance. "Close the door. It is about to become quite…noisy."

Saidi gave the order and men sprang to close the warehouse doors. One of them turned around quickly and shouted a warning. "There are cars out there! They have found us!"

Thabit stared at Saidi across the rifle muzzle. He spoke softly over the buzz of conversation that suddenly filled the warehouse. "You have heard about me, Saidi. You know how I do business. I am always one step ahead of those who would offer me harm. Now put the rifle down and wait."

"I should kill you right now." Saidi's voice was harsh and he glared at Thabit over the open sights of the rifle.

Calmly, Thabit nodded at his two bodyguards, both of whom had their weapons trained on Saidi. "If you do, you will be the next to die. I promise you that." Thabit had to force himself to appear relaxed. This was as close to death as he had been in a long time. "This trap was set by me, not my enemies, and they're about to find that out. If you doubt me, I can bury you here today, as well."

CIA Headquarters
Langley, Virginia

CIA Section Chief Brawley Hendricks stared at the large screen covering the wall in front of him in the ops room. In his early sixties, he'd been in this situation several times over the past few decades of his service. For the past fifteen years, he'd been chasing terrorist vermin like Habib ibn Thabit around the world. He'd gotten good at the job, but Thabit had been the most dangerous man he'd ever tried to corner.

The man was rising within the ranks of the known terrorists, filling the vacuum left by those they'd taken down in recent months. Terrorists were like the mythic hydra—cut off one head and two more grew in its place.

On the screen, several agents in vehicles converged on the warehouse where Thabit had gone for his meeting. The final destination of the Algerian trip hadn't been known. Thabit played things close to the vest. Now, though, it appeared they finally had him, and with Thabit they would get a key to the Muslim terrorist group the CIA had been tracking for three years.

"Keep breathing, Chief." Craig Morely, the CIA liaison reporting to Congress and the Joint Chiefs on this particular operation, stood nearby. He was in his late thirties, enough of a political animal to roll with the punches by now, and to be wary of results till the dust had settled.

Like Hendricks, Morely wore the tuxedo he'd had on the previous night when they'd found out Thabit was on the move. They'd been attending a meet and greet, jockeying to suck up to the right holders of the purse strings all agencies coveted now that budgets were being cut.

Nailing Thabit would be a big feather in Hendricks's cap. The section chief watched with increasing anticipation as the vehicles jolted to a stop and black-clad CIA special ops agents poured out. Hendricks had gotten to meet most of them, had handpicked and recruited them for the task force.

Hendricks pulled the headset microphone down to his mouth. "Okay, Swan Leader, let's get that flock into the air."

At the front of the room, near the wall screen but not looking at it because their attention was riveted on their individual computers, a handful of young agents monitored the operation. Three of those agents controlled drones. The spy vehicles were on-site to monitor the situation and intercept radio signals. And, if need be, they could track down anyone who escaped the invasion.

"Swan Team is online and is go."

On the screen, the three drones were in the air, marked in targeting triangles and identified with ID tags. They dodged and whipped across the rooftops toward the warehouse like oversize dragonflies.

Morely rocked from side to side nervously. He still had a headful of dark hair and years to go before his career was over. Hendricks had gray hair, wore bifocals and had noticed on some mornings an occasional tremor in his left hand that hadn't ever been there before. His game was about over.

He wanted to go out with a win.

"Agent Hendricks." One of the drone operators worked his controls quickly. "I thought I saw something in one of the surrounding buildings."

"What?" Hendricks's stomach dropped. He'd felt good about this op, but no one had ever before gotten this close to Thabit. Getting in this tight had taken time. There was no reason to doubt the intel.

"I think there are people in the surrounding buildings."

"Put it up on screen."

"I am. Moving from real-time to rewind…now."

A large section of the upper right-hand screen suddenly filled in with a view from one of the drones. The image slowed, tracking through the frames now, and finally stopped on a window of a nearby building just as a man dodged back inside. A curtain fell back into place, blurring the shadow behind the thin fabric.

Hendricks stared at the screen in sudden understanding and horror. "Give me access to the team. Do it now!"

"Yes, sir." The communications officer was a middle-aged woman who had worked ops like this before. "Patching you through now."

"Swan Leader!" Hendricks stepped toward the screen, then caught himself and realized that getting closer to the screen wasn't going to let those men hear him any better. "Swan Leader!"

Swan Leader was Special Agent Paul Gentry. He'd been a

bright kid with a bright future when Hendricks had recruited him from Virginia Tech. He could have been anything, but Hendricks had pulled him into the spy business. He wasn't even thirty yet.

"Paul! Get out of there! It's an ambush!" Hendricks looked at the comm officer. "Am I getting through?"

She shook her head and continued inputting keystrokes. "No. We're blocked. Someone has cut off the comm. Switching to direct sat-relays on handsets."

That was going to be too late. Those men were going to die today, and it was his fault.

Before the special agents in all their military gear could set up, they were hit from both sides by rocket launchers. The narrow alleys around the warehouse turned into a blistering battleground of explosive fury and flames.

Hendricks lifted a hand to his mouth and watched in helpless horror. "My God."

"PUT DOWN YOUR WEAPON." Thabit stared into Saidi's dark eyes. "You and your men are safe in this place. The CIA agents out there are going to die." He smiled grimly. "I decided to kill two birds with one stone."

Saidi lowered his weapon, then waved to his fellows to do the same. "How did you know they would be here?"

Thabit walked to the rear of his vehicle and gestured to the driver. "They put a mole into my organization seven months ago. It took me two months to figure it out, and five more months to figure out how I could best use him."

The driver reached into the car and triggered the trunk release. The lid rose slowly and revealed the man lying on his back inside the compartment. He was disheveled and bloody from the beating Thabit's security people had given him earlier. His lips were split around the gag in his mouth, and one eye was swollen shut.

"Since we were doing business together for the first time, I wanted to make sure you understood what I could do for you. And to you." Thabit reached into the trunk and hauled the man out.

The prisoner fell heavily on the floor. Plastic ties held his hands behind his back and bound his ankles. He writhed, looking up at Thabit and making pleading noises.

Thabit looked at Saidi. "You want the Moroccan government out of Western Sahara."

Saidi nodded. He was in the Polisario Front, the liberation group trying to increase the holdings of the Sahrawi Arab Democratic Republic.

"Today, you and I share a common goal. King Mohammed is a lapdog for the Westerners, and he will never allow Western Sahara to belong to the Sahrawi people. You are having trouble securing weapons with which to continue your struggles there. I can get them to you, and I can do it more cheaply than others who might want to take advantage of you." Thabit paused. "I work to strike back at the Western world the same as you, and I'm in a position to help you. All you have to do is accept that help."

"If I choose not to?"

Thabit shrugged. "Then I will find another rebel who is willing to do business with me. But I tell you now that no one else will be able to get you the weapons I have waiting for you in the harbor for less than what I am offering. I have chosen you because you are a committed man. I know you will use those weapons."

Saidi hesitated only a moment longer. "All right. It will be as you say. We have a deal."

"Good." Thabit smiled, then he reached under his jacket and took out his pistol. "Keep in mind, I am not a man who is afraid to get his hands bloody." He seized the prisoner's hair, tilted his head up, pressed the barrel into his forehead and pulled the trigger. The prisoner shivered and died, and Thabit felt warm blood from the dead man's wound on his cheek. He put the pistol away and took out a handkerchief to blot it from his face.

Sirens sounded outside.

Unhurriedly, Thabit nodded to his bodyguards. They picked up the dead man and threw him back into the car. One of them closed the trunk.

"We should go, my friend." Thabit pulled a card from his jacket and handed it to Saidi. "Call this number at eleven o'clock tonight. The final arrangements will be given to you then."

Saidi nodded. "Thank you. Your faith in me and my men is not misplaced."

Thabit smiled. "I did not think it would be." He stepped toward the car and one of the bodyguards opened the door. He slid into the backseat, then craned to check his face in the rearview mirror to make sure he'd gotten all the blood.

The bodyguards got in, then the driver drove them through the other exit. Flames still wreathed the dead bodies in the alley, and the driver didn't slow as he rolled over the corpses. Sanjay followed his escape route, easily avoiding the Algerian police.

Thabit relaxed in the backseat, taking a final glance at the carnage he'd wrought. The CIA might step up their efforts to get him. He didn't expect anything less. But that was fine. He had plenty of places to hide, and his fellow Muslim freedom fighters would respect what he had done. That not all of them were on the run. Thabit intended to put as many of his enemy as he could in his gun sights. His peers would relish that almost as much as he did.

His phone rang and gave him pause. He slipped the device from his pocket and glanced at the ID.

"Hello."

"A lost document written by Abdelilah Karam has just surfaced in Morocco."

Thabit's heart stilled for just a moment. Since before birth, he had been cursed. He had not even known of it until he was thirteen. For the past twenty years, he had dismissed the idea of a curse having power. Of a curse bringing him potential disaster. Yet…

Now here it was.

"Tell me what has happened."

"Have you heard of Annja Creed?"

8

Erfoud
Kingdom of Morocco

Inspector Khouri worked out of a tiny office, but it was an office, not a cubicle. There was a feeling of privacy that the cramped quarters couldn't quite expunge. The inspector sat in front of an archaic computer and typed with two fingers. He wrote in his own language, so the only things Annja recognized on the screen were her name and the names of the dig crew.

Waiting for Khouri to enter everything was mind-numbing and emotionally exhausting. Annja felt the need to be up and moving. She was certain Mustafa wasn't making life easy on his captives.

"They are British citizens." Annja struggled to keep the exasperation out of her voice.

"Yes, yes, Miss Creed. I understood that the first time you told me. And it is here in my report." Khouri tapped the computer screen. He glanced at her over his shoulder. He had to use glasses to see the computer, and he gazed at her over them now. "I must fill out this report if anything is to be done."

Annja made herself take a breath. "How long do you think it will take to *do* something?"

Khouri shook his head. "I do not know. You are talking

about the mountains. That is beyond the jurisdiction of this department. All I can do is forward this to the military. Perhaps they can do something."

"Perhaps?"

The inspector spun his chair around to better face her. "Miss Creed, you have to understand that what you are suggesting—"

"I'm asking for help for my friends."

"—is not simple. Those mountains are very dangerous. The bandits make that region even more so."

"Who can help them?"

"We can try. I am trying."

"Perhaps you could try the British consul."

Khouri frowned. "Surely you see the problems with that, Miss Creed. Imagine if I were to go to New York City and get mugged. Then, instead of letting the local authorities deal with the matter, I called in the Moroccan embassy. Do you think the New York Police Department would sanction that?"

Annja wanted to scream. She was beginning to believe she would have been better off staying to defend the dig team on her own. Except that she knew she'd been outnumbered. All she would have been able to do was get herself in deep trouble.

"No," she answered in a civil tone.

"Good. Then we are in agreement. You can see how the military would be reluctant to go into those mountains."

"I have their location on GPS. I've explained that."

"I understand, and I have put that in my report." Khouri took a breath. "Now, please, let me finish inputting all the details."

Unable to sit any longer, Annja stood and gathered her things. "You've got all the information I can give you, Inspector. Sitting here watching you type it into your report isn't going to help."

Khouri hesitated a moment, obviously wary that he might

be stepping into a trap, then nodded. "You have given me their pictures, their location and the name of the man you believe is behind this. Do you know where you'll be staying?"

"You can reach me through my phone. You have the number."

"Very good."

"Call me when you have news."

"The very minute, Miss Creed."

ANNJA WAITED TILL SHE cleared the police station before calling Garin Braden at one of the numbers he'd given her. Garin was the only man other than Roux linked to Joan of Arc's sword. At the time Joan of Arc had been burned at the stake, Garin had been a young man given to Roux, Joan's protector, as a slave, more or less. And then Joan had died, and the sword had been broken. That was over five hundred years ago. Garin had lived over five hundred years. Annja didn't know how long Roux had been around. Their longevity was a mystery.

They hadn't gotten along when Joan was alive, and the loss of her and the sword had been the final straw. They'd gone their separate ways shortly thereafter—relatively speaking, given the past five hundred years—and remained somewhat distant. On several occasions, they had tried to kill each other. Since Annja had equally mysteriously made the sword whole, and it had claimed her, they shared an uneasy truce.

An answering service picked up the call in German. "Hello, this is Mr. Braden's personal assistant, Inga. How may I help you?" The voice oozed sex and money, two things Garin idolized.

"Hi. This is Annja Creed." The personal assistant surprised Annja. The few times she had called Garin before, he had always picked up.

"Yes, Miss Creed. How may I help you?"

Annja walked along the street, keeping watch in the windows of the small shops she passed.

"I would like to speak with Mr. Braden, if I may."

"I'm sorry, but Mr. Braden is indisposed at the moment. Might I take a message?"

Indisposed? Annja's mind raced. Indisposed could mean he was in jail or off fighting for his life. Garin Braden owned legitimate companies, but he also managed several illegal operations, as well. One of his semilegal operations was fielding a mercenary group. Annja was hoping to call in a favor on that score.

"I would like Mr. Braden to return my call at his earliest convenience. The matter is life or death."

"I understand, and I will give him your message. Several of Mr. Braden's dealings of late have been life or death matters."

Annja frowned, wondering if the woman was trying to antagonize her.

"Might he reach you at this number?"

"Yes."

"Mr. Braden will doubtless return your call when he is able. Have a nice day."

Have a nice day? Annja fumed as she listened to the dial tone. She called Roux, but the old man wasn't any easier to reach than Garin had been. Reluctantly, she pocketed her phone and glared up into the distant Atlas Mountains.

Having no other choice, she flagged a passing taxi and headed for a hotel room. Any other time, she could have happily roamed Erfoud for hours. Now all she could think about was the danger the dig crew was in.

And that parchment scrap she'd managed to get her hands on.

IN THE SMALL HOTEL HALLWAY, Annja surveyed the door, checking for telltale signs that the room had been invaded. Seeing nothing immediately noticeable, she used her key and entered.

Erfoud didn't have five-star hotels, and those were generally something Annja didn't splurge for, anyway. Not on *Chasing History's Monsters'* budget. She preferred the smaller hotels because they gave her a chance to interact with people who weren't just going to shuttle her off to the nearest tourist attraction. While on her journeys, she'd gotten to know small, out-of-the-way places to eat, and had sometimes stumbled onto really good artifacts.

She wanted to take a bath. After days of living under primitive conditions, she wanted to be clean again. Instead, she set her backpack on the floor near the tiny desk, pulled out her computer and got to work. She had email addresses for Garin. She quickly sent messages, asking that he get in touch with her.

When she checked the GPS coordinates, they were still there, blinking patiently. She took solace in the fact that she hadn't lost track of the team.

Then, because she had no other choice yet than to wait, and because she was, at her best and her worst, curious, she opened up the responses she'd gotten from her blog postings.

The first six emails were from people who more or less agreed with her assumption that the writing was Kufic. Two of them thought it was a variant, but not one they'd seen before.

The seventh email, from tailorsboy444@houseoffirenze.org, provided more enlightenment.

Hey. I recognize the name Abdelilah Karam as a little-known historian of the Ridda Wars, which were also called the Wars of Apostasy. I'm sure you know those struggles came as a result of the argument over who would lead the Muslim people after Muhammad died.

I don't know if this is the same person named in your document, but it would be an incredible find if it was. Karam has a couple good pieces about the defense of Medina and the fallout that occurred afterward. Maybe he deserves more recognition? How did you find this? You didn't say.

That was interesting. Annja mused over that for a moment while she typed her thanks, but told tailorsboy444 she had to sit on the location of the find for the moment. The Ridda Wars had taken place in 632 and 633, and they were headed up by Abu Bakr, Muhammad's father-in-law. Bakr had been named the first caliph after Muhammad's death.

But if this was the same Abdelilah Karam, what was he doing in Morocco? Once the caliphate had been settled, or at least reasonably functional, the Muslims had begun the invasion of Persia. Surely historians would have been far more involved with that than whatever had brought Karam to Morocco.

And who had buried him in the foothills of the Atlas Mountains? And who had killed him? For what?

Questions buzzed through Annja's mind like fighter planes. She was grateful for the distraction, but she kept checking the GPS coordinates. They were miles outside of Marrakech. They had been traveling for the past few hours.

She was getting hungry. Starving herself wasn't going to do anyone any good. She gathered up her computer, regretted the fact that she still hadn't bathed and went to get something to eat.

9

Brawley Hendricks sat in his office and stared at the picture he'd taken with Paul Gentry only a few short years ago. The young agent looked so innocent and so sincere as he smiled back at Hendricks. Beside Paul, his young bride, Heather, was pregnant, carrying a baby bump, as the young people called it these days. She was blonde and beautiful, and as innocent as Paul had been when this photo was taken.

She'd been one of those good wives, able to accept that her man often disappeared to God only knew where to do the right thing in the world. And Hendricks had made her a widow today because he'd been prideful enough to believe he had had the upper hand on Thabit.

Hendricks's hand trembled as he touched the framed photograph. He had to make things right. Even it if meant stepping outside the lines to get it done.

"You doing okay?"

Glancing up, Hendricks saw Morely standing in the open doorway. The liaison still looked shaken himself.

Hendricks cleared his throat. "As well as can be expected, yes."

Morely seemed to want to say something else, but didn't. He patted the doorway. "If you need anything…"

"Sure."

"You should get out of here."

"I will."

Morely hesitated once more, then he left.

Quieting his rage, Hendricks shut down his computer, grabbed his coat and briefcase, and left the office. He knew where he had to go. After his earlier meeting with Heather, he knew what he had to do.

Curtain Bar
K Street, Washington, D.C.

THE BAR OCCUPIED A NICHE on Washington, D.C.'s, Fourteenth Street, not far from K Street. Back in the 1970s, the area had been the city's red-light district. Over the years, though, the neighborhood had been cleaned up. It was now home to small businesses that kept low profiles. Back in the day, Hendricks had gone there to get information, and to hire people for less than savory purposes.

Hendricks stood outside in the afternoon sun and lit a cigarette. He squinted through the smoke and looked out over the city, which had changed so much in the past few decades. It was going to change again, just keep turning over like a cesspool. As he filled his lungs with smoke, he realized he hadn't thought of D.C. like that in years.

In fact, he hadn't come calling on Sophie in almost a decade. He wondered if she'd changed. He knew he had, gotten older and more beaten down.

His phone chirped. He took it out of his coat pocket and looked at the screen.

Are you coming in? Or are you going to stand out there and brood?

Hendricks smiled. He dropped the phone back into his pocket, crushed his cigarette underfoot and walked toward the small bar.

A large black doorman stood in front of the plain wooden door with *Curtain* written across it in small bronze letters. A coiled wire in one of the man's ears indicated he was connected with someone inside. The guy was nearly seven feet tall and imposing in gangbanger clothing. As Hendricks approached, the man looked at something in one of his large hands, and Hendricks knew it was a smartphone that probably had his photograph on it.

The man nodded but didn't speak. He thrust his chin toward the door.

An electronic lock popped open. Hendricks entered.

The clientele at the bar watched Hendricks as he stepped into the small room. They were young, and had the hard eyes military people who had seen death up close tended to get. Hendricks recognized the look because he shared it.

The times had changed. Almost as many women occupied the room as men now, and they weren't there as arm candy. They had hard eyes, too.

The bartender was an older man, but still younger than Hendricks. That little fact made the CIA section chief feel even worse. A small television hung from the ceiling behind the bartender, and turned to CNN.

"Can I get you something, sir?"

"Scotch. Make it a double."

The bartender nodded, then poured and handed the drink over.

Hendricks raised an eyebrow.

The bartender cut his eyes toward the back of the room, but made no move. Hendricks knew the man would have a weapon behind the bar.

Turning, Hendricks looked down the row of booths at the back of the bar. No one sat there as far as he could tell, but the last couple booths weren't visible. No one would get past the people in the room unless they were cleared. He carried his glass, less shaky now than he'd been back in his own office, and knew that he was about to step across a line he hadn't crossed in nearly twenty years.

He found Sophie sitting in the last booth, and she didn't look much different from the last time he'd seen her. He guessed from their history that she was nearly as old as him, but could have passed for his daughter.

The dark hair was cut shorter, more in trend with today's styles, but it was the same color as it had always been. Her brown eyes stood out more, and her chin looked more forceful, more chiseled. Her lips were bright red and looked as if they were wet. Her long fingernails were the same color as her lipstick.

The tabletop turned out to be a computer monitor that currently showed a small gray kitten playing with a ball of yellow yarn.

"Hello, Brawley." She smiled at him as if she meant it. The skill of appearing sincere was what had made her so deadly.

"Hello, Sophie."

She pointed to the other side of the booth. "Have a seat."

Hendricks sat heavily as if the weight of the world was crushing him. He rested his forearms on the table. On the monitor, the kitten batted the ball of yarn over and over again, trapped in endless repetition.

"It's been a while." She picked up a coffee cup and sipped.

"It has. You look good."

"Thank you. I take care of myself. I have a personal trainer, a nutritionist and cook."

"You deserve it."

Sophie studied him, then leaned back in her seat. "From anyone else, I'd think that was sarcastic."

Hendricks took a breath and wondered how he was going to start this conversation. On the way over in his car, he'd had second thoughts. But in the end, he'd had nowhere else to go. Thabit couldn't be allowed to run free anymore.

"You're smoking again," she said.

"Just started back today. I'll quit again."

She smiled at him. "You always had the willpower to do things like that. Some of us have to live with our addictions. I heard about your protégé today," she said softly.

Hendricks wasn't surprised. If she hadn't been plugged into what happened in the Agency, she wouldn't have been the person he'd needed.

"I'm sorry."

Nodding, Hendricks took in a breath that tasted like tobacco fumes, then rinsed it out of his mouth with the Scotch. "I'm sure you didn't let him go in without telling him it was a hard business."

"I didn't."

"Sometimes things are just what they are."

Hendricks stared into her brown eyes. "I remember telling you that once upon a time."

A small, almost fragile smile flitted across her face. "When I was summarily dismissed from the Agency all those years ago, yes, you did."

"I helped you kill those men. Outside of CIA purview."

"You did. Only they didn't cut you loose."

Sophie sipped her coffee again, buying time.

Hendricks waved a hand. "I've heard the Agency hires you for black-bag jobs off the books."

"Flatterer."

"But it's true."

Some of the humor returned. "I can neither confirm nor deny. Isn't that how it goes?"

Hendricks took a deep breath. "I want Habib ibn Thabit dead."

Sophie tapped the monitor with her painted fingernails and brought up footage from the attack in Algeria earlier that day. "I took the liberty of searching through your casework to find out why you might be coming to see me today." Sophie regarded him. "This is all I could come up with."

On the monitor, the alley was still filled with dead men. His hand holding the Scotch shook slightly, but if Sophie noticed she was gracious enough to pretend she hadn't.

"The CIA wants Thabit alive," she probed. "They think he's the linchpin they can use to ferret out more terrorists."

"I lost a good man trying to do that very thing. I'm not prepared to accept that loss. I want him avenged."

Sophie leaned by and crossed her arms, sympathy in her eyes. "This isn't a revenge business. You told me that at the academy, as I recall."

"Revenge isn't the *Agency's* business. You and I know there are other things at work in the world. I helped you with yours. I need help with mine."

For a long, quiet moment, Sophie stared at him. "Thabit is a ghost. I don't have anything more on him than you do."

"I have something else." Hendricks had kept the link out of his reports. After Paul's loss, that omission would be almost understandable. And at any rate, he was on his way out. If things went badly, he could opt for early retirement. But the pieces would have already been put into play to take down Thabit.

"What?"

"Thabit has a special interest that no one else knows about. It fell into my lap today. I've kept it out of the reports for the moment. I think he'll expose himself."

"And if you're wrong about that?"

Hendricks shook his head. "Then I'm out of options and the man is untouchable."

"What do you have?"

He didn't even hesitate. "There's a female archaeologist, Annja Creed, who seems to have discovered something in Morocco that has captured Thabit's interest."

"What?"

Hendricks shrugged. "A body. Some kind of document. At this point, that's all I know. And that Thabit is starting to move heaven and earth to find out more about her discovery."

Sophie didn't take notes. But she touched the monitor and brought up a website featuring Annja Creed and the cable TV show *Chasing History's Monsters*. "A very attractive young woman."

"Yes."

"If I agree to this, you're going to be putting her in harm's way."

"She's already in Thabit's sights. She could very well be in harm's way now and this effort could save her."

"This is a mercenary business, as you know. Where's the payday?"

"Thabit *is* the payday." Hendricks had anticipated this. "I can give you some of the particulars of Thabit's bank accounts. We have identified some of them in the Caymans and in Zurich, but we can't touch them. You can."

"Once I have Thabit, perhaps. But only if we take him alive."

"Keep him alive long enough for that."

"How much money are we talking about?"

"Upward of nine million. And that's only what we've been able to discover. There will undoubtedly be more."

Sophie tapped a fingernail on the monitor, then caught herself and stopped. "It's an intriguing proposition. Do we have an in for Annja Creed?"

Hendricks let out a slow breath and felt some of the weight shift off his shoulders. He was almost confident he had Sophie where he wanted her.

"The archaeological team she was working with has been kidnapped by raiders. The Erfoud police and the Moroccan military haven't exactly been forthcoming with help."

Sophie nodded. "Good. I like that." She smiled a little. "A search-and-rescue mission is always a good place to start."

Hendricks spread his hands. "That's what I have. That's all of it. If it's not enough, tell me."

She looked at him quietly. "It's enough. You knew that before you came here. But you need to know something in return."

He waited.

"I want the paycheck here. I'm not emotionally involved in this thing. The man I put on it won't be, either."

"Who do you have in mind?"

"Are you sure you want to know?"

Hendricks immediately understood she could only be talking about Rafe MacKenzie. MacKenzie had also been cut by the Agency a few years ago. They'd used him primarily for wetwork, and MacKenzie had developed a taste for it that bordered on the psychopathic. Hendricks had handled the man, and had later taken point on ousting him from the CIA.

If Paul Gentry was the good son that Hendricks had never had, Rafe MacKenzie was the bad one. Annja Creed wouldn't just be in harm's way. He would be trapping her between two forces that could crush her.

"Either way, I'm taking this deal," Sophie said matter-of-factly. "At this point, you don't have a choice. With or without those bank account records, I'm sending MacKenzie after Thabit. He's already in Mauritania. He can be in Erfoud by morning. After he finishes up his current assignment."

10

Rafe MacKenzie stared through the mud-and-bug-smeared window of the twenty-year-old Toyota SUV they were using for the op. Beneath the dented and paint-splotched exterior, a specially enhanced engine and transmission were protected by a reconditioned frame and underbody that had been strategically lined with bulletproof armor.

Beside him, in the driver's seat, Yahya bore down on the accelerator.

MacKenzie patted the slight man on the shoulder. "Slow down."

"But I will lose the car." Yahya was young and he loved the hunt. He reminded MacKenzie of a jaguar, sleek and dark and deadly. He didn't mind scaring those who fell into his clutches, and he was skilled in torture. He was also a good driver, but he lacked patience in traffic.

"You will not lose the car." MacKenzie settled back into his seat and watched the gridlock along avenue Abdel Nassir. They were following the street in from Nouakchott International Airport to the center of the city.

"The traffic is impossible."

"The traffic is normal. Besides, we know where the diplomat is going."

"Unless he stops somewhere."

"Where would he stop?"

Yahya tightened his fists on the steering wheel.

"Just breathe. Everything is going to be fine." On most days, MacKenzie didn't let the Mobile, Alabama, accent surface. Every now and again, though, he heard it when he got tired or when he got close to someone.

At thirty-four, he wasn't old enough to be Yahya's father, but he often thought of the younger man as a little brother. For the past three years, he'd trained Yahya's rage into something more focused. A weapon.

Yahya had raised himself on the streets of Cape Town, and MacKenzie—raised by a single mother in poverty in the U.S.—had taken a shine to the young man while on an op there. Yahya was the only one of MacKenzie's current mercenaries who stayed with him on every operation. With the others, it was only business.

"We have another job after this one is finished." MacKenzie brought that up only to give Yahya something to think about while he drove.

"We do?"

"Yes."

"Where?"

"Morocco."

Yahya changed lanes smoothly and pulled past a slower moving truck. Growing up as he had, he worried about the future, about the next job. He checked his mirrors, then pulled back into the lane he'd left, making space for himself. The truck driver behind them laid on his horn.

"Patience."

"I will not lose that car."

The diplomat's black sedan glided through traffic. The

driver was obviously skilled. He was Chinese, according to the intel packet MacKenzie had gotten from his ops broker, and had driven for the diplomat for three years. Some of that time had been in Hong Kong. The traffic there was bad.

During the years MacKenzie had worked for Sophie since getting kicked out of the CIA, he had never known her to give misinformation. That was why he never contested her percentage of the take. She was worth every cent.

The next job presented the biggest payday MacKenzie had ever stood to receive. Not that he was looking to retire anytime soon. He enjoyed his work.

"I have not been to Morocco." Yahya was distracted now, and that curbed some of his impatience.

"I have."

"What is it like?"

"Not much different than this place." MacKenzie waved at the city.

"The languages?"

"Not so much different, either." Yahya's facility with languages was another reason MacKenzie had taken him on. Like MacKenzie, Yahya learned languages phonetically, picking them up almost as if by osmosis. Of course, he could neither read nor write in them, but for what they did, those skills were not so important. Surviving inside a culture or community long enough to take down a target was all that was necessary.

"Sounds good."

"It is good." MacKenzie reached under his seat and brought up the H&K MP5 he'd hidden there. He kept the machine pistol in his lap at the ready, hidden under a jacket. He had a 9 mm pistol holstered at his waistband in back.

His sat phone rang and he answered it because it was Sophie and she would have news.

"Yes."

"Can you speak?"

"This line is not secure." MacKenzie told her that out of habit. She never said anything over any phone line that could be used against her.

"I have eyes on your package."

"Good." That meant someone was watching over Annja Creed. MacKenzie wasn't truly interested in that and thought it was overkill. From what he'd seen of the woman's file, she was nothing. A minor celebrity who had stumbled onto something too big for her.

Habib ibn Thabit presented the true danger. The man had to be handled just so, before he got a chance to establish himself or take the woman.

"Shall I set up an appointment?"

"Tell her I will be in touch no later than tomorrow morning."

"You can make the meeting?"

"Yes. What I have to do here won't take much longer." MacKenzie watched the speeding car ahead of them.

"Keep me apprised of the situation."

"Of course." She always said that, too, but she knew he wouldn't tell her anything unless he wanted to. The click in his ear told him that she'd broken the connection. He put the sat phone away and nodded to Yahya. "All right."

Yahya grinned and bore down on the accelerator.

11

Erfoud
The Kingdom of Morocco

Dining out turned into a working dinner. Annja found a small restaurant not far from her hotel and settled in. Beautiful and ornate teal, yellow and maroon tile covered the inner court-yard floor and walls. There were no windows on the first floor because all that would have been within view were the nar-row, twisting alleys that separated the businesses and dwell-ings. The restaurant was off the beaten path, so there were only a few adventurous tourists among the patrons. The rest were Moroccan families.

The restaurant provided dining inside, as well, but Annja preferred the open spaces. There was more room, and al-though there was a chill, it wasn't cold enough to be uncom-fortable. With her phone and her computer fully charged, and with the mini satellite receiver functioning, she was in total work mode.

She wore a microphone headset but kept one of the ear-pieces off center so she could hear the activity around her. She didn't like being deaf anywhere outside her loft, or in an area where she didn't trust the security.

She opened up her Skype account and called Dr. Ernest

Woolcot, an acquaintance at Harvard who specialized in Middle Eastern history, particularly the caliphate.

The call didn't go through immediately, and she was about to leave a message and log off when Woolcot accepted the connection and the computer monitor opened to a picture-in-picture. The professor was in his late sixties, dark skinned from his Saudi Arabian mother and his African-American father. His father had been a lawyer working with the Kingdom of Saud when he'd met and fallen in love with Woolcot's mother, a much-removed member of the House of Saud. Once, on a lark, Woolcot had worked out how many "mishaps" would have to occur for him to be anywhere near the throne. He'd explained it to Annja over lunch during one of her visits to the archives there, and went on to say it would be easier to put together a moon landing.

"Annja Creed, this is an unexpected pleasure." Woolcot was bald but had magnificent eyebrows over his dark brown eyes and a carefully trimmed gray beard. He wore a dark turtleneck with the sleeves pushed to midforearm.

"Am I interrupting?"

"Not at all." Woolcot waved idly to a stack of papers beside him. "Grading students' work. Separating those who actually put some time and effort into their assignments from those who watched something on the Discovery Channel." He lifted an eyebrow. "You'll be happy to know that I seem to have quite a few fans of your television show in my classes these days."

"That's a good thing?"

"When they're quoting *most* of your pieces, yes. When they're sourcing that Kristie Chatham woman, not so much. And I have the distinct feeling that some of your content has been…molested."

"*Molested* is a good word." Annja grinned.

"I thought it might be."

Annja took a sip of her tea. "As you might have guessed, this isn't a social call." She felt guilty. Woolcot was a friend and she had a bad habit of only calling friends when she needed something.

"A social call usually involves some kind of meal. I see you're in the midst of one."

"Sorry, I had to eat."

"Not a problem. So, if this is not a social call, let us agree that this is at the very least a pleasant diversion. What can I help you with?"

Quickly, Annja outlined yesterday's discovery, but left out the ambush by the Bedouin raiders. "Have you heard of Abdelilah Karam?"

Woolcot leaned back in his chair and laced his fingers behind his head while he mulled the name over. Then he shook his head slightly. "Should I have?"

"If you haven't, then he couldn't have been very important."

"Yet someone killed him and left his body in Morocco."

"Yeah."

"Curious."

"That's what I'm thinking, too."

"Would you like me to do some legwork on this fellow?"

"I don't want to be an imposition."

Woolcot smiled and shook his head. "One thing you definitely are not, Annja, is an imposition. Surprising, yes, challenging, yes, but never an imposition." He paused and took a breath. "I would like to propose an addendum, in return for my services."

"What?"

"You can have the glory of the find. That's already yours. But, if possible, I would like to coauthor a paper on what we may turn up. I'm afraid the publish-or-perish life of an educational functionary is never quite finished. The wolf is always at the door, and this sounds promising."

Annja grinned. "Claim that all you want. I happen to know you like seeing your name in print."

The professor sighed with good-natured acceptance and spread his hands. "Permit me at least a little ego."

"Does an ego come in that size?"

Woolcot chuckled. "Probably not, but this way I will get to have my cake and eat it, too. My colleagues will be scandalized if this turns out to be something and my name is on a paper with Annja Creed, cohost of *Chasing History's Monsters*. I would enjoy tweaking some of their noses. There are people in this department who are entirely too full of themselves."

"Not worried about being tarnished by association with pop culture archaeology?"

"I relish the opportunity and pray that we meet some kind of success. Those selfsame colleagues who would be looking down their noses at me would also be insanely jealous."

The coming night had started to filter darkness into the courtyard, and the air had grown considerably chillier. Annja thought again of the bath she'd put off and wanted to get back to her hotel room.

The loud voices of muezzins from the surrounding minarets broadcasted over speaker systems around the city, calling all the Muslim faithful to worship. Around Annja, several of the families got up to go, carrying their prayer rugs with them.

On the computer screen, Woolcot checked his watch. "I should probably let you go. I have a dinner date with a woman who loves me and puts up with me for God alone knows what reason."

Annja smiled, thinking of Woolcot's petite wife, an English professor, who shared his love of learning and teaching. "Tell Miriam I said hello."

"I will, and the next time you are here, you should stop in for dinner. She would love to see you."

"I will." Annja said her goodbye, then broke the connection and gathered her things.

OUT IN THE ALLEY, ANNJA spotted a man watching her from the deepening shadows. For half a block on her way back to her hotel, the man kept pace with her.

She studied him in the glass windows she passed. He was too well dressed to be a mugger, but he wasn't a professional man by any means, either. He looked like a nicely dressed thug in slacks, a light jacket and walking shoes. Guessing from the look and the clothing, the man was American or European, with an easy way of walking. He kept his hands in his pockets, but there was plenty of room under the jacket for a weapon.

Annja settled her backpack over her shoulders and turned at the next alley, moving quickly now. Once in the shadows next to an overflowing bin, she shucked out of the backpack and pressed back into the wall.

The man came around the corner still at the same easy pace. That told Annja he already knew where she was ultimately heading. That was unsettling. She stepped out of the shadows behind him. Before she could say anything, he whipped around, spinning to his right with a short-bladed knife glinting in his fist.

Annja deflected the knife blow with her right forearm, bent her knees to slide beneath his arm and delivered a left jab to his short ribs that felt as though she'd struck a side of beef. The man's breath puffed out in a ragged gasp, but he stayed on his feet and danced back.

He dropped the knife to the cobblestones and smiled. He was good-looking and he knew it. Possibly in his early thirties.

"Hey, hey, no foul, Miss Creed."

Annja held her fists up, ready to close or retreat if she had to, though she had no intention of retreating. She also kept listening for footsteps in case the man hadn't been as alone as she'd thought. Or if he'd been in radio communication with someone.

"Who are you?"

He shook his head. "You don't need to know me. I'm just a messenger. Don't kill the messenger."

"You came around with that knife pretty quickly."

"You surprised me." He winked. "Not a wise thing to do."

"Neither is tailing someone."

"I came to deliver a message."

Annja waited.

"The local police aren't going to do a lot to get your friends back. I have a...an associate...who can help you."

"Why would your associate do that?"

"It's his story. I'll let him tell you."

"Does he have a name?"

"You got a favorite?"

"Hortense."

The man chuckled and lowered his hands. With slow deliberation, he bent, picked up his knife and made it vanish inside his jacket. "Good enough. He'll love that. *Hortense* will be in touch tomorrow morning. If you're nice, he might even buy you breakfast."

"Am I going to see you again?"

"No." The man tipped his head. "Good night, Miss Creed." He turned and walked away, whistling.

Reluctantly, Annja watched him go, wondering just exactly what she had gotten herself involved with. The dig had already gotten complicated enough.

12

"I have some information for you regarding Abdelilah Karam." Ernest Woolcot sounded tired but excited the next morning.

Wearing a robe, with a towel wrapped around her wet hair, Annja checked the time on her computer. It was 7:47 a.m. locally, which meant it wasn't yet three o'clock in Boston. "Seriously? You haven't been to bed?"

"I couldn't sleep. I started making calls to friends as soon as I got home from dinner."

Annja walked over to the window and peered out at the city. Erfoud was already bustling with the morning crowd and the influx of tourists. From her hotel she could see the crowd swelling at the souk. Today was Saturday. The marketplace was going to do massive business. Vendors had set up tents, pushcarts and roped-off areas filled with rugs, fossils brought in from the Sahara Desert, olives, spices and handmade clothing.

"You kept other people up, as well? I'm betting Miriam was *so* glad I called last night." Annja checked the front of the hotel visible from her room and tried to spot the man she'd encountered the night before. She couldn't see him, but that didn't mean he wasn't there.

Or someone else.

The possibility left her feeling a little cold. But so did the fact that Inspector Khouri hadn't called with any news of an immediate rescue of the archaeological team.

Annja had returned to the hotel and slept. She'd been without rest for too long, and sleeping no matter what was going on was something she'd learned to do in the orphanage and in the foster homes she'd been subjected to while growing up. Each of them had had their own cultures and languages and challenges. She'd been forced to learn to disassociate herself to keep from being overwhelmed.

"I got consumed with the hunt for Karam."

Annja understood that. She'd liked that about the professor, and had, in fact, been counting on that when she'd called him.

"Would you care to know what I found out?"

Retreating from the window, Annja sat on the edge of the bed. "I'd love to hear what you found out."

Annja took one of her journals from her backpack and opened it to a fresh page. She took out a pen from the case she carried. Later, she'd transcribe the notes to her computer, but the notebook shorthand worked when she didn't have access to electricity. Or in case she got separated from her backpack. Redundancy was a necessary evil in the field. "I'm ready."

"All right. From what I have learned, Karam was a historian of Muhammad and the first three caliphs."

"That period of history covers at least from 630 CE to 661 CE, right?" Annja clarified. "When Ali died after being attacked in the Great Mosque of Kufa."

"By Abd-al-Rahman ibn Muljam, one of the Kharijite assassins who tried to assassinate the three rulers of Islam at the time, yes. You know who the Kharijite assassins were, don't you?"

"Kind of a catchall phrase for Muslims who rejected Ali ibn Abi Talid's assumption of the caliphate. Loosely translates to 'those who went out.'"

"Yes."

"Karam wasn't a young man. Assuming he might have started as an historian apprentice at thirteen or fourteen years, he had to have been in his eighties when he was traveling through Morocco. That could well account for why he didn't finish his journey."

She snorted. "He didn't finish because someone bashed in the back of his skull."

"Oh, yes. That fact had escaped me. But that does beg a question, doesn't it?"

Annja wrote down the dates. "Who would murder an eighty-year-old man? Yeah, that one's occurred to me, too."

"The motive could have been robbery."

"Robbers wouldn't have left the coins on him."

"Maybe there was something else Karam was carrying that the murderer wanted."

"Okay, let's go with that for a moment, but let's turn it around. What was an eighty-year-old man doing so far from home? Did Karam have a family?"

"Unfortunately, we don't have that much information on his personal life. He wrote more about the Umayyad caliphs and Muhammad than he did about his own affairs."

"How much of his material did you uncover?"

"There's not a lot to be had, unfortunately, but it is all detailed. That's why, if your hunt turns out to be productive in turning up other documents, many historians will be interested."

"We'll cross our fingers." Annja was. She was more hopeful than she dared, but she knew at least part of that scroll was still out there waiting to be recovered. Unless Mustafa had destroyed it. "What do we have from Karam?"

"Surprisingly, one of the best finds was discovered on a Spanish galleon that washed up on the Scottish coastline in 1987. Ship's records and artifacts led to a confirmation that the ship was one of those that was lost in the August storms that wreaked havoc on the Spanish Armada."

"What was a document written by Karam doing on a Spanish ship? Not only is there a separation of hundreds of miles, but you're talking about almost nine hundred years of history."

"One of those passengers was an historian who had an interest in Muslim affairs. His papers had been locked up with the captain's manifests, and all of that largely survived the storm and over four hundred years of being sunk."

"It's amazing what the sea holds on to."

"And what she gives up. The historian wrote that he'd gotten Karam's papers from Morocco while taking passage on the Spanish vessel."

"How?"

"Think about the time frame, Annja. The British and the Spanish were fighting each other over control of the Atlantic Ocean, and privateering was rampant, but they weren't the only pirates sailing those waters."

"The Barbary corsairs." Annja shook her head. She should have remembered that.

"Exactly. The corsairs were operating from Tunis, Tripoli and Algiers, which are not so far from Morocco."

"Throw in the fact that a lot of the Barbary corsairs were actually Europeans, and it's easy to make a case that your Spanish historian spent time here."

"His name was Philip Gardiner, and he was actually an Englishman."

"An Englishman on a Spanish pirate ship?"

"Yes. That's not so unbelievable. Have you heard of Henry Mainwaring?"

Annja thought for a moment. "The English privateer turned pirate who got pardoned by King James I."

"Mainwaring was indeed an English pirate, but he was

also awarded Letters of Marque by Philip II, the then-king of Spain. King Philip planned the attempt to overthrow Elizabeth I after she supported the Dutch Revolt against Spain in 1587. He used Mainwaring against the British, before King James offered royal forgiveness."

"So Gardiner was on a Spanish ship when it went down in the Atlantic?"

"Yes. One of my colleagues works at the University of Aberdeen and has been a prodigious researcher of Muslim history. He was quite excited when I told him you'd possibly found Karam's body and part of a document. I sent him a copy of the scroll that you sent me. He's quite good with Kufic. He managed to translate what you had."

"He did?"

"Yes, but I'm afraid there isn't much. In the fragment you have, Karam sets up his case that he was chased from his home by assassins."

"Why?"

"The document doesn't say. That's part of the missing information. But Robert told me that if you could get your hands on the rest of it—or any more of it at all—he'd be deeply indebted to you if he could see it."

"That's not a problem. My Kufic is a little weak."

"So is mine." Woolcot yawned. "At any rate, that's where we stand at the moment, but I shall endeavor to keep digging. We still have to figure out how those documents came into Philip Gardiner's hands, and why the one you found was left in the Atlas Mountains. You'll contact me when you find out more?"

"Definitely. And can I get the translation your friend sent you?"

"Of course. I'll email it to your cloud address as soon as I hang up."

ANNJA FORCED HERSELF to finish getting ready before sitting down at the computer. Within a few minutes, she was dressed in jeans, good hiking boots and a green pullover.

She pulled up the use.net accounts first. There had been some chatter, but nothing definite had emerged. She'd gotten more information from Woolcot.

A quick check for the GPS markers showed they were still in place outside Marrakech. Seeing them gave Annja hope. She was just about to call Inspector Khouri to check on a potential rescue effort when a knock sounded at the door.

Instantly on alert because it was early and she didn't know anyone in the city, Annja approached the door and resisted the urge to peer through the peephole. People got hurt doing that. Even though no one could see in through the fish-eye lens, they could still see the shadow of someone standing there under the door.

She took hold of the door and pulled the sword into the room with her. "Who is it?"

"Hortense."

The man's voice sounded flat. Annja tried to place the accent but couldn't.

"What do you want?"

"You have friends in trouble. I am here to help."

"Why would you do that?"

The man paused and shuffled his feet. Even that small noise sounded irritated. "Because you need help. They need help. And if you don't get it to them soon, they're going to be dead. If they're not dead already."

"Why should I trust you?"

"Do you have anyone else in mind for this job, Miss Creed? If so, I'll be on my way. Otherwise, let me into the room so we can speak."

Annja considered that for only a moment. The bottom line

was that she *didn't* have another choice. The police and the military weren't likely to help, and Garin hadn't yet returned her phone call. Reluctantly, she opened the door.

13

The man standing in the hallway was tall, dark and handsome in a cold, distant way. He wore khaki cargo pants, hiking boots and a shirt unbuttoned over an olive-drab tank top. His hair needed cutting and his mutton chops were thick. There was a cruel curve to his full lips. Wraparound metallic green sunglasses covered his eyes.

He showed her his empty hands and she noticed the scarring over the knuckles and the old knife scar across his right palm that left the flesh puckered.

"Invite me in?" His voice was a rumble that came from deep inside his chest.

Annja let go of the sword, stepped back and opened the door.

He walked into the hotel room alone, then stood with his arms loosely folded.

Annja faced him, not giving an inch, but staying just out of his reach. "You know who I am."

He smiled at her, but it was cold and empty. "Call me Mac."

"Is that your name?"

"I'll answer to it."

"That's not exactly reassuring."

Mac dropped the smile. "Your friends don't have a lot of time. That's not reassuring, either. I thought you'd be more worried about them."

"How did you find out about me?"

"I know a guy at the police department who keeps me informed about out-of-towners who get into troubles they can't handle. If I think I can do something, I offer my services."

Annja got the sense that what he'd told her was close to the truth, but not the exact truth. She also knew how news could spread regarding foreigners. "I guess that guy's name is another name I don't get."

"That's how this works."

Annja studied the man. The accent sounded more American now, and there was even a hint of the Old South in there. "You're a mercenary."

He smiled a little, as if surprised. "That's blunt."

"I like blunt."

His shoulders lifted and dropped a fraction of an inch. "Sure. I'm a mercenary. That means I do what I'm paid to do. The fact that I'm still alive should tell you I'm good at it."

"How much would you charge for something like this?"

"An extraction from a hostile situation?" Mac's lips pulled back to expose his white teeth and a gold-capped incisor. "A lot."

"I don't have a lot." Even as she said that, Annja wished that she had a means to raise money that would interest the man.

"I understand that. I had you checked out. You've got a little, but it would take time to get it. Anyway, I'm not after your money." Mac walked over to the window and peered out, keeping himself pressed against the frame to present a low profile.

"I've known a few mercenaries. Generally they don't volunteer their services for free."

"I'm not. But you're thinking about what you can raise yourself. There are other avenue streams involved in this operation."

"What other *avenue streams?*"

"Mustafa doesn't just trade in slaves. His group also sells guns. Guns, especially in this part of the country, have an immediate resale value." Mac talked as if he was distracted, as if the sales pitch had already been presented and he was just running through it.

"How do you know about Mustafa? The police inspector I talked to yesterday didn't mention that."

"Because it's my job to know things like that. And because that police inspector isn't just going to volunteer information. If you want your friends back, you'll have to trust that I can do what I say I can do. That I'm a professional." Mac turned back to her. "When was the War of 1812?"

Annja didn't answer.

"I know it started in 1812, but that's about it. If it was important to what we're going to do, I'd trust you to know everything you needed to." Mac smiled like a cat, lazy and condescending. "We're both experts."

"I concede your point."

"Good. What I'm suggesting is this—we both have something to trade. I have a team capable of extracting your friends from a bad situation. You have the means of guiding me to them, and Mustafa. And Mustafa is rumored to travel with a sizable nest egg in gold and jewels, which I'll take as payment for my team's services. That way you're not out a nickel and you get your friends back." Mac paused. "If they're still alive." He eyed her speculatively. "Is that too blunt?"

"No. That's fine." That thought hadn't strayed far from Annja's mind.

Mac returned his attention to the window. "How soon can you be ready to go?"

"I'm ready now."

"Good, because I think you've got company."

"What do you mean?"

Mac pointed through the window and Annja joined him. Down in the street, a pair of black SUVs braked to a stop in front of the hotel. Men in suits got out, and from their complexions, Annja felt certain they were Middle Eastern. The drivers stood beside the vehicles and chased away the valets and bell boys. Eight other men strode toward the hotel's front door.

"Do you know them?" Mac remained calm and unhurried as he let go of the window drape and freed a semiautomatic pistol holstered at his back.

"No. And why do you think they're here after me?"

"Maybe they aren't. Maybe they're after some other American pop culture star who's staying at this low-rent hotel. You want to hang around and take the chance?"

"Not really." Annja had a bad feeling about the men. She'd learned to trust her instincts. However, she wasn't too happy about trusting Mac. She got the distinct impression he knew more than he was telling.

Still, he offered a chance at getting to Smythe and the others. If that didn't work out, she still intended to do what she could to free them.

"If I'm wrong, we've got an early start and you can chalk me up as paranoid." Mac looked around at the room. "You need much of this stuff?"

"Not really." Annja folded her computer and stuffed it into her backpack. The mini satellite dish went into a protective pocket. She hauled the backpack over her shoulders.

Mac stepped past her to the door. He grinned at her. "Never met a woman who could pack so fast."

"I'm feeling inspired."

Keeping his hand on his pistol under his shirttail, Mac opened the door and filled the opening so that Annja couldn't pass. Close on his heels, she peered over his shoulder.

Two maids with pushcarts occupied the hallway. No one else was around.

"All right, let's go." Mac took the lead and headed toward the back of the hotel, moving quickly toward the steps.

Annja moved with him. Her phone rang and she silenced it at once, noting the caller ID.

Garin.

She accepted the call and pulled it to her ear. "Now may not be a good time," she said quietly.

"I'm returning your call." Garin sounded irritated. "Do you know how many people are waiting for me to call them back even as we speak?" His voice was deep and strong, and it conjured up images of him. He was an imposing man, six feet four inches tall, broad and powerful, with straight black hair, dark eyes and a square jaw. He was an attractive man, and that part of him that was pure outlaw made him even more so.

"Is there going to be a test?"

Mac flicked an irritated glance at her as he opened the stairwell door and went through. "Put the phone away."

"Give me a minute." Annja didn't like being told what to do.

"A minute for what?" Garin covered the mouthpiece to talk to someone else and Annja knew she didn't have his full attention.

"I'm in Morocco."

"Am I supposed to be interested?"

"I was calling to ask for help."

Mac headed down the stairs and Annja shadowed him.

"Still not interested."

Garin was lying, though. Annja heard that in his voice.

"Some friends of mine have been captured by Bedouin slavers."

"Then write them off or set them free." Garin's reply was

blunt and matter-of-fact. "If they don't have anything you want, there's no reason to take the risk."

"Not exactly the answer I was looking for."

"I'm not the yellow pages. You're not the only person with problems." Garin sighed. "What do you need?"

Incensed now, Annja refused to even think about Garin helping. She had Mac and his people now. They could be in Marrakech within hours. She didn't know how long it would take Garin to mobilize a team. "Nothing. You called too late." Annoyed, she broke the connection and pocketed the phone, turning to follow Mac as he reached the first floor.

Mac wasn't happy with her, either. Annja read that in the man's body language. Her phone conversation hadn't worked out all the way around.

"Who were you talking to?"

"A friend."

"Does your friend have a name?"

"Yes."

Mac shot her a look. "Holding back information isn't smart."

"He doesn't have anything to do with this."

For a minute, Mac looked as if he was going to argue with her. Then he focused his attention on the rear door out of the hotel.

In other countries, the rear door would have had security locks. Some of the better hotels in Erfoud had security measures. But this one didn't. Annja had been in and out this one during the days she and Smythe had prepared for the dig. She'd liked the freedom to come and go whenever she wanted.

Opening the door, Mac peered out.

Behind Annja, footsteps crept into the hall. She glanced back and saw three of the men in black suits come around the corner from the main lobby. They spotted her at the same time and reached under their jackets.

The lead man spoke loudly. "Annja Creed! Stay where you are!"

Well, that confirmed they were there for her. Annja reached for the sword.

With a quick lunge, Mac caught Annja's elbow with his free hand and yanked her toward the door, throwing her off balance. She was halfway through the exit before she knew it. At the same time, he took one step in front of her and raised his pistol, firing a quick succession of shots that filled the hallway with thunder.

Morning sunlight slanted down into the narrow alley between the hotel and the building behind it. Erfoud, like many Moroccan cities, was a maze of alleys and buildings that offered blank walls at the first-floor level. Locked doors barred entrances to buildings and to outer courtyards.

The alley was so narrow that the black SUV hurtling down it almost scraped on both sides. The throaty roar of the motor echoed within the narrow space.

At a glance, Annja thought the vehicle looked a lot like the ones that had parked in front of the hotel. Through the dark windshield, a Middle Eastern driver kept both hands on the wheel and accelerated.

Mac stepped out into the alley and fired his pistol at the SUV. The bullets cracked the windshield in several places and skipped from the hood and roof. Then he put a hand in the middle of Annja's back and shoved.

"Run!"

Annja ran, knowing the alley was too long and that they'd never reach the other end of it before the SUV overtook them.

14

Annja spotted an arched doorway only a short distance ahead of her. She ran and hoped that she didn't trip over a cobblestone, trying not to think about how close the SUV was getting. She dodged to the right and fit herself into the doorway, pressing up hard against the wooden barrier as she slid her backpack off one arm and to the side.

She reached out and caught Mac, pulling the man into the doorway with her, his body slamming into hers as the SUV caught him a glancing blow. She held on tight to his jacket, hoping he wasn't badly hurt.

The SUV driver braked and the tires squealed.

Annja peered into the alley, thinking maybe they had time to sprint back to the other end. At the same time, though, the men inside the hotel boiled out into the alley, spotted her and opened fire.

Ducking back into the recessed door, Annja tried the door. It was locked. Beside her, Mac changed magazines and released the slide of his pistol. He was breathing hard but didn't appear to be injured, and he looked calmer than she felt.

"The door's locked."

He glanced at the door, then took aim at the lock. He fired three times, ripping splinters out of the wood and reducing the locking mechanism to broken metal.

He pushed the door and it swung inward.

Annja bolted into the courtyard, a larger, ornate *riad*. Moroccans designed their interior gardens so Islamic women would have privacy. Their "little Edens."

Evidently whoever owned this one did quite well. A fountain in the center of the space created a rainbow of spray before trickling down into the recessed basin. The traditional orange trees occupied one side of the courtyard. The sides of the *tadelakt* plastered walls were covered with *zellige* tiles. Quotes from the Koran were written on the tiles in flowing calligraphy.

The *riad* fronted three stories of personal dwelling space. Wrought-iron railings ran around the floors and stairs led to the upper floors on two sides. The walls were yellow and red.

Mac's pistol cracked behind Annja. "They're here."

"Did you come to me by yourself?"

"No."

Annja yanked the straps of her backpack back on. "Where's your team?"

"I've got a driver waiting, a couple of extra men. But they're not ready for something like this."

The SUV backed up to the open door. A man rolled down the window and took aim with a machine pistol. Mac fired a few shots and drove the man back into hiding.

"Come on." Annja sprinted forward, ignoring the stairs, and leaped for the second-story landing's edge. She caught hold and hauled herself up, climbing the railing and lunging for the next. Mac cursed loudly, but put his pistol away and climbed up after her.

Bullets slapped the front of the home and Annja felt sorry for whoever lived there. She hoped no one was home.

On the second floor, Mac flipped over the railing instead of following Annja up to the third floor. He drew his pistol, took deliberate aim at the man firing at them from the SUV and fired twice.

Hauling herself up, Annja glanced over her shoulder and saw the gunner in the SUV fall backward, already limp in death as his face gushed blood. She chinned herself onto the rooftop, then swung herself sideways to get a leg up on the edge and stay low. Her breathing came hard, but she was in good shape and moved easily.

Mac holstered his weapon again, stood and climbed to the railing to haul himself up to the third floor. He glared at Annja. "As far as exit strategies go, this one sucks."

"Only if we don't make it."

In the alley, men yelled commands. The SUV pulled forward, away from the front door, and the gunners from the hotel swarmed into the *riad*. They opened fire at once and bullets thudded into the house, scarring the walls and shattering the windows.

One of the bullets struck the roofline near Mac's right hand. The roof crumbled in his grip and he swung wildly, barely maintaining his one-handed grip. Even if a fall didn't kill him, it would probably leave him too injured to get away, and he'd be a sitting duck for the men hunting them.

Annja reached down and caught a handful of Mac's jacket, then pulled as hard as she could, adding her strength to his. His feet scrabbled for purchase and he came over the roof's edge, immediately sprawling across the curved roof tiles. A few of them shattered under his weight. Bullets hammered some to pieces.

Pushing herself up into a crouch, Annja headed toward the peak. Her boots occasionally slipped and shattered tiles slithered away. The steep angle of the roof made the going harder and even more dangerous.

When she reached the peak and spotted Mac struggling to come up behind her, Annja caught hold of one of the tiles, set her feet on either side of the summit and whipped her body as though she was throwing a Frisbee. The half-pipe tile whirled through the air and caught one of the gunmen in the face. The man collapsed backward as the broken tile tumbled down his body.

Mac hauled himself across to safety. Once they were on the other side of the roof, they had shelter from the gunners. Bullets still cracked the tile, then quickly stopped.

Annja crept out to the roof's edge and looked across. The next house was within easy jumping distance. She looked back at Mac and discovered he'd assumed a prone position with his pistol pointed before him.

"Are you coming?"

He didn't move as he said calmly, "Give me a sec."

One of the men clambered up the roof after them.

Annja hated watching what was about to happen. She'd killed before, but in the heat of battle, when her life—and the lives of others—was on the line.

As soon as their pursuer's head cleared the roofline, Mac put a bullet between his eyes, snapping his body back. He fell without a sound.

Mac turned toward Annja and carefully crossed the roof. "That'll hold them for a minute, but they'll be circling the building, and I don't know how many there are."

Without a word, Annja took the lead. They raced across the rooftops, moving across five other houses before dropping into another alley. Mac took out his sat phone and spoke rapidly in a voice too low for Annja to overhear. He finished his conversation and put the phone away.

"Who was that?" Annja shouldered her backpack and walked toward the end of the alley. The street looked clear.

"A friend. I'll introduce you in a minute. He's coming to pick us up."

"Then what?"

"Then we get my team together and go get your people."

Mac glanced at her with new awareness. "You had some good moves back there for an archaeologist."

"We were lucky."

"Yeah." Mac nodded, still studying her. "We were."

"Do you know who those men were?" Annja stared into his deep brown eyes and waited for him to lie to her.

Mac hesitated. "Yeah. They work for a guy named Habib ibn Thabit. Do you know him?"

Annja shook her head. The name held no meaning for her.

"Guy's a terrorist. One of the really bad ones. The CIA's tracking him all over the place. They want him as much as they ever wanted Osama bin Laden. Thabit networks money for other terrorist organizations, puts cells into motion to strike big targets."

"Did he follow you here?"

"Not me." Mac scratched one of his muttonchops. "Guy must have been after you. I barely beat him here. If I hadn't gotten to you when I did…" He shrugged.

Annja kept walking and thought about that. "Doesn't make any sense. I've never had any contact with this guy. Why would he come after me?"

"I don't know."

"Then how do you know those guys belonged to him?"

Mac gave her a cold grin. "Me and Thabit, we've traveled some of the same circles. This isn't the first time we've traded paint."

"Traded paint?" Annja considered what she knew about the man. "You're American. The accent is from the South. I guess you're a NASCAR fan?" The term came from the sport, from when two cars bumped into each other during a race and "traded" paint.

Mac's expression turned frosty. "A word of advice, Miss Creed?"

"Sure."

"Don't get to know me any more than you need to. We've got a business transaction, nothing more. I get your friends out of trouble. I keep you safe. I get Mustafa and his treasure cave. We keep that straight, we're going to do fine. Understand?"

"Yeah. Crystal."

Once they stepped into the street, a small sedan that had seen better days pulled to the curb. A young black man with a South African accent sat behind the wheel and looked anxious. He eyed Annja, then Mac.

"Are you okay?"

Mac nodded and opened the back door, then waved Annja in. She slid over. Mac got in beside her. "I'm good."

"I saw those guys getting out at the hotel. I almost came after you, but you told me to stay with the car." The young driver glanced over his shoulder, took his foot off the brake and edged into traffic.

"You did as I told you to do. Everything was fine."

The driver paused at a corner and glanced over his shoulder. "So you're Annja Creed?"

Annja nodded and offered her hand. "I am."

The young man smiled, but his expression remained cold, his eyes dead. He took her hand, and his flesh felt hot and rough. "I am Yahya. Do not worry, Miss Creed. Mac and I will take care of you." He took his hand back and accelerated.

Annja leaned back against the seat and looked at the street, but she remained acutely aware of Mac sitting beside her. He was quiet and contained, but she felt his energy. He was like some kind of wild animal poised and waiting for the next prey.

Annja had to focus on getting Smythe and the others back, but she couldn't help wondering about Habib ibn Thabit and why a man she'd never heard of might be so interested in her.

LESS THAN THIRTY MINUTES later, Annja stood in a warehouse at the edge of Erfoud. Mac had chosen the place as a staging area for his troops—he'd gathered eight more people to fill out his team. Six of them were men with obvious military training. Two were women, one African and the other Middle Eastern. The men wore street clothes and the women wore *hijabs*. Annja didn't think that necessarily made them Muslim, but it disguised them. In Morocco, women tended to be invisible.

The team moved as though they'd all worked together before. They had an easy camaraderie, a confidence.

Mac and Yahya were obviously the most familiar with each other. Annja had picked up on the mentor/apprentice relationship. The others were purely professional.

She had expected the mercenaries to be heavily armed, but they mostly carried personal weapons: pistols and knives, though the Middle Eastern woman carried a cut-down pump shotgun under her white wool burnoose.

They weren't exactly outfitted to take on Mustafa and his raiding party.

Annja held her sat phone to her ear. It rang four times before the other end picked up.

"Annja?" Bart McGilley sounded exhausted, and she thought perhaps he'd gotten a case late in the day that had lasted through most of the night.

"Yes. Look, I know I'm calling at a bad time."

Bedsprings squeaked at the other end of the connection, and sheets rustled as Bart rolled over. "What time is it?"

"Here or there?"

"What?"

"It's early there—4:00 a.m. or so."

"Are you in trouble?"

"No."

"You don't make a habit of calling me at 4:00 a.m. when you're not in trouble. That would end a friendship quicker than just about anything I know that didn't involve fire or killing a pet." Bart paused. "You still in Morocco?"

"Yeah. I ran into a guy here. I'd like to have him checked out."

"A guy in Morocco? And you want me to check him out here in New York?"

"Trust me. If this is who I was told he is, he'll show up when you start looking for him."

"Let me get a pencil." Bart was gone for a moment, then he was back. "Now give me a name."

Annja did and Bart put her on hold a second time. She listened quietly and watched Mac put his group through their paces. One of the team was already working at a notebook computer.

Bart came back to the phone. "This guy you're wondering about? He's trouble, Annja. The killing kind. Thabit's got his photograph on every major wall through the intelligence arena. I'm talking CIA, NSA, FBI, NCIS, the works. *Everybody*. He's real popular with the alphabet groups. How did you run into this guy?"

"Some of his men came after me this morning."

"You're sure about that?"

"Pretty sure." Annja believed Mac about that.

"What did they want with you?"

"I don't know. I didn't stick around to ask. Can you do me a favor? Can you check into this Thabit guy and let me know what you find?"

"Sure, but if you want my best advice, I'd say get out of there. Drop whatever you're doing and head home." Throughout their friendship, Bart had always spoken what was on his mind, but he'd never tried to guilt Annja.

"I can't."

"Annja, whatever you're working with, it's probably centuries old. Trust me, it can cool off for a while. At least until you regroup."

He didn't know about the rest of the dig team.

Bart sighed. "Let me do some digging. I'll get back to you as soon as I can."

"Thanks." Annja hung up as Mac started over to her. He'd seen her talking on the phone, but he didn't question her.

His eyes met hers. "I've booked passage for us on the grand taxi line. It's a three-hundred-mile trip across the desert to Marrakech." Mac glanced at the expensive watch on his wrist. "It'll take seven or eight hours to get there, at least— but there's no guarantee of safety along the way. Thabit will know about the dig team. He'll know about Mustafa."

"The police will give him that information?"

"They won't know it's Thabit asking. He'll work through a go-between."

Annja nodded. "I understand, but what I don't get is why Thabit is interested in this."

Mac shook his head. "I don't know. That part of this little tea party is your specialty. I'm just going to work on keeping us alive." He glanced at his watch. "We're pulling out in thirty minutes. Is there anything you need?"

"No. Thank you."

He excused himself and returned to his team, and Annja pulled out the piece of the scroll she'd managed to escape with. She didn't know if the answer to Thabit's interest was there, but the scroll was all she had. What secret had Abdelilah Karam carried to his grave?

15

Habib ibn Thabit stood inside the pilothouse of his two-hundred-and-ten-foot yacht and watched over the harbor. The number of boats had increased out on the water as shipments had come in, and some of those were doubtlessly manned by CIA agents or their assets. They didn't know about his boat, and the true ownership was hidden beneath a snowstorm of paperwork, so he felt safe enough. The main flurry of searches for the attackers on the warehouse the previous day had died down.

Dressed and fresh from the shower, Thabit drank sparkling water from a champagne flute. On a low hill overlooking the harbor, the Casbah looked like something out of a fantasy story. The *coupolettes* were covered with beaten metal that gleamed in the afternoon sunlight.

Thabit had visited the Casbah a number of times when he'd been a younger man, little more than a boy. Getting lost there was easy, but the sights were always worth seeing. The Citadel, as it was also known, was divided into the high city and the low city, and that division had continued until present time.

The structure was scarred by time and violence. As long as it had been on the hill, the structure had been a place of refuge and struggle. Damage from spears and arrows, from cannonballs and from rifles and small arms fire during the Algerian struggle for independence scarred the walls.

Thabit pulled his gaze from the old buildings of the Casbah and glanced at the satellite-fed television that hung in the corner of the helm. Reporters were still on the scene at the warehouse where the CIA agents had been ambushed. Fire had spread through the building, but it had been quickly brought under control. Still, the warehouse had suffered major damage.

According to the reports, several people were dead, including a handful of rescue personnel. Once it had been discovered that many of the dead were suspected of being American intelligence operatives, the Algerian police and military had closed in rapidly. Journalists still got tipped to the story and the probable identity of the dead men, and the story was blazing across the news services.

The CIA would have its hands full trying to contain the event, explain the men there and spin damage control.

"Mr. Thabit, if I may."

Turning, Thabit found Rachid standing behind him. Rachid was one of Thabit's chief sources of information. Slim and dapper, with a blue velvet eye patch covering his right eye, Rachid had spent half of his forty years in the United States, learning technology as well as how the Western minds worked. Not once had he forgotten he was a Muslim living in a land of enemies. During that time he had gone to college, worked in Washington, D.C., as a political aide to garner the American Muslim votes and had gotten to know several people within the intelligence communities.

A few years ago, his cover had been blown when the CIA had been on a fishing expedition. He'd barely gotten away with his life, and he'd lost his eye. When he was on a mission, he wore a prosthesis instead of the patch, but when he was around Thabit, Rachid wore the patch. It was his badge of arms.

"Yes?"

"I have some bad news, sir." Rachid stood stiffly at attention.

"What?" Thabit was splitting his time watching the live newsfeed and Rachid.

"Our agents in Erfoud were unable to take Annja Creed into custody."

Dark anger stole through Thabit. "What happened?"

"Someone else was there and aided her. If you wish, I can show you."

Thabit nodded and followed the smaller man to the inner offices of the yacht. The operations room had been set up like a military command vessel's CIC. Everything in the wheelhouse could be operated from inside this room, and there were no windows. Computer hardware covered the walls.

Rachid stood in the center of the room and held the small tablet PC that allowed him to control the computer. At his touch, a sixty-inch monitor rose out of a recessed area in the floor.

"The hotel where Annja Creed was staying had no security cameras." Rachid's voice was flat and factual. "Nor did any of the buildings on the other side of the streets that surrounded the building. However, there were a few people who saw what happened and took video on their phones and cameras, which they later uploaded to YouTube, Facebook and other social networks. My data miners sought them out and I patched them together."

The resulting video was patchy and jerky, and it jumped from place to place. Thabit watched in silence as the interception team strode into the hotel. Within minutes, gunshots played over the recording.

"They escaped through the rear of the building." Rachid

touched the tablet again. This time the image on the monitor magnified, showing Annja Creed in the alley behind the hotel. She stood near a tall black man.

"They escaped?"

"Yes. Annja Creed and this man." Rachid stroked the tablet PC again, and the image on the large screen magnified, losing some of the sharpness. "After enhancing this image, I have managed to identify him through facial recognition."

A yellow rectangle suddenly framed the man's face and lifted it out of the screen. Over the next few seconds, the features became clearer. Once the image looked clean, a window on the other side of the screen opened and began flicking through images faster than Thabit could follow.

The image froze on the new picture, which showed the man standing in an office building with an assault rifle canted in the crook of his arm. He looked fierce and hard edged, a dangerous man, with few scruples.

"His name is Rafe MacKenzie. From all accounts, he is a mercenary, but he also moonlights for the CIA. I believe they brought him into this situation."

"As an agent?" That interested Thabit.

"I believe so."

"Then the Americans have not yet given up their hopes of running me to ground." Thabit smiled at that. He'd bloodied their noses yesterday. He wouldn't mind doing it again. "What do we know about MacKenzie?"

"He's worked as an asset for the CIA in years past."

"In what regard?"

"An assassin. An extraction specialist. Anything the Agency wanted that requires guts. MacKenzie works on the contracted hits and operations."

"Why would the CIA involve MacKenzie with this woman?"

"I can only assume the Americans realized you were interested in the discovery Annja Creed has made in Morocco."

Thabit took a deep breath. If MacKenzie had been sent to Morocco to meet up with Annja Creed... Of course, they couldn't know the secret that had been buried for fourteen hundred years.

"How would the CIA have discovered my interest in Creed's find?"

Rachid shook his head. "I have no immediate answer to that, but I will look into it."

"Do so."

"At once."

Thabit turned and walked out the door, heading for his private rooms on the yacht. He tapped the headset that linked him to the yacht's control center. "Captain Abu."

The captain responded at once. "Yes, sir."

"Get us away from here."

"Yes, sir. What heading would you like?"

"Make for Morocco. Put us up in international waters."

"Yes, sir."

In his suite, Thabit poured himself a fresh glass of sparkling water and got out his prayer rug. He took off his shoes and knelt facing the east. For a moment he merely sat there and breathed while his mind wrestled with everything going through it. He had solved one problem rather easily, but now he had another before him.

His phone rang and he pushed the call through to his television. The screen shimmered, then revealed Mirza Almodarresi. A few years older than Thabit, Mirza was going gray at the temples, and a little heavier because he no longer took care of himself as much as he had when he'd been younger. Like Thabit, he preferred Western clothes, but he also wore a keffiyeh because he did business with the Europeans and Americans and did not want them to forget what he was.

Almodarresi sat at a massive desk, leaning back in his chair, his fingers steepled before him. Behind him, a small shark swam restlessly through a huge aquarium amid brightly colored coral. "Hello, Habib. I trust you are well."

"I am, Mirza. Thank you. I trust you are also well."

"Yes." Almodarresi nodded. "I see that you have been busy."

Thabit sipped his water. He knew what was coming and looked forward to getting it over.

Almodarresi frowned. "Are you going to tell me that you are not responsible for the deaths of the CIA agents in Algiers?"

"Have they been confirmed as CIA agents?"

Almodarresi waved that away irritably. "We are friends. Please do not insult me."

"As you say. In answer to your question to the deaths of those CIA operatives, yes, I am responsible."

"You are valuable to us. We would not see you lost."

Thabit smiled slightly. They could talk freely because the satellite phone connection was heavily encrypted. "I would desire not to be *lost* even more than you wish it."

"Then why do you antagonize the Americans?"

"They planted a mole within my organization."

Almodarresi was quiet for a moment. "You did not know this?"

"Of course I knew this. The work we have been doing has not been compromised. God looks out for us, as He always has."

"Why did you not simply get rid of the mole?"

"I did. I shot him myself yesterday."

Almodarresi frowned. "You could have done that quietly."

"The CIA has been closing in on some of my operations. I wanted to create some breathing space. It would do you and the others no good if I allowed myself to be hemmed in."

That was true. Thabit did what the other Shiite leaders would not: confronted their Western enemies and killed them where he could. Those like Almodarresi took comfort in their fortunes and spent money to have other people fight the war against the West. Thabit respected them for what they could do, but he detested them for what they didn't do. They were at war with the West, and with the current economy in that part of the world, great strides could be made.

If they weren't so afraid.

Mirza Almodarresi resided in Bahrain in wealth and privilege. Thabit had lived there, too, only without so much wealth and privilege—until he had decided to take it for himself. Almodarresi and his ilk depended on the oil industry that fueled the Bahrain economy. During his early years, Thabit had lived off that, too, only not so well.

Twelve years ago, Thabit had made his decision and he had charted his own course. His personal fortune was not so grand as that of Almodarresi and others, but Thabit had more power. They all knew it and hated that fact as much as they envied it.

Most of all, they loathed the simple truth that they needed him. He was the hard fist they reached for when they wanted to leave a mark on the Western world.

Almodarresi placed his hands on the desktop. He tapped a forefinger and struggled to look calm. But his bright eyes told Thabit the man was angry.

"Do you truly think you were becoming hemmed in, my friend?"

Thabit sipped his water. "I am closer to the situation than you are, so yes, I believe I am the authority in this matter." He paused. "And I will never make a habit of checking in with you before I choose to do something, Mirza. Do not do yourself the disservice of ever thinking that. You are no fool."

Almodarresi tapped his finger again, caught himself and

drew his hands back into his lap. "People worry that you are becoming too aggressive, Habib."

"I am convinced we are not being aggressive enough. We need to strike back now while the West is afraid and while they're fragmented."

"To follow that course of action is to further reveal ourselves. This mole you killed is proof that they know who you are." Almodarresi met Thabit's eyes directly. "Once the West knew who Osama bin Laden was, his days were numbered."

"Are you saying my days are numbered?"

"All of our days are numbered, my friend, but bold moves will shorten the number of those you have left. Be more patient."

"You do not fight a war patiently."

"No, but you change the world patiently. We are working God's will. We need to keep that uppermost in our minds."

Anger stirred Thabit. He put his hands behind his back and clenched them into fists. He did not need to entertain that discussion at this moment. Although he had emerged the victor, the skirmish with the CIA had created repercussions. The discovery Annja Creed had potentially made in Morocco might prove damaging.

And now Almodarresi was daring to call him on the carpet.

"I am a holy warrior, Mirza. I am a tool for God. I am a weapon He uses to strike against the unbelievers."

"I know this, my friend. I—we—are also worried that you will draw the wrath of the Sunnis upon yourself. Iran and some of the other nations fear Western and Israeli aggression as a result of the attacks."

"No, the worst aggression that the West sees is the alliances being made between Muslim warriors and criminal organizations. They have seen through the curtains you and your people have tried to pull over funding. The Western powers are targeting those endeavors more than they are targeting anything I am doing."

Almodarresi frowned and pursed his lips, obviously holding back a retort.

"Greed is baring the bones of those operations. That is what is making them more vulnerable."

"There are many who would not like it that you take it upon yourself to say such things."

Thabit stared at him. "Tell me I am wrong."

Almodarresi hesitated just a moment. "You are wrong." But the declaration was made without any fire.

Thabit smiled, knowing he had scored a victory even though it would never be acknowledged. "The men I lead against the West are true Shiites, Mirza. They are not infatuated with wealth found in this world. God has their fortunes waiting for them in the next for dying in battle with their enemies."

Thabit had allied himself with desperate men whose belief in the words of God was the backbone of all that they were.

Irritated with the conversation, Thabit squared his shoulders. "I must take my leave, Mirza. There are many things I must attend to."

A frown formed on Almodarresi's face, then quickly disappeared. But it was there long enough to let Thabit know the man was not pleased about being dismissed so casually. "As you will, Habib. But do take my words into consideration."

"Of course. May God watch over you."

"And you."

Thabit ended the call and the connection to the television. He turned his thoughts to Annja Creed and the problem she presented. Even though he did not presently know where she was, there was a way to find her.

He punched up Rachid's ops room on his phone. The computer specialist answered at once.

"We have lost Annja Creed." Thabit walked over to one of the windows and looked out. The Algerian harbor receded and they motored past a sailboat with a full-bellied canvas taking advantage of the wind. The yacht's powerful engines vibrated the floor beneath his feet and the vessel rose and fell slowly as it pushed out to sea.

"For the moment. I expect to have her whereabouts soon."

"She is going to Marrakech, is she not? You said she was trying to find help for the archaeological crew kidnapped by Bedouin slavers."

"Yes."

"Put a team in Marrakech. Let them seek out these Bedouins. Perhaps we can get ahead of this woman and she will come to us."

"Of course."

Thabit hung up and turned from the window. Rafe Mac-Kenzie was a mercenary. Mercenaries, as Thabit knew, were not prompted by duty to country or God. They lived on cash.

Perhaps an arrangement could be made. If not, Thabit would be prepared for that, too.

16

R702
Between Erfoud and Marrakech
Kingdom of Morocco

Cramped and uncomfortable, Annja sat in the grand taxi's rear seat squashed between Mac and two of his men. The taxis weren't built for luxury. The vehicle was an old Mercedes sedan that had been converted to diesel fuel, and the fumes had ignited a dull, percussive headache between Annja's temples that was working into her shoulders. The vehicle had no air-conditioning so the dust-laden wind whipped through the windows and the constant taste of alkali lingered on her tongue.

Mac sat to Annja's left and the butt of the pistol he carried on his right hip dug into her side. She'd tried shifting several times to find a more comfortable position, but that seemed beyond her. She struggled not to look at the dashboard clock to see how much time remained on the trip.

Outside, darkness crept across the eastern sky and stretched toward the west. They were due to arrive in Marrakech at midnight, so relief was still hours away. To make matters worse, the driver—a lean older man with a gray beard— chain-smoked and listened to the same Taylor Swift CD over and over, adding occasional refrains in a strange mix of English and his native tongue.

She occupied herself with the information Bart had sent her regarding Habib ibn Thabit. As Bart had said, the man was dangerous, and wanted in a dozen countries.

Thabit had been born in Bahrain, had grown up there, then, twelve years ago when he'd been twenty, he'd disappeared. It hadn't been until Thabit's name had started turning up in terrorist-related counterespionage operations that anyone figured out who he was.

Mac gazed at the tablet PC over her shoulder. The battery was getting low. She'd have to charge it soon.

"Where did you get your information on Thabit?" Mac's voice carried just enough above the wind whistling through the windows to reach Annja's ears.

"I've got a good friend on the New York police force." Annja felt a little self-conscious looking at the information. She'd also sent Bart a picture of Mac and discovered that the mercenary's real name was Rafael MacKenzie and he'd been born in Mobile, Alabama. He'd graduated high school. Then—like Thabit—the man's background grew sketchy, a mix of half truths, outright lies and cover stories. His background as a mercenary was solid, but he'd been a lot of other things over the years, as well. He hadn't returned to the United States very often.

Bart hadn't been thrilled to discover that she was with MacKenzie.

"What did your friend tell you?"

Annja looked at MacKenzie in the fading light as Taylor Swift sang "And I can't breathe without you" while accompanied by the off-tune driver with a Moroccan accent. The ludicrousness of the moment struck her and she couldn't help smiling.

MacKenzie frowned. "What do you find so amusing?"

"The serenade. The fact that your gun is poking me in the ribs. Has been for hours. And we're both bored as we're racing toward a dangerous encounter."

"Sorry." MacKenzie shifted and leaned more into his door. The movement helped some, but the gun butt wasn't going away.

"As for Thabit, he led a very affluent life in Bahrain for a while." Annja nodded at the tablet PC. The image there showed a young Habib ibn Thabit. "Then, when he was twenty, he left college, left Bahrain and went to Afghanistan."

"Joined up with Osama bin Laden?"

"No, but he did join up with Shiite terrorists training inside Helmand province. He was identified by U.S. Marines and he barely avoided getting killed when the United States attacked the Taliban and al Qaeda."

Something ghosted through MacKenzie's dark eyes. "Those were...interesting times." MacKenzie smiled but there was nothing friendly in the expression. "Couldn't go home again."

"Thabit could and did, but it wasn't to hide out. He started recruiting hard-core Shiite believers to his cause to bring the West to its knees."

"Ambitious."

"I'm sure he's not trying to do it all at one time."

"It's guys like that who keep me in business." MacKenzie studied her. "You know all that, but you have no idea why the man would be interested in you or what you found out there in those mountains?"

"No." Annja sighed. She shifted and tried to get comfortable again, but it was impossible.

For a moment MacKenzie looked out the window and studied the countryside. "Are your GPS locaters keeping track of Mustafa and his group all right?"

"They are."

"Maybe when you get to see the rest of that scroll, you'll know more."

"Possibly." Annja took a deep breath. "The main thing is getting those people safe." When MacKenzie didn't answer her, she felt disappointed and slightly irritated. Trying to relax the tension in her neck, she laid her head back and closed her eyes. With the driver crooning Taylor Swift over the sound of the whirring tires and the wind rushing through the windows, she drifted off to sleep.

Marrakech

"HEY." A ROUGH HAND shook Annja awake. "Hey, wake up."

She curled her right hand into a fist and almost smashed it into MacKenzie's face before she realized what was going on. His eyes widened in surprise, but he'd already caught her fist in his.

The car was stopped in darkness out in front of a small building. A few streetlights lined the thoroughfare, but to the north—she got her directions from the compass app on her phone—she saw a large pool of light. It must've come from Djemaa El-Fna, one of the main squares in the city.

Around her, the men climbed out of the taxis. MacKenzie paid the drivers and the vehicles immediately headed in the direction of the square.

MacKenzie nodded toward the few suitcases his team had brought with them. "Let's get the rooms squared away, then go see about dinner."

"Sure."

"I'm going to assign a couple men to watch over our things and the rooms. Would you like them to keep your bag?"

Annja hooked her thumbs in the backpack straps and shifted the load between her shoulders. "No. Thanks, anyway." She didn't know if MacKenzie made the offer out of thoughtfulness or wanted the chance to go through her notes and computer.

"Okay." MacKenzie leaned down and picked up one of the bags. He led the way.

THE CHECK-IN PROCEDURE was a breeze. Within a few minutes, Annja was in her room. This one was even smaller than the one she'd quit that morning, but after being packed into the taxi for eight hours, it seemed expansive.

Knowing she had a few minutes before meeting with MacKenzie, she retreated to the bathroom, stripped off and took a quick shower. She washed her underwear and sports bra in the tub and hung them up to dry, then dressed in the spare set she had in her backpack and put the same clothes back on.

She had to get more clothing soon.

By the time she heard a knock on the door, she felt somewhat refreshed, but she knew she was going to sleep hard that night when she returned to the room. She regretted leaving the bed, but her stomach wouldn't be denied.

THE CITY SQUARE WAS awesome to behold. People lined up at the food stalls from a dozen different countries, judging from their dress. The smell of spices and cooked meat and fish overpowered even the scent of dust that hung in the air. Conversations in a half-dozen languages floated all around Annja as she waited for her turn at a kiosk.

MacKenzie stood nearby, but his attention wasn't on her. His gaze roamed the crowd.

She purchased a *tajine,* a clay pot filled with lamb and vegetables and seasoned with *ras el hanout,* a mixture of spices that included cinnamon, cardamom, cloves, peppercorn and paprika. There were probably more ingredients, but that was all Annja could detect. *Ras el hanout* was made differently from family to family, business to business. She also ordered a *halwa shebakia,* a dessert of twisted deep-fried bread covered in honey and sprinkled with sesame seeds.

After thanking the vendor, she waited till MacKenzie had ordered his food. Together, they proceeded to the street and flagged down a taxi. Two of MacKenzie's men, also supplied with their meals, rode with them.

They returned to the hotel lobby. Annja removed the conical covering over the *tajine* and inhaled the pungent aroma. She picked up her fork and set to work without a word as MacKenzie did the same.

For a time, they ate in silence. Annja watched MacKenzie out of the corner of her eye and caught him watching her, as well.

"Something on your mind?" MacKenzie blew on a forkful of food.

"No." Annja was lying and she knew he knew it.

A few minutes later, as Annja was tearing her *halwa shebakia* into more manageable bite-size pieces, MacKenzie's sat phone rang. He answered it, talked cryptically for a moment, then put it away and glanced at Annja. "One of my team has found a man who has information about Mustafa. I'm going to talk to him in a few minutes."

"No." Annja popped the last of her dessert into her mouth and chased it down with tea. "*We're* going to speak to him."

MacKenzie didn't even try to be polite. "That's not a good idea."

"Perhaps not, but that's how this is going to happen."

For a moment Annja thought MacKenzie was going to argue. Then, slowly, his hackles fell and he gave her a grudging nod. "All right. If that's how you want it."

17

"You do realize this could be a trap." Annja walked a step behind MacKenzie as they entered one of the many alleyways that threaded through the city. The alleys weren't always signed, but she'd learned to memorize locations by landmarks.

The mercenary had his hand on a pistol tucked into his belt at his back waistband. His shirt disguised the weapon. He moved like a big cat, easy and sure-footed. "Yeah." He grinned mirthlessly. "That's pretty much the reason I wanted you to stay behind."

Point, Annja conceded. She knew he was probably better at handling himself in situations like this than she was, and that her presence there made things harder on him, but she couldn't have stayed back in the hotel without anything to do.

One of MacKenzie's men walked thirty feet ahead of them. Two others trailed them. Two more sat in rental cars on either end of the alley, prepared to speed to the rescue if necessary. MacKenzie had planned the operation quickly and succinctly. Annja had been impressed. When he'd finished, no one had asked questions.

The point man walked past the target doorway and stood against the alley wall, hidden in the shadows and holding a machine pistol beneath his light jacket.

"You ready to do this?" MacKenzie stopped in front of the door.

There was no name or number. The blemished surface showed a history of violence and disrepair. Not too long ago, someone had tried to liven up the entrance by painting it maroon. Enough light came from the street to reveal the color, but only just.

"Yes." Annja hitched her backpack a little to one side with her left hand and closed her right around the hilt of the sword in the otherwhere. One good yank and it would be in the alley with them.

MacKenzie kept his right hand on his pistol, turned sideways to make himself a skinnier target and rapped on the door. The sound echoed down the alley.

A moment later, a peephole slid open in the center of the door. Weak moonlight danced in the whites of the man's eyes as he peered out.

"You are Walker?" The man spoke in heavily accented English.

"Yes."

The man peered past MacKenzie and stared at Annja. "How many men did you bring with you?"

"Three."

The man considered for a moment. "Only you and one of the men can enter. And the woman."

"The woman stays out here."

The eyes narrowed. "This is a mistake."

"What's a mistake?"

"Leaving the woman out here. It is not safe for a woman so beautiful."

Said by someone else and under other circumstances, that might not be so creepy. Annja waited, deciding then and there she wasn't going to remain in the alley. There was already too much out of her control.

MacKenzie started to speak, but was interrupted by the man behind the door.

"If you wish the information you requested about Mustafa, the woman must enter. This is—how do you say in your language? A deal breaker."

Annja stepped forward. "Let's go." She nodded at the man on the other side of the door. "I'm coming."

"Good. We have cheese and bread. Very good cheese and bread." The eyes vanished and the locking mechanisms holding the door closed started ratcheting open. There were enough of them to be impressive.

MacKenzie shot Annja a look. "Do you know what you're getting yourself into?"

Annja kept her voice pitched low so she wouldn't be heard. "With me, that gives us three people on the other side of that door. Shouldn't you be feeling a little better about that?"

Cruel humor twisted MacKenzie's lips. "You like taking risks, don't you, archaeologist?"

Before Annja could decide whether or not she was going to reply, or whether or not she was going to lie, the door opened. The arched entrance was dark, but light gleamed off to the left. In the center of the courtyard, she spotted a garden and water shimmering on a small pool. At least two shadows patrolled on the upper floor walkway across from the entrance.

The gatekeeper stood revealed in the dim light. He wore a white shirt and white pants and a tan keffiyeh. His short beard split to reveal his bright smile as he half bowed and waved Annja inside. "Please to enter."

Annja did, with MacKenzie and Yahya following her along the narrow stone path that led to an enclosed dining patio. The candlelight came from the table, and now that she was closer she could smell their spicy scent.

A lean, wolfish man with a neatly cropped black beard and moussed locks stood up from behind the table as Annja approached. He wore an elegant suit and she would have bet money that he'd gotten dressed to meet her. It was proof that the man sitting there had known exactly who he would be talking to when he contacted MacKenzie or his people.

"Ah, welcome to my humble home. I am Houssine." He held his hands wide and smiled. In the candlelight, he loomed large against the stone wall behind him. He reached for Annja's hand. "I know who you are, Miss Creed. I have enjoyed your show on several occasions."

Annja didn't know if that was a lie or not, but the words came out easily enough. She took his hand and felt the calluses along his palm.

"It's a pleasure to meet you."

Houssine released her hand and turned to MacKenzie. "And you are?"

MacKenzie took the man's hand. "You can call me Al."

The name struck Annja as humorous even though this was not the best time for humor.

"Please. Sit." Houssine gestured to the chairs around the table. As the gatekeeper had promised, there was bread and cheese, and several selections of fruit. "Help yourselves."

"We just ate." MacKenzie's voice was neutral. "And we don't have much time."

"All right." Houssine poured tea into cups sitting near Annja and MacKenzie, then into his own. "What do you wish to know?"

"Where Mustafa is. How many men he has." MacKenzie sat in the proffered chair, but he was anything but relaxed. "I was told you were the one who would know."

Houssine picked up his tea and sipped, then held it in both hands, elbows resting on the tabletop. "I do know about such things."

"My friends were kidnapped by him three days ago." Annja didn't touch the tea. She slid out of her backpack, but set it close to her chair.

"The archaeological expedition, yes, I had heard of that.

Most unfortunate." Houssine's voice took on a timbre of sympathy, but emotion didn't touch his dark hazel eyes. "But you're here to rectify that, are you not?"

MacKenzie ignored the question. "Tell us what you know about Mustafa."

"Do you have a map?"

The mercenary reached into his shirt pocket with his left hand. His right hand had never left his hip. Yahya had remained apart from the table and had taken up a position across the enclosed space from the man who had answered the door. The young man's attention was directed solely at Houssine's apparent major domo, who had also stayed away from the table.

Other than the open front of the dining enclosure, a door behind Houssine led into what Annja guessed was the main house. Above them, a latticework held a thick mesh of flowering vines that filled the area with sweet scent. Despite the glimmering candlelight and their effusive host, she couldn't help but feel a little cornered.

One-handed, MacKenzie brought out the map, shook it once so that it unfolded with a whip-crack and laid it on the table.

Houssine smiled and gestured to the map. "May I?"

"Be my guest." MacKenzie slid the map across.

Studying the map, Houssine took out a gel pen and his cell phone. He thumbed a few buttons, then studied the screen as the soft blue glow played over his hard features. The light revealed that he was older than Annja had believed, probably in his mid- to late forties.

"I have map coordinates for Mustafa. Longitude, latitude. Of what was his last known location." Houssine wrote quickly and his handwriting was surprisingly clean and uniform.

"How did you get those coordinates?" MacKenzie watched the man write.

"I had business with him."

"What kind of business?"

Houssine looked up and gently pushed the map back across the table. "The kind of business that I do. I sold him guns."

Again using one hand, MacKenzie refolded the map and put it back in his shirt pocket. "How many guns?"

"Several."

"What kind?"

"Military grade."

MacKenzie scratched his chin with his free hand. "That's going to make our job harder."

"I wasn't doing business with you at the time or I might have curtailed my sales." Houssine shrugged. "Of course, from Mustafa's point of view, my telling you where to find him isn't going to help him any."

"You have a point. What about the number of men?"

"Thirty. Possibly thirty-five. If the group gets much larger, Mustafa is going to find it hard to remain hidden out there. He doesn't have a lot of supporters. He has lived a violent life, and I expect him to meet a violent end." Houssine leaned back in his chair. "As for yourself, *Al,* you have a choice."

MacKenzie lifted an inquisitive eyebrow. "A choice?"

"About whether you meet a violent end."

As Houssine's voice tailed off, the ruby-red disc of a sniper scope dawned on MacKenzie's chest. Annja spotted the light immediately and couldn't help checking her own chest to see if another had formed there. Nothing.

Smiling and self-assured, Houssine brought up a pistol from under the table. "Mustafa didn't just buy my guns. He also bought my services. He wants Annja Creed alive, but he doesn't care whether you live or die. So, which will it—"

MacKenzie uncoiled like a striking rattler. He lifted his boot and drove it into the table, knocking it into Houssine's chest and driving the man over backward. Pushed back by the force he'd used on the table, MacKenzie went over backward before the gunner with the scope could fire.

The gatekeeper brought out a pistol, but before he could even get it up, Yahya pulled out his own weapon and shot the man twice in the chest before dropping into a loose roll and coming to his feet beside the houseman. He pointed the pistol at the man's head and squeezed the trigger one more time to ensure the kill. Then he rose up in a half crouch against the stone wall as running feet slapped against the stones.

18

Bailing from her chair, looking back along the stone pathway leading through the courtyard, Annja closed her hand on the sword's hilt and yanked it from the otherwhere. Moonlight gleamed along the razored steel as she brought the weapon around in front of her. She leaped onto the table, crossed it in one stride and jumped down again to confront Houssine. The man lay stunned on his back.

Annja kicked the pistol from his hand and fisted his shirt. He tried to reach for her but Annja ducked forward quickly and yanked him upward, driving the top of her head into his face. When he fell back, he looked dazed again, and this time blood streamed from his nose and mouth.

Behind her, MacKenzie rolled to his feet with his pistol in both hands. He and Yahya laid down cover fire that bought them a brief respite from the men closing in from the courtyard.

Still in a crouch, Annja reached out and tipped the heavy table over. Judging from the weight and the solid wood construction, it would provide a brief barrier from flying bullets.

"MacKenzie, back here."

The mercenary glanced over his shoulder as he changed out magazines in his weapon. He understood at once. "Yahya."

Together the two men crouched behind the shelter with her

as a hail of bullets ripped into the table. The deadly leaden storm didn't penetrate, though.

Annja felt certain from the muzzle flashes she saw that eight or ten gunmen were closing on their position. Getting back the way they'd come was out of the question. She glared down at Houssine.

"Get on your feet."

Groggily, Houssine tried but couldn't quite manage it. Annja pulled him up. Almost immediately, bullets slapped into the wall beside him, driving stone splinters into his face.

"Stop shooting! Stop shooting!" Houssine wrapped his arms around his head and ducked.

Sudden silence filled the courtyard.

Annja shoved Houssine toward the door. "Open it."

Houssine cursed and fumbled with the door, finally getting it to open back into the adjacent building. Dim electric light filled the eight-foot hallway that led into the house's main room. Houssine started forward.

Annja held on to him by his shirt collar as she grabbed her backpack from where she had left it, then followed. "How many men are in the house?"

"I don't know."

Annja yanked on Houssine's shirt collar at the same time she kicked the man's rearmost foot sideways, causing him to trip. Using his momentum and the leverage she had, she rammed Houssine's face into the wall. He cursed and covered his face.

She let him feel the razor-sharp sword's edge against his neck. "Don't lie to me or I'll kill you right here." She wouldn't, of course. But Houssine had been prepared to do that, so he couldn't imagine that anyone wouldn't do the same if they had proper motivation.

"Five or six. I don't know. I don't keep track of all of them."

"Sloppy management. Guess you missed the *Villainy for Dummies* book."

Houssine wiped his face and didn't say anything further as Annja propelled him forward. She glanced over her shoulder and saw that MacKenzie and Yahya were following. Both men held their pistols up before them and remained in crouches as they backed toward her.

As they stepped into the main room, Annja spotted the sniper up on the second-floor landing, crouching behind his rifle at the railing. Only forty feet away, the sniper didn't have to be good to hit his target.

"MacKenzie!" Annja kept Houssine in front of her despite his attempt to get away, but two more men in the room were closing in on her fast.

Desperately, Annja shoved her captive forward, keeping him upright for only another five or six steps. Houssine went down, tripping over his own feet. Knowing she didn't have much time to act, Annja released her hold on the man, let go of the sword and sprinted across the room as a bullet clipped her cheek.

The harsh crack of the weapon pummeled her hearing. The two men who had closed on her were suddenly behind her, lifting their weapons.

Annja sprinted for all she was worth, veering to her left. When she reached the wall there, she put her left foot up against it at an angle, gained momentary purchase and shoved herself up as though she was running up the wall. She managed two steps, then gravity started to reassert itself over her momentum and she shoved toward the second-floor landing.

Catching the railing in one hand, Annja swung forward, caught hold with her other hand and managed to vault over the railing without it tearing away. The sniper tried to whirl around, astounded that she'd managed to get up there with him, but he was too late. Annja set herself, spun and delivered a roundhouse kick to the man's head that knocked him over the railing.

The rifle, abandoned as he fell, teetered on the railing for an instant before Annja seized it. She didn't bother with the telescopic sights. She just pointed at the nearest man downstairs as the sniper crash-landed, then pulled the trigger.

The rifle bucked against her shoulder and the bullet caught her target somewhere in the chest. Surprised, the man staggered for a moment, tried to shoot his weapon, then sprawled over Houssine.

The other man already had Annja in his sights, but before he could pull the trigger, MacKenzie shot him through the head. The corpse dropped bonelessly into the pool in the middle of the room and blood fanned out through the water.

MacKenzie put a foot on Houssine as the man tried to get up, then shot him in the face. Houssine slumped back as MacKenzie brought out his sat phone and talked hurriedly.

Annja tossed the rifle aside and raced down the steps on the side of the room near the main door. Yahya exchanged bullets with the men in the hallway, keeping them pinned down, while MacKenzie opened the front door.

A moment later, MacKenzie led the way outside, immediately turning right to face the oncoming car driving without its headlights on. He opened the door and ushered Annja inside, then Yahya. When he closed the door, he took the front passenger seat for himself and the driver got under way.

MacKenzie reloaded his weapon and slid it out of sight just as they roared out onto the street.

BACK AT THE HOTEL, Annja felt hollowed out and was regretting eating so heavily at dinner. She walked through the lobby expecting more of Houssine's gunmen—or the local police— to jump her at any moment.

MacKenzie walked her to her door. "You going to be all

right?" His warm brown eyes met hers and he seemed genu-inely interested.

"I'm fine." But Annja kept remembering how MacKenzie had so cold-bloodedly killed Houssine. That was something Roux or Garin would have done without a second thought, as well. Trained killers.

She hoped she never grew that callous, but she knew she was already a far cry from where she'd been when she first picked up Joan's sword. Would Joan have turned out like Roux and Garin if she had lived long enough? Annja had never wondered that before, and she didn't like thinking about it now.

"I'm fine. Thanks."

MacKenzie nodded. "That move up the wall, that was pretty awesome."

"Adrenaline." Since she'd picked up the sword she'd be-come capable of feats of strength, speed, endurance and agil-ity that she'd never been capable of before. She didn't know if the sword gave her those skills or if it had simply unlocked those abilities within her.

MacKenzie rubbed his stubbled chin with the back of his hand and dried blood flaked away. He nodded toward the room. "Are you okay in there by yourself?"

"I'm fine. But what about the police? Or Houssine's men?"

"Houssine's people are going to be looking for a new em-ployer. A lot of them will scatter back to the streets. That's where he got them from, and they haven't learned anything better working for him. As for the police…" MacKenzie shrugged. "They're not here now, so I'm betting they don't know anything about us. Strangers wander in and out of this city every day. We get through tonight, we're gone by first light. Nothing left of us but a vapor trail." He smiled. "Get a good night's sleep. You'll need it tomorrow."

"You, too."

MacKenzie turned and walked away. Annja watched him

go, noting the bloodstains on his pant leg from when he'd shot Houssine on the ground. She made herself turn away and open the hotel room door.

WHILE ANNJA HAD BEEN OUT, things had developed with the document on the user sites. Annja was grateful for that. As tired as she was, she was still buzzing with adrenaline and knew she wasn't going to be able to sleep for a while.

She sat cross-legged on the floor and cradled her notebook computer in her lap. Freshly showered, she felt somewhat better, but she wanted to be back in her loft in Brooklyn surrounded by all her things.

With all her electronics plugged in and charging, she went through the research sites and forums she usually haunted, but came up with nothing but speculation about Abdelilah Karam's work. Demonscientist@blackartsbedone.org had the strangest theory.

Everybody knows how Solomon locked all the demons in his seals, but not everybody knows that Abdelilah Karam was doing the same thing for the Muslims that Solomon was doing for the Jews. Do you really think that Christianity named all the demons? No! There were lots of them in the Muslim world, too. Muhammad believed he'd been possessed by demons. Check it. Abdelilah Karam was locking away all the Muslim demons unleashed by the writing of the Koran.

Annja sorted through the rest of the emails and most of the forums and didn't find anything new. However, when she checked her personal email and phone log, she discovered messages left by Dr. Khadija Zayd, a historian from Aligarh Muslim University's Centre of Advanced Study.

Ms. Creed, what an amazing discovery! I congratulate you on your good fortune. I only just learned of your interest in

Abdelilah Karam through a mutual acquaintance, Dr. Wool-cot. Ernest is a dear friend.

Also, I know he has Professor Manning working with you regarding the translation of the manuscript you found. I can't wait to hear what he has to say once he has finished. This must be very exciting for you.

I believe I am in possession of some information you and my esteemed colleagues lack. Abdelilah Karam was "encouraged" by Muhammad himself to work to keep the Muslim people together. You see, Muhammad knew—in the days of his failing health—that his succession would be most troubling. Given that the Muslim community—my community, in fact—has fractured as much in its own way as have the various other religions, he was, of course, most prophetic.

I jest. But I would like to talk to you about Abdelilah Karam at some point. Perhaps I could offer you new insight into what he was possibly doing in Morocco.

Yours most warmly,
Khadija Zayd

"Well, well, Professor Zayd, I would like to speak with you, too." Annja opened her sat phone's address book and entered the professor's information. It was too late to call now, but Annja resolved to do that first thing in the morning. Waiting till then was going to be hard.

19

"Do you know who the woman is talking to?" Yahya sat across from MacKenzie at the breakfast table in the small restaurant only a few blocks from their hotel. Filled with nervous energy, he unconsciously tapped the table with this right thumb.

MacKenzie glanced through the window and watched Annja Creed as she leaned against the building and talked on her sat phone in the morning shade. The woman had seemed distracted this morning, and he'd gathered it had something to do with that scroll she wasn't talking about. She ate out there, as well, dipping her hand occasionally into her take-out bag.

"No." MacKenzie turned back to the *bissara* he was having for breakfast. He wasn't a fan of split-pea soup mixed with olive oil first thing in the morning, but the idea of trying to get to lunch on a piece of bread and jelly wasn't something he wanted to deal with this morning. It was times like this that he missed his granny's breakfasts: biscuits and gravy, ham hocks and scrambled eggs. Something that would stick to a man's insides.

"She seems very excited." Yahya frowned as he watched her.

"She is very excited."

"She doesn't even know if her companions are still alive."

"She hopes they are. You can see it in her eyes." Mac-

Kenzie sipped his tea. "It's not about those people the Bedouin have. She's an archaeologist. It has to do with that scroll they found when the Bedouin took them prisoner. She hopes to recover the rest of it." Even though Annja had not mentioned this, he knew it was true.

Yahya looked at him and was quiet for a moment. "Do you think it's a treasure map?"

MacKenzie had to fight to keep from grinning. Yahya didn't open up to many people, but when he did, he could get his feelings hurt easily. And hurting Yahya's feelings could be dangerous. MacKenzie had seen the young man kill over the slightest affront. He didn't think Yahya would ever try to kill him, or that the young man could if he tried, but he didn't want to test either theory.

"No."

"Why?"

"She has never referred to it as a map. Neither have the people who sent us here."

"Do you think they would know?"

MacKenzie chose to give the impression he was giving that possibility some thought. "I do."

"Or that they would tell us?"

"That would be another matter."

Yahya shook his head, then slurped more of the thick soup. "It must lead to a treasure."

"Why?"

"Nothing else would be so important. This man, Thabit—"

"Yahya, listen to me," MacKenzie said in a low-pitched command.

The young man quieted at once.

"Never mention that name. It is a very dangerous name to use carelessly in public."

After a moment, Yahya bowed his head. "Of course. I am sorry." But his right hand was out of sight beneath the table's edge. MacKenzie was certain there was a weapon curled up in those calloused fingers. Yahya didn't react well to harsh tones or direct commands, and he always went on the defensive when criticized. If he'd tried to take up with someone else in MacKenzie's line of work, he'd be dead already.

MacKenzie adopted a more casual tone. "I'm telling you this only for your own protection."

Yahya nodded. "I understand." But the hurt in his tone relayed that he really didn't.

"I understand that you don't trust the woman. You shouldn't, and I don't. But you should trust that you know what she is after, what she can do. She wants whatever secrets are in that scroll, and her mission isn't done until she gets her hands on what she is missing."

"As you say." Yahya relaxed a little.

They sat quietly at the table and watched Annja Creed through the dirty window. If she knew they were watching, she ignored them.

A man entered the restaurant and stood in the doorway for a moment to acclimate his vision. He was dark enough to pass for a Moroccan, but his suit was expensive and European. He slipped off his sunglasses and glanced around the room until he saw MacKenzie.

The man's gaze unsettled MacKenzie at once. He'd felt the same way when he'd found himself face-to-face with a cottonmouth in the swamplands as a kid.

Leaning back slightly, MacKenzie dropped his left hand to the pistol holstered at his hip under his shirt.

A moment later, the man approached the table and stopped just out of reach. He smiled politely. "Mr. MacKenzie."

MacKenzie didn't like that the man knew his name but he was in the dark about the man's identity. "I don't know you."

"I was sent here to speak with you."

"Who sent you?"

"Someone who would pay most handsomely for your time."

MacKenzie picked up the hot tea he was drinking, thinking that he could throw it on the guy and keep from shooting him if possible. "I'm not interested."

"You're making a mistake."

MacKenzie glared at him. "Go away."

The affable smile disappeared like coke up an addict's nose. "The person I work for could also have your life snuffed out in an instant for your insult."

Shifting only a little, MacKenzie freed the pistol he carried and pointed it at the other. He hid all but the muzzle beneath his arm. "Not by you. You'll be dead as soon as you give the order. If your boss has told you anything about me, he's told you I don't mind killing."

The man's sneer vanished completely at that point. Yahya also had his weapon trained on him and was searching around the room for anyone who might be in collusion. MacKenzie took pride in the young man's skills.

"I was told to offer you twice what you're being paid."

MacKenzie grinned. "Why not make it three times that amount?"

The other hesitated a moment, then gave a short nod. "I was told that can be arranged."

"Do you even know how much I'm being paid?" MacKenzie knew that if he tried to break his deal he'd never work for Sophie again. Business was business, but it often became personal.

A sigh escaped the man before he caught himself. "No."

"Then go away." MacKenzie waggled the pistol.

"I was told to get a definitive answer from you."

"Would a bullet through the lung be definitive enough?"

Grimacing, the man turned and walked back the way he'd come.

Yahya watched him go. "He is not happy."

"Neither am I." MacKenzie kept his pistol hidden and didn't put it away.

"He seemed very serious."

"I believe he was." Picking up the teacup again, MacKenzie sipped the hot liquid and added more sugar. His granny used to brew the tea and the sugar together, steep it as dark as soot, then add water to lighten it up. He hadn't gotten tea like that since he'd left Alabama.

"Do you know who he works for?"

"Yes."

"The one whose name you do not wish me to speak?"

"I believe so."

Yahya considered that. "This is a very dangerous man, and you have just offended him."

"He offended me first. Thinking I could be bought off." MacKenzie smiled. "Besides, Yahya, a man who offers to buy you off *after* he's tried to kill you isn't sincere. Or trustworthy."

"No, I suppose not." Yahya studied the room. Then he looked back at Annja Creed on the other side of the window. "However, the lengths the man is willing to go to in order to get whatever Annja Creed is after makes me think it must be worth quite a lot."

"Yes."

Yahya folded his napkin. "I am curious as to how much it is worth. And if it is worth enough for us to consider retiring from the business we're in after taking it."

MacKenzie blew on his tea. "It's something to consider."

McLean, Virginia

THE PHONE VIBRATED against Brawley Hendricks's chest and woke him from an uneasy slumber. He'd been having nightmares about Paul Gentry. They had been in the hospital awaiting the birth of Paul's daughter, Jenny. Heather had suffered through a long and exhausting pregnancy that was about to pay off.

A middle-aged nurse with frizzy brown hair had stepped through the door of Heather's room. "Agent Hendricks?"

Hendricks had stood, just as he had when Jenny had been born. "I'm Hendricks." He knew her calling him "Agent" Hendricks was odd. The hospital hadn't known he or Paul were with the CIA. The nurses had thought Hendricks was Paul's father. Paul's actual father had died in the first Gulf War.

"It's time. Where's the father?"

Hendricks looked around the room. Paul had been with him only the moment before, sitting in the chair next to Hendricks. But Paul wasn't there now.

"I don't know." Hendricks had known something was wrong. Paul had never left Heather's side during the delivery.

Someone called from inside the room and the nurse looked anxious. "You need to find him. Now."

In the nightmare, Hendricks had started for the waiting room door, thinking he might find Paul in the hallway. But he'd known that Paul was dead in Algiers, his body waiting in a morgue while the State Department struggled to get through the red tape.

Before Hendricks could begin to search, the nurse had returned. This time blood covered the front of her green scrubs. Horror etched her face as blood dripped from her gloves and misted from her mouth. "Something has gone horribly wrong!"

Hendricks shivered, then he realized it was the phone vibrating against his chest. He came fully awake and sat up in the darkness of his bedroom.

Caller ID showed Blocked—2:18 a.m.

Only one blocked caller could be reaching him on this line. He punched the answer button and held the handset to his ear. "Hendricks." He didn't worry about the line being secure. That made as much sense as wondering if he'd taken his last breath.

"Contact was made."

The icy grip around his heart loosened slightly. He had known MacKenzie was forcing Thabit's hand, and he'd been expecting contact. "Good."

Sophie sounded the same as she always did even at this late hour. He'd always wondered how she'd managed that. "Evidently your target is getting antsy."

"Because of your people?"

"No, because of whatever the woman is doing."

"Do you know what that is?"

"No."

Sitting on the edge of the bed in the darkness, Hendricks tried not to feel frustrated. He'd researched Annja Creed. Sophie had done the same thing. The woman was nothing more than she appeared to be—a television celebrity who had achieved some international recognition—but she should have been nothing to a man like Thabit.

"What happened?"

"One of your target's men tried to bribe my agent."

"And?"

"My agent turned the offer down. We're pushing the ball back in your target's corner. Let him make the first mistake."

And what if he doesn't make a mistake? What if he kills Annja Creed and your man? In the darkness, he could see the blood-covered nurse. "All right. Keep me apprised."

"Of course." Sophie hesitated. "Get some sleep, Brawley. You sound horrible." She didn't wait for a reply. The phone beeped as she disconnected.

Realizing he was thirsty and his throat was dry, Hendricks left his phone on the bed and went into the bathroom. He took down the small medicine cup he kept there and got a drink, doing it all in the dark because he knew where every-thing was.

As soon as his thirst was sated, though, the harsh, fierce anger over Paul's death returned. He considered asking Sophie to bring in the Creed woman for her own protection, thinking maybe they could sweat out whatever knowledge she had of whatever it was that interested Thabit.

But he wasn't sure they could manage that, either. Based on the information he had gathered about Annja Creed, the woman was quite capable of taking care of herself. For the moment, they had MacKenzie with her. Hendricks hoped that would be enough.

20

Marrakech
Kingdom of Morocco

Even standing in the shadow of the building eaves, Annja felt the city heating up around her. It would only be a matter of hours before Marrakech was once more in full fever. Thankfully, the city was high in the Atlas Mountains.

As she leaned against the wall behind her and kept watch of the foot-and-vehicle traffic around her, Annja knew MacKenzie observed her from the small restaurant at the corner. She made certain she didn't step out of his view because she didn't want to worry him while she talked with Professor Khadija Zayd.

"How much do you know about Philip Gardiner and his service aboard the Spanish ships?" Khadija had a soft voice, but she was a direct person.

"Not much." Annja referred to her journal and flipped through the notes she'd taken while talking to Ernest Woolcot. "I've been on the run and I haven't actually been in the best place to research what I've found."

"That may not be true." The woman had a curious blend of Indian and British accents. "Philip Gardiner's work caught the eye of a rather skilled Syrian historian, Dr. Ulker Bozdag. Have you heard of him?"

"No. Can you spell it?"

"Of course."

Annja wrote the name down in her journal.

"I'm not surprised that you haven't heard of him, Miss Creed."

"Call me Annja, please."

"If you were not interested in the caliphs immediately following Muhammad, you would never run across his name. Even at that, he would be hard to find. Bozdag was trained at Oxford in the 1960s and fell in love with pop culture. I have been told he loved the Beatles and favored esoterica bordering on conspiracy theory. Adored the notion of hidden puzzles lying about in history."

"There appear to be no shortage of those kinds of puzzles. I've tripped across a few myself."

"I think most of what people believe are puzzles are nothing more than events, people and objects that have been forgotten over the years. But in the case of the Middle East, the battles between Christian and Muslim forces have never been out of the international eye since the Crusades. And many people are interested in what happens there, and what *has* happened there. You're familiar with the Battle of Bassorah, yes?"

"Yes. The Battle of the Camel. Muhammad's widow Aisha rallied forces around her to chase down Uthman's assassins."

"So it is written in some histories. In other histories, Aisha was making her bid to control the caliphate by naming Muhammad's true heir after Uthman's death."

"As I recall, that didn't work out for her. Ali ibn Abd Munaf became the fourth caliph despite her protests. Ali let her live, but he banished her."

"To Medina, yes. And she lived there for the rest of her life. Probably as a very bitter woman."

"As one of Muhammad's wives—"

"Purportedly his favorite."

"—she had everything. Then she was left with nothing."

"She was still referred to as the Mother of the Believers. But while Muhammad had been alive, she had led more of a life than women in that day could be expected to have. She was an expert politician and theologian. When she spoke, men listened. Then, with Muhammad's death, all of that was lost. Except for one thing."

Annja waited.

"Aisha still had the services of Abdelilah Karam, the historian. She died in 678. Did you pinpoint the time that Karam was in Morocco?"

"He was here at earliest in 698. There were gold coins with his body that were struck in 79 AH."

"Twenty years after Aisha's death."

"Yes."

"Interesting."

"But what does any of this have to do with Bozdag?"

"You are familiar with the Yazidi?"

"Sure. Kurdish people living in the Mosul region in Iraq."

"There are also groups of them living in Transcaucasia, Turkey, Armenia and Syria."

"Syria. And Bozdag is from Syria."

"So you see how this begins to come together," Khadija said in amusement.

"I do."

"Have you heard of the Melek Taus?"

Annja thought back, but even with her prodigious memory she couldn't remember having heard the term before. "No."

"I'd have been surprised if you had. The Melek Taus is also called the Order of the Peacock Angel. They also have another name, Shaytan, which is the same name the Koran has for Satan."

"Living in Muslim countries, I'll bet the order wasn't popular."

"No. And it still isn't. They have a story about a *jinn*, a genie, named Iblis, who refused to acknowledge Adam as superior over him. In the Muslim belief, Iblis became the leader of the fallen angels, the Devil in Christian terms. Bozdag became fascinated by the Melek Taus while in London. One of the books he read was *Secret Societies Yesterday and Today*. He was a young man at the time and was convinced that he'd found his calling in history. His university was not so enchanted as he was, and he was ultimately released from his contract. However, he had been traveling back and forth to Fes, Morocco, to continue his studies."

Annja understood immediately. "The University of Al-Karaouine."

"Exactly. The university there is one of the most influential areas of study in the Muslim world. So if anyone would have information on the Melek Taus, Bozdag felt certain that university would."

"Does it?"

"No more than any other place, that I know of. And none of that ties directly into your search. But Bozdag does. He secured a teaching position at the university and worked there until he died in 1983. Some of the papers he left behind mention his follow-up work on Philip Gardiner's investigation into Abdelilah Karam."

"Bozdag couldn't have found the scroll that was with Karam. That scroll was still buried."

"No, but he did find another. This one was written by a young historian from Persia who claimed to have been learning his craft from Abdelilah Karam. That scroll, written by Allal Khaldun, was included in the papers kept at the university. Bozdag wrote a small monograph that underscored the thought that Philip Gardiner had been with the Barbary pirates and had gotten his Kufic scrolls from Morocco. Of course, at the time no one really cared." Khadija was silent for a moment. "But if you can find papers written by Abdelilah Karam detailing events during the caliphate wars, this could be a spectacular discovery. The Battle of Bassorah divided the Muslim people, splitting them into the factions that have become known as the Sunnis and the Shiites."

Annja burned with excitement. "Khadija, I really appreciate your time this morning."

"Do not just appreciate my time." The professor laughed. "You have made me most curious. When you have the story, please tell it to me. And if you ever find yourself in India someday, let me know. I would love to meet you."

"I will." Annja thanked the woman again and disconnected. She turned and walked back to the restaurant, hoping she could get her hands on the missing piece of the scroll.

And that Smythe and the others were still in one piece.

LESS THAN AN HOUR LATER, Annja was leaving Marrakech by camel. MacKenzie had purchased the animals from a local merchant. Outfitting his team had cost quite a lot, and she had to wonder again at how MacKenzie was so free with his money. She wasn't convinced Mustafa was sitting on a treasure trove out in the mountains.

The sun burned down and she was certain the temperature had gotten up to nearly ninety. By noon it would be close to unbearable. She wore khaki shorts she'd purchased in the market and a white tunic top. Sunscreen covered her exposed skin and face. She'd pulled her hair back in a ponytail and wore a baseball cap and aviator-style sunglasses.

Her gear was rolled behind the saddle—additional clothing, water and food—but she wore her backpack. If things somehow went sideways, she didn't want to be separated from her things.

MacKenzie had given her a Glock 17 and made her show proficiency with handling the weapon before he was satisfied. She'd kept it hidden when they'd ridden through Marrakech, but now that they were out in the wilderness she wore it on her hip.

She wasn't really comfortable wearing a weapon. Bart McGilley had tried to get her to carry one in New York, but she'd declined. Of course, he didn't know about the sword.

And if she hadn't had such easy access to the sword, she sometimes wondered if—based on the things she faced on a fairly routine basis—she would carry another weapon. But she never wanted a gun to be the first solution she reached for.

MacKenzie rode his camel up next to hers. He didn't look exactly comfortable riding the beast, and Annja had to struggle to keep from smiling at him as he fought against rocking back and forth.

Annja had settled back into the camel's awkward gait within a few minutes.

"How far out from the Bedouin camp do you think we are?" MacKenzie tried to take a drink from his canteen and ended up sloshing water on his shirt. He cursed and tried again, this time more successfully.

"Thirteen-point-two miles." Annja had just checked the GPS on her notebook computer.

"How fast do these things travel?"

"Anywhere from twenty to thirty-five miles a day."

"So we can look forward to six or seven hours in the saddle before we find your friends."

Annja nodded.

MacKenzie glared at his mount. "I hate these things. I hate the way they walk. I hate the way they smell. I hate how stupid they are."

"Beats walking."

"Yeah, I know. I wish we could bring vehicles out here."

"You could. Of course, those vehicles could break down and leave you stranded with a long walk home. And they'd definitely stir up more dust and make more noise than these camels will." Annja grinned. "Camels have ninja mode."

MacKenzie sighed. "But that doesn't make them smell any better."

21

Two hours later, MacKenzie called a stop to rest and water the camels. The animals didn't need much water to survive on, but he was sensible about taking care of them. He didn't have any feelings for the pack animals. They were valuable tools he was using as part of the job he'd undertaken.

Annja sat cross-legged in the shade created by the camel she'd been riding. She'd watered the animal and it had hunkered down immediately. The shade wasn't much because it was almost noon, but sitting on the mountainside helped.

A gentle wind stirred up small dust devils that whirled like dervishes across the dry land.

After consulting her notebook computer to get the GPS coordinates, Annja shut the device down and put it away. Charging the battery wasn't going to be a problem because she'd also picked up a solar charger and a hand-crank charger in the marketplace. Technology was getting more and more available, stripping away some of the Old World feel of cities like Marrakech. The architecture of the cities was the same, but with satellite dishes outside a lot of the homes and buildings.

MacKenzie walked over, his boots crunching on the ground. He looked at her from under the wide brim of the hat he'd purchased. He wore his wraparound sunglasses.

"Did you water your camel?"

Annja nodded. "First thing."

MacKenzie looked around for a moment and Annja instinctively knew that he didn't like being out in so much open space. "How far are we from Mustafa now?"

"Seven-point-six miles."

MacKenzie's eyebrows lifted in surprise from behind the sunglasses. "We're making better time than I'd thought."

"And we've been across terrain we would have had to avoid even in Jeeps equipped with four-wheel drive."

Taking a handkerchief from his back pocket, MacKenzie mopped the sweat from his neck. "We should catch up to Mustafa in another three, four hours."

"Probably."

MacKenzie returned the handkerchief to his pocket. "I'm going to have to think about that. We come up on them in the daytime and they see us, they might open fire without checking who we are." He looked at her. "Plus, we'd have to keep you out of sight."

The moment Mustafa saw her, the Bedouin chief would know something was amiss.

"Even if they don't drop us, Mustafa could start killing hostages. We wouldn't have any leverage at all." MacKenzie frowned. "All we've got out here is surprise, and the only way to maintain that is to creep up on them in the middle of the night."

"So we need to stop somewhere between here and there."

"Yeah." MacKenzie reached into his shirt pocket and took out a map of the region. "I need to find a place we can stay to wait for night that's not far from the Bedouin camp."

"There's an old fort about six miles up. It's practically on the way, maybe a quarter mile north of our heading."

MacKenzie looked at her in surprise. "You've already been looking?"

"Yep."

"Not bad for a television star."

"Archaeologist first, then television star. And as an archaeologist, I've studied a lot of battlegrounds. I've learned a few things."

"Like finding out places to cold camp."

"Like that."

MacKenzie grinned. "We can live with a quarter mile out of the way." He started studying his map.

"The fort isn't on that map. I found it on satellite imagery I downloaded of the area. I stored files on my computer."

"Did you, now?" MacKenzie looked even more impressed. "Girl Scout when you were a kid?"

Annja shook her head. "I was raised by nuns. I'm better prepared than a Boy Scout."

MacKenzie laughed and refolded the map. "All right. You lead the way to this fort you found."

ANNJA RODE AT THE FRONT of the caravan after they remounted, with MacKenzie to her right and Yahya on her left. Both of them carried assault rifles, the buttstocks resting on their thighs.

The others on the mercenary team behind them carried their weapons the same way. Annja couldn't help thinking that they looked like a military expedition. If they'd crossed paths with any of the small-trade caravans that still carried goods back and forth across the mountains, they would have scared them away.

Annja didn't like the presence of the weapons. They reminded her of how much danger Smythe and the others were in.

Three hours later, she spotted the ruins of the old fort ahead of them. Three of the stone walls still stood, but the fourth lay loosely scattered inside and outside the original perimeter. When it had stood, the fort had held three rooms.

They settled the camels on the north side of the building

against one of the walls and watered them again. Although they weren't thirsty, the camels drank. They knew to take advantage of resources. This time MacKenzie also made sure the animals were fed.

With the camel behind her quietly chewing the food she'd given it, Annja studied the GPS readings on her notebook computer. They were only a mile and a quarter from the Bedouin campsite.

Satisfied, she powered the computer down and replaced it in her backpack.

MacKenzie walked over to her and nodded at the ground. "Mind if I sit?"

"Go ahead." Annja took out a water bottle and drank. One of the biggest threats in desert country was dehydration. She reminded herself to keep sipping water at regular intervals.

Slipping the assault rifle off his shoulder, MacKenzie sat cross-legged. One of his knees cracked, but Annja knew it was from an old injury, not age.

"How far we are from Mustafa?"

"A little over a mile."

"The moon's going to be bright tonight."

"Three-quarters. A new moon would have been better, but we didn't get to pick the timing."

MacKenzie shook his head. "Maybe I should stop being so surprised at what you know. And what you pay attention to." He took out a trail bar, then offered it to Annja.

She shook her head and produced one of her own. She peeled the bar open and took a bite as he did the same.

"You pay attention to a lot."

Annja looked back at him and felt an undercurrent of unease stirring. Despite what they'd been through, she couldn't quite bring herself to trust MacKenzie. She often felt the same way around Garin, so the feeling wasn't new to her.

"It's part of my job."

"Right. Archaeologist."

Annja remained silent and took another sip of her water.

MacKenzie waved a hand at the fort. "What can you tell me about this place?"

Glancing over her shoulder, Annja studied the fort for a moment. "What do you want to know?"

"It was built in the middle of nowhere. Why would they do that?"

"How much do you know about Moroccan history?"

MacKenzie smiled at her. "Unless something really big happened, I don't remember what I saw on the news the previous day."

Annja leaned back against the camel. The beast shifted a little and blew out a short breath, popping its lips in displeasure, but didn't object too much. "Morocco was a center of trade activity. Merchants formed caravans during the months when they had crops and goods to sell. Salt and gold flowed from North Africa to South Africa, then made its way into the Western world."

"And slaves. They were sold, too."

"Yes. Later. In the beginning it was salt and gold, and crops specific to this part of the world. Those caravans crossed incredible distances as the merchants took chances to become wealthy. A ship crossing the ocean wasn't as vulnerable as those caravans because they carried warriors and fortifications with them."

"Makes sense." MacKenzie studied the structure with more interest. "So somebody came up with the idea of sticking warriors out here to protect those caravans."

"Yeah." Annja brushed a crumb off her shirt. "Probably guys you'd relate to better than you think despite all the centuries that have passed since this outpost was manned."

MacKenzie pursed his lips. "How did these guys make their money?"

Annja warmed to the subject because of MacKenzie's obvious interest. "Donations from kings and merchants who wanted safe passage for their goods. Some of them probably bought things and did some speculating on their own as they traveled back and forth. The same way you're speculating on Mustafa's gun collection."

A wolfish smile curved MacKenzie's lips.

"Some of them probably hired out to journey with the caravans to the seaports, then brought back things to sell locally to the other men stationed here. Maybe those warriors went north or south to small villages where they could sell those items for inflated prices."

"A guy who pays attention to things could set himself up with a nice side business."

"Exactly. That's the way it's always been. A market gets created. People have to ship goods there, and an enforcement arm comes into being out of necessity. The gravitation from enforcer to merchant for someone that's clever was a natural thing."

"It still is." MacKenzie folded the wrapping from his trail bar and put it in his pocket. "I know a lot of guys who figured they were smarter than their bosses and decided to take over." He shrugged. "It's not always a good move. Just because you can pull a trigger doesn't mean you have the smarts to run a business."

"I'll take your word for it."

"I don't think you have to take my word for it. I think there's been a lot of that in history. I'm sure you could tick off stories without even working up a sweat."

"Just sitting in this heat is working up a sweat." She pulled at her shirt and let go, creating a momentary cooling breeze.

"Let's say your friends are still alive and we can get them all away in one piece."

That was a dark what-if. "I don't want to think it'll go any other way."

"Then don't. My team and me, we're good at this. But what comes next for you? Are you going to keep chasing whatever it is you're looking for on that scroll?"

Annja didn't hesitate. "I am."

"Do you know what it's about yet?"

She studied him. "Do you mean, is it a treasure map?"

MacKenzie sat with his forearms resting on his knees, hands clasped together, and shrugged.

"As far as I know, this isn't a treasure map."

"But it could be."

"Are you a betting man?"

He favored her with a lopsided grin. "Nature of the business, girl. Nothing I do is without risk, and when I risk, I'm all in."

"I wouldn't bet on this being a treasure map."

"Then what are you betting on?"

Annja considered that for a moment. "I'm not betting. I'm curious. So we find this old guy—he's got to have been in his eighties when he made the trip to Morocco, which was only then coming under Islamic control under Uqba ibn Nafi for the Umayyad caliphate. I can't help wondering what he was doing out here. Why would he leave his home and come all this way to die on a trip to…where? More than that, why did someone kill him?"

"He was murdered?"

"I guess I didn't tell you that."

"No."

Annja pointed to the back of her head. "Somebody crushed his skull."

"To get what he had?"

"Maybe."

"Do you know what he was carrying with him?"

Annja sighed. "I don't. This man was a historian, not a politician or person of wealth. He was just an old man."

MacKenzie was quiet for a moment. "He wasn't just an old man to everybody. Whoever killed him? They thought he was a threat." Grabbing his rifle, he used it to help push himself to his feet. He resettled his hat on his head. "When you get the story, let me know how it goes. I'm interested."

"But not enough to go chasing after it with me?" Annja wasn't sure if she felt relieved or anxious that MacKenzie would be leaving. She still didn't understand why Habib ibn Thabit was interested in her or what they had found buried with Abdelilah Karam.

"I'm a risk taker, but only when I know there's a potential payday involved." MacKenzie looked over the surrounding mountainous terrain. "We've got a few hours before night. Try to get some rest. Once it gets dark, we're going to be busy." He trudged back to his team.

The young man, Yahya, had remained at a distance, watchful. Annja had wondered if he was related to MacKenzie, but gathered that they weren't. They looked after each other, though.

The sun soaked into her as she lay back against the camel. She'd long ago blocked out the animal's stink. After a while, feeling warm and relaxed, she slept.

22

Garin pulled the Melkus RS 2000 up to the curb in front of the gothic club in the Mitte district. Dozens of people wearing leather and rubber and all things vampire stood in line against the side of the three-story warehouse that housed Club Ravenswing.

A valet dressed in black trotted over to the sports car as the driver's-side door gulled up and Garin stepped out.

"Keys, sir?" The valet held out his hand.

"No. The car is staying here." Garin clicked the key fob and the door gulled back down.

"Sir, you can't park here." The valet tried to sound firm about that.

Garin stood straight, towering over the younger man. At six feet four inches tall and built broad, Garin was an imposing figure. He wore black pants, a black turtleneck and a black duster that dropped to midcalf, nicely concealing his weapons. His black eyes flashed.

"The car is staying here." Garin ripped the valet's identification card off his lapel. "Furthermore, if it's not here when I get back—" he checked the card "—Joachim, then I'm going to hold you personally responsible. Do you understand?"

The valet didn't hesitate. "Perfectly. I understand perfectly."

"Good." Garin took a five-hundred-euro note out of his coat pocket and shoved it into the valet's hand.

The valet closed his hand reflexively.

Garin brushed by him and strode toward the club's entrance. Two large men kept watch over the doors, which had been remodeled to look like folded bat wings. The handles looked like gargoyles that had popped out and were trying to climb from inside the doors. The men were dressed in black clothing with *Security* written on their chests in German and English.

One of them stepped forward. A baton shot out of his right hand but he kept it close to his leg. "You cannot go in."

Garin hit the man in the throat with two fingers, pulling the blow just enough to keep from crushing the trachea and killing him. Choking and gasping for breath, the man dropped to his knees. Garin caught the abandoned baton before it hit the ground. The man's partner, stunned for a moment, moved too slowly to do more than set up in a defensive position. By that time Garin had brought the baton up between the man's legs, then shoved him aside as he collapsed and threw up.

Still in motion, Garin opened the door and dropped the baton at his feet.

The inside of the club looked like hell. Digitized flames cascaded around the walls as laser lighting flickered out over the gyrating crowd. Spinning spheres that resembled flaming asteroids swung from the ceiling and projected the lasers. Garin was surprised the repeat clientele hadn't gone deaf from the high-decibel death-metal music.

Cocktail waitresses wearing shimmering red camisoles, tiny thong shorts, high heels and horns circulated through the crowd. Bars occupied both sides of the club. At the other end of the expansive dance floor, a DJ dressed as a young Dracula ran the sound. Every so often he took a drink of something, then spat flames into the air above the crowd.

"Can I get you something to drink?" A young waitress stood to Garin's left.

Garin laid a hundred-euro note on her serving tray. "No. Thank you." He strode past her, knowing without asking that Eniko would be in the back of the club holding court.

The dancers on the floor parted ahead of him as he crossed. A few of the men frowned, but the women gazed at him with interest. He ignored them all, watching for shifting that went against the grain of the whirling bodies.

Eniko was expecting him. She had to be.

Three men converged on Garin before he reached the other end of the club. Cameras mounted on the flaming asteroids captured video of the crowd and mixed it with the fiery footage on the walls. He saw himself, and he also saw the aggressors coming for him. They cut through the dancers like sharks through an ocean.

Evidently the security crew at the front had radioed ahead. Tracking their movement, Garin saw that they came from the left. That was where Eniko would be, back in the area cut off from the dance floor by one-way glass.

The first man to reach Garin was nearly seven feet tall, a steroid-induced giant that would have intimidated a lesser man. Garin had stood against armored knights as well as British Mark I tanks during the Battle of Flers-Courcelette in World War I. The giant threw a straight punch, whipping his other hand back to his hip in a martial-arts swivel. Garin slipped the blow, feeling the wind of the man's fist passing his cheek, and threw his right arm up at the same time he lifted his right leg. Pivoting and shifting his weight, Garin drove his right foot against the side of the man's right leg, snapping the knee. He also trapped the man's right arm before his opponent could recover it, then slammed his left forearm into the man's elbow, shattering that joint, as well.

Crying out in pain, the man tried to stay erect. Garin spun him long enough to use him as a human shield against the second attacker, a black man only slightly smaller than the first, then shoved him forward. Although the second man tried to escape the first, the giant caught his comrade in a one-armed bear hug that effectively put him in a straitjacket.

Mercilessly, Garin stepped in behind the second man before he could turn and clapped both hands over the man's ears. The twin blows ruptured the man's eardrums. Fighting vertigo, he stumbled and went down with the first man clinging desperately to him.

Garin had lost track of the third man, but as he started to turn, the Asian's fist exploded against his jaw. The blow had been aimed at Garin's throat. If it had landed, it would have disrupted the blood flowing from his carotid or possibly broken his larynx. As it was, the force split his cheek. Warm blood trickled into his goatee.

Taking a step back as the dancers fled the floor, Garin grinned at his opponent. "Try that again. When I'm looking this time."

The man launched another flurry of blows, all of them capable, and all of them coming within millimeters of striking home. Garin had to move quickly to escape. Nearly five hundred years of battling, brawling and banging heads stood him in good stead. He didn't think about fighting. He simply reacted. Just as a pebble was worn smooth in a river, Garin's fighting prowess had matured, becoming effortless. It was a combination of instinct and experience, a concoction that left him incredibly lethal.

Keeping his elbows in so as not to telegraph his blows, Garin used a combination of *krav maga* punches, snapping jabs and elbows into the man's face. When the man staggered back, Garin followed with a fist into the man's face, pulling the power up from his toes and through his body, twisting his hip to get everything lined up.

Unconscious, the man fell backward and sprawled to the floor. Garin stepped over him and headed toward the small room at the back of the club.

Security personnel boiled out from behind the bar.

Garin reached under his jacket and took out the nickel-plated Desert Eagle .50. The laser strobe lights glinted rainbow-colored fire from the pistol's shiny finish. He pointed the big muzzle at the approaching men.

They froze where they were.

A woman emerged from the darkness of the back room. She was tall, statuesque, with a face that had been emblazoned on the covers of magazines and tabloids around the world. Sultry and contemptuous, her brilliant red hair a stunning alchemy from a hairdresser's palette and barely reaching her shoulders, Eniko was in her early thirties but looked ten years younger with her pale skin. Contact lenses turned her eyes a wicked acid-yellow, electric in the darkness of the club as they reflected the light. Curved horns jutted out from her forehead, expertly placed by a makeup artist.

Eniko waved the security away as she regarded Garin. She wore a shimmering emerald dress that barely covered the full breasts and threatened to become immodest around her hips at any moment. Calf-high boots almost the exact shade of green sheathed her long legs.

"Garin." She smiled.

He didn't put the pistol away, but he did lower it to his side. He ran a hand through his hair, pushing a few errant strands back into place. "I came for the amulet you stole from me."

"Stole?" She raised an eyebrow. "Such a harsh word between friends."

"I said harsher ones a few hours ago when I discovered

you'd switched out the amulet. And there were a few others while I tracked you down. Then there were more on the way over here."

"Are you certain the amulet is a fake?"

Garin stared at her.

Crossing her arms over her impressive cleavage, Eniko shrugged. "Well, I suppose you would."

Garin lifted his hand to her face and thought how easy it would be to smash her beauty. That was the thing about him that Annja Creed didn't understand. He was capable of doing whatever he needed to or wanted to. She was bound up in her own morality. Roux, to a lesser degree, was, as well.

But pain had set Garin free when he was a boy. His father, the man who had raised him, had insisted that Garin was a bastard, born to his mother from some other man. Garin had never known the truth of that, but he favored what he remembered of the man. Sometimes Garin wondered if his father would have changed his mind if he had seen him grown into adulthood.

That wasn't how things had worked out, though.

Today, he was the man all those yesterdays had built, and he had been betrayed.

Instead of hitting the woman, Garin leaned forward and kissed her gently on the cheek. He pulled back and looked into those acid-yellow eyes. "You are lucky I have decided to let you live."

She smiled at him, still secure in her own fantasy. The light caught her horns and they glinted. "You could never kill me."

Garin rested the Desert Eagle's barrel in her cleavage. "Don't bet on that."

Eniko almost lost her grin then. But she clung to the mask of self-satisfaction fiercely. He knew her own upbringing and personal tragedies would allow her to do nothing less. She searched his face. Finally she lifted her hand and touched the blood on his cheek, then licked it off her fingers.

"Is there no one you love, Garin Braden?"

"No."

"A man shouldn't live without love."

"Where's my amulet?"

"In here." She turned and he let her go, then followed her.

The room was small, filled with couches and comfortable chairs. The wall with the one-way glass looked out over the dance floor. Another wall held several monitors, many of them trained on the club's interior and some of them showing various television channels.

A half-dozen young men and women, Eniko's playthings, sat frozen, like prey before the predator. A central table held several bottles of wine and liquor, and a smorgasbord of elegant finger foods.

Eniko walked to a couch, shooed a couple young women away and reached into her purse. Garin took a slow breath and readied himself to lift the Desert Eagle if it came to that.

Keeping her movements in view, Eniko pulled a small jewelry box out of her purse. With a tight smile, she opened the box to show him the contents.

The amulet, a design dug deeply into the gold, revealed an ankh with blue sapphires at the four points. Egyptian hiero-glyphics Garin had barely translated were on the obverse. The object roughly measured three inches by two inches.

Eniko offered the box to Garin. He plucked the amulet from the soft bed and felt the weight of it, heavier than it looked because of the gold. This was real. He couldn't explain how he knew that, but he did. It was some shadow of the gift Roux had for sniffing out such things.

"What *is* the amulet?" Some of her composure back now, Eniko gazed at Garin with a small amount of belligerence.

"Mine." Garin pocketed it but didn't put the pistol away.

"What's so important about it? You had me go to the trouble of getting it for you."

Only because having Eniko get the amulet was the easiest path. If she hadn't done it, Garin could have gotten it himself. But there would have been a lot more bloodshed. Eniko had played on another man's emotions, the same way she'd tried to play on his.

"Nothing you'd be interested in."

"Then tell me why you're so interested in it."

"No." The amulet was actually a key to something else that he hadn't found. For the moment all that mattered was that he had the amulet. It would lead him to the next thing. He gazed around the room.

"Looking for the back way out?"

"No. I'm walking out the way I came in, and if any of your little friends show up, I'm going to put a bullet in their heads and let you explain it to the police."

"They'll arrest you."

"No, they won't. And you know that." He took her by the arm and led her back toward the dance floor. He had barely started across when his phone rang. When he glanced at caller ID, he saw that it was Annja.

He answered the phone but swept his gaze over the club crowd. Most of the people stood back, warily watching him. "Yes."

"Are you busy?" Annja sounded distracted.

"Not terribly. What do you need?" Garin kept moving.

"Have you heard of the Melek Taus?"

"The angels of destruction?"

"Those are the ones."

Garin gazed around the club at all the men and women in their make-believe demon costumes and vampire dress. He couldn't help but laugh.

"Something funny?"

"It's a location joke. What do you want to know about the Melek Taus?"

"Everything. There's a new angle on this dig that might require further exploration."

"Can't you do that yourself?"

"Normally I could, but we're about to stage a rescue and my time is limited. Especially since we could be running for our lives shortly. I thought maybe you could take a minute and have some of your research people send me a background portfolio."

"I don't live to serve at your beck and call."

"We'll chalk it up as a favor. I'll owe you one."

Garin thought of the curious amulet and the secrets it protected, and he thought having Annja owe him one might not be such a bad thing. "All right." He was almost to the front door. "Call me when you're ready."

"I will. I have to go."

"Keep safe." The phone clicked dead in Garin's ear. He pocketed it and headed through the door, his hand once more around Eniko's upper arm.

The bouncers gave Garin a wide berth.

Garin used the key fob to open the Melkus RS 2000's door before he reached the vehicle.

"Nice car," Eniko said calmly.

At the door, Garin turned to her and leaned down to kiss her. She turned her face up to meet him. They had been lovers recently, and he felt she was expecting to be again. Instead of kissing her lips, though, he kissed her on the forehead.

She looked at him in shock and spoke in a whisper. "What was that?"

"Goodbye." Garin slid into the car and closed the gullwing door.

"Goodbye?"

Garin thumbed down the window. "You betrayed me."

"I was going to give you the amulet after I figured out what it was and what it meant to you."

Shaking his head, Garin started the car's powerful engine. "What it meant to me was that I can't trust you."

"This was a test?" She wrapped her arms around herself.

"No. An unfortunate circumstance." Garin paused. "I liked you well enough, but sometimes these things don't work out."

"Garin…wait. You can trust me. I swear."

"No. Never again." Garin raised the window, and put the transmission into first gear. Pressing the accelerator, he let out the clutch and roared into the street. He left her standing in the past.

He pressed a button on the dash as he whipped through the streets.

"Mr. Braden, how are you this evening?"

"I'm fine, Sepp. And you?"

Sepp Welker was one of Garin's primary researchers. The young man had a way with computers and the internet that was decidedly criminal. He was involved with several of the contracts Garin's international black ops teams dealt with.

"Actually, I was about to call you. In the past you've professed an interest in Annja Creed."

"Yes."

"One of the search and seizure assets we've used in the past gave me news about her. A tip he only just received from one of his contacts in the Middle East."

Traffic passed in a blur around Garin. "What news?"

"Apparently Creed is involved with some clandestine CIA operation in Morocco springing from repercussions in Algeria. Maybe you knew that?"

"I know she's in Morocco." Garin always played things close to the vest.

"Well, if this man is correct, Creed is heading for an ambush there."

"What do you mean?"

"She's working with a mercenary. The man she's currently with—"

"Rafael MacKenzie."

"Yes." Sepp sounded surprised, but only a little. "MacKenzie is being tracked by a Habib ibn Thabit, who is also being sought by the CIA for an ambush that took place in Algeria and resulted in the deaths of several CIA agents. Thabit has men following Creed and MacKenzie, and there's a Bedouin named Mustafa waiting for her."

Grimly, Garin held on to his temper. "Find out all you can about her, and also an organization called the Melek Taus. This comes first. Do you understand?"

"Of course."

Garin hung up and immediately dialed the number Annja had called from. The phone rang and rang.

There was no answer.

23

North of Marrakech
Atlas Mountains
Kingdom of Morocco

Annja moved silently through the darkness only a few steps behind MacKenzie. The three-quarter moon hung overhead, but it was dimmed by scudding clouds. Still, even then their shadows were sharply defined and dark against the ground, letting her know they were more visible than any of them would have liked.

They had left the camels back at the abandoned fort. If things went badly, it was a long run back to an escape route.

The weight of the AK-47 across her shoulders was a grim reminder that things were definitely going to get worse before they got better. MacKenzie had insisted that she take the assault rifle and she hadn't argued. She carried extra magazines for the weapon in the tactical Kevlar vest she wore.

They crept through the mountainous land and took advantage of the boulders and stunted trees that grew in sparse patches. Mustafa would have sentries posted. MacKenzie hoped to spot those men before they were spotted. The fact that there were so few mercenaries was both an asset and a liability. There was less likelihood of being seen, but there was also considerably less manpower.

The minutes passed as Annja counted the steps they took. She was up over a thousand. They should be coming up on the Bedouin camp soon. The GPS locators were still working and had remained fixed.

They crested a ridge and she spotted a soft bubble of light to the west of their position. Her heart lifted and filled with dread at the same time. They were going to know shortly if Smythe and the others were alive.

If they had been sold and were still alive, she'd find a way to go after them.

MacKenzie turned to the team and waved them into position.

Lying on her stomach, Annja took her microbinoculars and focused on the glowing light bubble only a little more than a hundred yards away. The images blurred for a moment as she adjusted the magnification, then she brought the camp into focus.

Several campfires lit up the site. Bedouin warriors sat hunkered around the fires or near tents. A makeshift corral lay to the east where the horses grazed on grass and leaves. The men went armed.

Annja made herself breathe slowly as she gazed around the camp. After a moment, she spotted David Smythe sitting just inside a lean-to against one of the foothills. He sat leaning forward, his hands bound behind his back. He looked worse for wear, haggard, his clothing disheveled. Bruising stained one side of his face, and the deep purple coloring told Annja the injury was fresh.

MacKenzie touched her arm, drawing her attention. He pointed at one of the other tents. Annja trained her binoculars there and saw the woman inside. Theresa Templeton. A moment later, she spotted other students from the dig. Annja let out a breath, realizing then that the Bedouin would have kept the women segregated from the men.

She worried about Cory Burcell and Souad and Nadim. Smythe and Templeton would have been seen as worth ransoming. Burcell was black and might not immediately have been recognized as American or European even with his accent.

Smythe was talking to someone inside the tent. A moment later, a Bedouin warrior pulled the tent flap back and went in with a pot and a handful of bowls. During that brief moment, Annja caught sight of Cory and Souad and several other members of the dig team.

"Are they all there?"

Annja lowered the binoculars. "It looks like it."

"Then you got lucky. The Bedouins must have taken quite a few supplies from your dig site. That's the only way they could have supported this many hostages."

That thought sent a shiver through Annja even though she'd been thinking it herself. She also couldn't help wondering how many times MacKenzie had found himself in similar situations regarding people he might have taken on operations.

She decided she didn't want to know.

Yahya lay on the ground beside MacKenzie. The younger man was quietly counting to himself as he surveyed the camp.

"How many Bedouin?" MacKenzie adjusted the focus on his binoculars, rolling the wheel with his forefinger.

Yahya answered immediately. "Thirty-one."

Annja tracked the men. "I count twenty-nine."

MacKenzie smiled. "I count twenty-nine, as well. Very good, Annja."

Yahya scowled and spat a curse. "Some of them are always moving."

"Yes, they are." Retreating on his hands and knees, MacKenzie climbed back from the ridge. He put his binoculars back in his chest pack.

Annja followed him, trailed by Yahya.

MacKenzie sat still for a moment. "We have our work cut out for us."

"Outnumbered almost three to one?" Annja nodded.

"Three to one doesn't bother me." MacKenzie trailed fingers over his stubbled chin as he thought. "We have surprise on our side. For a little while. We can cut down the odds with that. The problem remains whether they decide to fight us or kill their hostages."

Annja totally understood what MacKenzie was saying. "We don't have a choice. We can't leave them here."

MacKenzie took a deep breath and let it out. "All right. Then let's get to this." He stood and called his team over.

Curtain Bar
K Street
Washington, D.C.

THE BAR HAD A FULLY EQUIPPED op room in the basement. Hendricks knew he should have expected that, but he was still surprised. He supposed he should have been more surprised that Sophie had showed it to him.

The latest computer equipment filled the room, leaving little space for the casual observer, though Hendricks was certain nothing casual ever took place in that room. Two people, both young, one male and one female, sat in front of an array of monitors. Their hands darted back and forth across their touch screens, gesturing to pull up files rather than typing things in.

The images cycled very quickly, showing exploded views of a desertscape at night as well as views from high overhead. Human forms glowed on the main screen that filled one whole wall. There were two groups, and the illuminated forms stood revealed in red and blue. Hendricks quickly deduced that Annja Creed and Rafe MacKenzie's group ringed the Bedouin camp.

As he watched, a man inside a lean-to was suddenly limned in yellow. Immediately following, a rectangular space popped open on another screen and quickly filled in with a head-and-shoulder shot of a guy who looked worn to the bone. Beside that rectangle, another opened up and hundreds of photos started cycling through. An instant later, the image froze, producing one that looked a lot like the captured image from the Bedouin camp. Data scrolled underneath the picture.

The female tech spoke up as she continued to gesture at the computer console. "I have one of the dig team identified."

"Ping them separately. We want to keep track of everyone there." Sophie sat beside Hendricks at a small observation area in the back of the room. As always, she looked stylish and elegant. Her attention was divided between the operation in the room and the tablet computer in her hands.

Hendricks glanced at her. "Who is that?"

Sophie flicked a finger at her tablet. An instant later, an image floated onto the computer monitor set in the table in front of him.

Hendricks studied Professor David Smythe in both pictures. "At least he's still alive."

"Yes."

"What about Thabit?"

Sophie tapped her tablet again and an image of the camp and the surrounding countryside opened up.

"No one followed Creed or MacKenzie out of Marrakech." The soft light from her tablet glinted in her eyes. "The man isn't as interested in your archaeologist as you believed he was."

Hendricks shook his head. "That can't be. Thabit's communiqués about Annja Creed were very detailed."

"He could have been baiting you."

"Why?" Hendricks waved a hand at the screens at the other end of the room. "I don't have an investment in this mission other than to reach Thabit."

Sophie pulled a lock of hair behind her ear. "I don't know. If I'd had more time to properly plan this, I might have found another angle we could have played."

"No." Hendricks glared at the screen and kept seeing the ambush over and over again in his mind. "This is the only thing we've had on Thabit in years. The man is a ghost. We only see him after he's struck, or when he wants us to."

Sophie looked up from the tablet. "What do you want me to do?"

"What do you mean?"

"MacKenzie might not represent much to the CIA these days, but when things turn bloody, he's one of my top operators. I don't want to lose him on a wild-goose chase. I could scrub this before we lose anyone."

Hendricks looked back at the haggard faces of the archaeologists. "And just leave these people to their fates?"

"They might catch a bullet during the ensuing confrontation, anyway. There are no guarantees how this will turn out." Sophie paused. "I'm not running a charity here. If we proceed, this will still count toward that favor I owe you."

For a moment, Hendricks didn't respond. He didn't want to lose the chance at taking Thabit down. But leaving those people to their fates wasn't an option. "Let's go."

Sophie smiled. "I'm glad you said that. I'm still willing to pursue Thabit another way if you can come up with one. I don't mind having a high-profile agent in the CIA owe me one."

If he did end up owing her, he wouldn't be the only CIA agent who did.

She tapped the earwig she wore. "Dove, your operation is

cleared. Begin extraction." She glanced back at Hendricks. "This should be entertaining."

Hendricks tried to ease some of the pain in his stomach by stretching, but it was nerves and the pain wouldn't go away until the action brewing in the Atlas Mountains was resolved. Silently, he watched as Rafe MacKenzie and his men crept in. He'd lost track of which of the red figures was Annja Creed.

24

North of Marrakech
Atlas Mountains
Kingdom of Morocco

Two snipers remained at the ridgeline, each armed with heavy-caliber Barrett rifles capable of shooting holes in cinder-block walls and armored vehicles. The rest of the mercenaries advanced with MacKenzie. They followed the incline of the hill and stayed behind boulders and scrub grass as much as they could. The proximity of the campfires would dull the Bedouin warriors' night vision, as well.

All small things, but they were the edge MacKenzie planned to capitalize on.

Carrying the AK-47 in front of her, Annja stayed to MacKenzie's left as she crept down the incline. Although the day had been fiercely hot, the night had cooled considerably, dropping into the high fifties. The wind chill dropped that even further. Her boots crunched in the arid soil despite her attempts to remain silent.

Thirty yards ahead of them, a Bedouin guard sat on a rock and stared out at the night, looking right at them. Except he couldn't see them. Then, abruptly, his body language changed as he sat up straighter and took a new grip on his assault rifle.

The earwig in Annja's ear picked up MacKenzie's quiet

order. He had given her the device only moments ago and told her to stay off the frequency unless she needed him. None of the mercenaries talked, but Annja had heard a woman's voice briefly acknowledge MacKenzie and inform him the operation was clear.

Annja had been told the woman was "tech support." It made sense that someone would need to manage the satellite uplink, but she couldn't help wondering where the uplink was coming from.

"Take the sentries down *now*," MacKenzie repeated.

Annja wanted to shut her eyes. It was one thing to respond in defense to violence, but it was another to know that it was coming, and that it was about to take the lives of unsuspecting victims. Not that these Bedouins were victims.

The sniper in front of Annja suddenly dropped in his tracks as his head burst like a dropped pumpkin. A split second later, the harsh cracks of the sniper rifles rolled down the incline, but the bodies had already fallen, taken out before they heard the bullets that killed them.

"All right, everybody dig in." MacKenzie sounded calm as he took up position behind a rocky shelf. "Make your shots count."

Annja lay on her stomach as she pulled the AK-47 to her shoulder. She hated fighting this way. It was one thing to be in the heat of battle, but it was another to deliberately take out targets—*people*—from a distance. Tactically, it made sense, but it appalled her.

You're saving your friends.

She followed a Bedouin running for cover, settled her sights over him and squeezed the trigger. The rifle bucked slightly against her shoulder. The bullet caught the Bedouin somewhere in the chest and spun him off balance, sprawling him to the ground.

Inside the lean-to, David Smythe fell forward, his hands

still bound behind him. Nadim lurched up, then quickly fell on Souad, covering the boy with his body.

Unwilling to leave those people undefended, Annja took two more shots and put down a second man but missed a third. Then she got her feet under her and ran in a wide circle around the camp.

MacKenzie's voice popped into her head through the earwig. "Creed, what do you think you're doing?"

"Saving the people we came here to save." Annja ran through the darkness as fast as she could.

Curtain Bar
K Street
Washington, D.C.

HENDRICKS STRUGGLED to keep track of all the movement on the large monitor, but in the end there was just too much happening. It was like that in battle. The red and blue figures, and the yellow hostages, moved too quickly for him to follow. He forced himself to take deep, slow breaths. He clenched his fists under the table.

"What is she doing?" Sophie said in disbelief. "She's going to get herself killed."

Suddenly, the image on the screen flickered and changed. The Bedouin camp shrank and immense darkness pooled around it as the view telescoped back.

"There's a bogey in the area," the male tech said in a flat voice.

"What bogey?" Sophie snapped.

"An airplane has entered the encounter zone."

Even as Hendricks searched the monitor for an airplane, the craft lit up. The coloration changed to a uniform steel-gray that lifted the plane out of the night.

"Do we know its origins?" Sophie continued attacking her

tablet. She reached up and clicked the headset that hung in her ear, speaking rapidly in Russian, a language Hendricks was familiar with but not competent in.

Shadows tumbled from the plane as it maintained a heading that would take it near the Bedouin camp. Parachutes. He leaned forward in his chair. "It's Thabit."

Sophie swore in a handful of languages.

"Thabit has access to these kinds of people and hardware?"

Hendricks clenched his fists. "This is why we were after the man, Sophie. We don't know everything he has. All we know is that he has a personal fortune and is tied to several Shiite movements."

Sophie grimaced. "Well, then, this little fishing expedition of yours is going to cost us more than we had anticipated. MacKenzie and his people might be able to handle the Bedouin, but not this." She turned her attention to her headset. "Dove? We have a problem."

Paralyzed with helplessness, Hendricks felt his heart and his hopes sinking as quickly as the parachutists gliding toward the Bedouin camp. "Have MacKenzie get Annja Creed out of there. If we can hold on to her, we might still have something."

North of Marrakech
Atlas Mountains
Kingdom of Morocco

THE ASSAULT RIFLE WEIGHED her down and Annja almost considered throwing it away as she ran. But then she'd be left defenseless. Except for the sword. And she didn't want to show up to a gunfight with a sword unless she had to.

She circled behind the lean-to, watching the Bedouins go down under the withering fire of MacKenzie and his troop. Bodies lay sprawled among the large tents while the combatants tried to hole up around natural defenses like boulders and low ridges.

As Annja closed in, bullets ripped through the fabric and she hear someone cry out. Two Bedouin sprinted for the lean-to. Neither was Mustafa.

One of MacKenzie's people, a woman, ran toward them firing at another Bedouin behind a small rock pile on the other side of a fire pit. She didn't see the two Bedouin running toward the lean-to until it was too late. They lifted their weapons.

Knocked off balance by their bullets, the woman tried to find cover, but the Kevlar body armor only protected her to a point. She managed three steps, then collapsed.

By that time, Annja had her rifle up and the first of the Bedouin in her sights. She stitched a handful of rounds across the man's chest and he looked down at his body in surprise, as he fell.

The other Bedouin managed to slide behind a hill. Annja fired a few rounds into the ground along the ridge to keep him pinned down as she raced for the back of the lean-to.

Transferring her rifle to her left hand, she seized the sword out of the otherwhere and slashed vertically through the thick canvas. Another slash, this one horizontal at chin height, freed the canvas to fall in on itself as she released the sword.

The darkness inside was splintered by the fires in the center of camp. David Smythe, Cory Burcell, the other graduate students and the *khettara* craftsmen lay on the ground. One of them held his hands to his wounded leg.

Souad recognized their rescuer first. "Annja!" The boy tried to push up from the ground, but his father kept him down and growled a warning.

A Bedouin appeared in the doorway and brought up his rifle. Annja managed to get her weapon up first and squeeze the trigger. The rounds froze the man in place, then he dropped.

Annja stepped to one side of the opening and covered the front of the lean-to with her weapon. "Come on! Get out of there!"

Nadim released his son and Souad bounded out, followed immediately by his father, who stepped on the slashed canvas and ripped it even further. The others poured from the structure, with Smythe and Cory Burcell bringing up the rear.

"Where do we go?" Smythe asked.

"Into the mountains. Anywhere away from here." Annja fired again as two more Bedouin approached.

Smythe got the graduate students moving.

Cory paused at Annja's side as she reloaded. "They've got Theresa."

"I know. I'll get her." Annja slammed a fresh magazine home.

Cory shook his head. "*We'll* get her." He stayed low and ran parallel behind the row of Bedouin tents.

Groaning as she watched her rescuees scatter, Annja glanced up at Smythe and saw that the group was getting away easily. No one had spotted them. She ran after Cory.

Then she heard the woman's voice again over the earwig. "Dove, we have a problem."

"What?" MacKenzie replied.

"Airborne troops headed your way."

In disbelief, Annja looked up and almost tripped over loose rocks. She caught herself and kept moving. For a moment she didn't see anything, then—only because the parachutes blotted out the stars behind them—she spotted the arrivals.

She paused beside Cory at the back of the tent that housed the women.

"Where's your knife?" he asked.

Annja bent as if she was picking something up from the ground, then pulled the sword from the otherwhere and slashed through the tent.

Surprise filled Cory's dust-covered and bruised face. "Where did you find that?"

"On the ground."

"I don't know how I missed it."

"Get them out of there. We have to go."

Cory tore away the fabric.

Annja felt sure their situation was about to get a lot worse.

WHEN HE SPOTTED THE parachutists, MacKenzie swore with inarticulate rage. "Who are those people?"

"We believe they belong to your target."

MacKenzie counted eighteen parachutes. There were probably more he missed. If they had been sent by Habib ibn Thabit, the man wasn't wasting time. Overhead, he heard the faint drone of airplane engines only now reaching him through the battlefield gunfire.

"Is he with them?" MacKenzie sighted through his rifle's sights and bracketed another Bedouin's head as the guy ran toward a tent. That was the last place MacKenzie had seen Annja Creed headed. He squeezed the trigger and watched the Bedouin spill forward in a jumble of arms and legs.

"We don't know."

MacKenzie got up and ran toward the camp. "But it's not very likely, is it?"

"No."

Trust Sophie to give it to him straight. She was never one to beat around the bush. Judging from the descent rate of the parachutes, they'd be among them in short order.

"That's too bad, because the rescue op here was going so well."

"You have a casualty."

That surprised MacKenzie. "Who?"

"Jane Doe." Sophie gave him the cover name of one of the female mercenaries. MacKenzie hated to hear it. He'd worked with the woman on a few other missions and she'd always been dependable.

"Given the changing parameters of your current mission, we've chosen a new objective for you."

MacKenzie went into the camp in a crouch, half stepping quickly the way the military had taught him, keeping the rifle up while keeping himself mobile and as small as he could. "What?"

"Get Annja Creed out of there."

MacKenzie knew Annja wasn't going to agree to that. "That could be a problem."

"You're not paid to point out problems." Sophie's voice held a dangerous edge. "You're supposed to solve them."

And survive. But MacKenzie didn't mention that. He changed his course and headed for Annja Creed's position behind the tent. She was linked in over the comm. She would know he'd be coming and what he intended to do.

25

Get Annja Creed out of there.

A chill passed through Annja when she heard the order. It was the first true indication she'd had that MacKenzie wasn't calling his own shots.

"Let's go, let's go." Cory reached through the back of the tent, grabbing for the graduate students and hustling them along.

Annja had been looking out for the Bedouin warriors; now she had to add MacKenzie and his crew to that list.

And the parachutists. You can't forget about them.

When one of the graduate students slipped, Annja caught the young woman by the arm to steady her.

Annja sensed the presence above her before she saw the parachutist and brought her rifle to bear as she looked up. He swooped in on her like a predatory bird, letting go of one of the guide controls and reaching for the machine pistol holstered across his abdomen.

Bracketing him in her sights, Annja squeezed the trigger. The bullets caused him to jerk reflexively. Thinking that he might, like her, be wearing Kevlar body armor, she put her next burst into his face, then barely had time to dive to the side as he fell.

She rolled to her feet and awkwardly came up with the rifle, but she still had it. Swiveling, staying low, she wheeled around to where the parachutist lay on the mountainside twenty feet away. The parachute twisted in the breeze for a moment, then gave a final flutter and draped over the man. He didn't move.

"Annja!" Cory was on his way up the mountain. "Come on!"

"More are coming!" Theresa pointed into the sky.

Annja spotted ten or fifteen more parachutists dropping out of the night. Few Bedouin warriors remained to engage them, and most were trying to escape.

She thought wistfully of Abdelilah Karam's scroll, the part she didn't have, and wished she knew where to look. But the first priority was the safety of the archaeological team. She turned and ran.

Only a short distance ahead, though, she saw that there was no place to run. More parachutists landed ahead of them, dropping from the sky like ravens. Several of them fired bursts over their heads, driving them to the ground.

Annja pulled up behind a ridge with Theresa and Cory.

"Oh, man!" Cory peered over the ridge at the airborne troops who were already shrugging out of their parachute harnesses. "We are *so* screwed. Until you shot that guy, I thought they were here to rescue us." He looked at her reproachfully. "Who are they?"

Annja shook her head. "I don't know."

"And who are the guys you're out here with? Friends of yours?"

Get Annja Creed.

"Not exactly." Annja peered over the ridge, searching for an escape route. The parachute arrivals were digging in, setting up a perimeter and cutting off any forward advance.

"Annja," MacKenzie said over the earwig.

Annja didn't reply. She was angry at him, but mostly at herself. She wished she had waited for Garin. Part of the reason she hadn't was because she didn't like having to ask for anything. Especially from him. Their relationship, and the relationship they each had with Roux, was complicated.

But waiting on Garin's help might have taken too long. Of course, given her present circumstances, late or early didn't seem to matter much. Nobody was safe.

"Annja, I know you can hear me." MacKenzie sounded slightly out of breath.

"It would probably be better if you stayed away from me right now." Annja peered through the darkness, searching for MacKenzie. She didn't know who she felt more threatened by, him or the new arrivals.

"Help!" Theresa called.

Annja turned to see MacKenzie standing behind Theresa. He had his left arm wrapped over her throat, holding her back against him. A flat black pistol in his right hand was pointed at Annja.

Cory launched himself at MacKenzie. Maybe he didn't see the pistol, or maybe he thought he could overwhelm MacKenzie. Either way, MacKenzie swung the pistol in a blur and laid the barrel along Cory's temple when he got close. Poleaxed and out on his feet, Cory toppled and lay at Theresa's feet. She struggled against MacKenzie, but it didn't do any good.

Annja pointed the rifle, but only the barest profile of MacKenzie's face showed past Theresa's head. He held his pistol against the young woman's neck. In the moonlight, even if Annja had been an excellent shot, she couldn't have guaranteed success. And she still didn't know if MacKenzie was the enemy. Or if he worked for one.

"You can't shoot me, Annja. You're not that good. You also don't want me to accidentally pull this trigger. Even if you miss me, I can't say that I won't shoot. These aren't exactly stress-free moments we're enjoying here."

Even though she decided she wasn't going to shoot, Annja

didn't lower her weapon. "She doesn't have anything to do with this. Let her go."

"If I let her go, you might try something stupid."

"I was stupid when I took you on for a partner."

"Pains me to hear you say that. Matter of fact, if this present situation hadn't gone toxic, I'd have gotten your friends out of here, and I'd be a hero."

"Who are you working for?"

"Can't say. I subcontract for a woman who organizes jobs sometimes. This is just something she took on from somebody else. A handoff."

"Are you there?" Annja spoke sharply as sporadic gunfire echoed around them. "I heard you talking to MacKenzie earlier."

No response.

MacKenzie shook his head. "She doesn't like talking to people."

"She's going to talk to me."

"I don't think so."

"I'm not going to leave these people here to die."

"If you come with me now, they can live. Once those guys figure out you're gone, those men will walk away."

Doing the math on that didn't take long. Annja stared at MacKenzie over her rifle sights. "So those people are after me, too?"

The woman at the other end of the commlink cursed.

MacKenzie blinked. "We haven't got a whole lot of time. Those men are closing in. I'm the only chance you've got."

Beyond MacKenzie, Yahya dropped into position and pointed his rifle at Annja's face. The young man looked grim and merciless behind the weapon.

"Annja Creed!" A man's voice rang out over the mountain. He had a Middle Eastern accent.

Not taking her gaze off MacKenzie, Annja spotted one of

the parachutists out of the corner of her eye. He was standing in the open. David Smythe, gripped by the hair and on his knees, sat on the ground beside him.

"Annja Creed, I am going to shoot this man. Then I am going to shoot another one. Show yourself."

"You're not the only way out of here," Annja told Mac-Kenzie.

MacKenzie's expression hardened. "Don't be a fool. You can't go out there."

Annja tossed the AK-47 away and rose to her feet with her hands over her head. She raised her voice. "Over here."

The unknown woman's voice crackled over the earwig. "Those men will kill you when they're done with you."

"I don't know that you people aren't planning the same thing."

"We want the man responsible for sending them here."

"Who would that be?"

No reply.

The parachutist holding David Smythe waved her forward. "This way, Creed."

Conscious of the rifles trained in her direction, Annja started walking.

MacKenzie's voice was flat in her ear as he asked, "Do you want me to kill her?"

A chill spread between Annja's shoulder blades, but she kept walking. If she turned around now, the man holding Smythe might either kill the archaeologist or her. She was committed.

"No." The woman sounded angry. "Get your team out of there, Dove."

"Roger that."

Annja kept walking till she reached Smythe's captor. She studied his features, but she hadn't seen him before. The

Middle Eastern heritage was apparent in his dark skin, black hair and dark eyes.

"I'm glad you are being sensible," the man said softly. He released Smythe, who fell to the ground.

Annja knelt slowly to examine the professor. "David?"

"I'm all right." Gingerly, Smythe straightened, but only managed to get to his knees before their captor dropped a gloved hand on his shoulder and kept him down.

"Stay there, Professor Smythe. You are going, as well." The gunman swept his gaze over the mountain. "I suppose the men you were with abandoned you?"

"I don't know."

"Well, we will find out soon enough." He looked at her. "You may call me Hamez."

"Do you work for Habib ibn Thabit?"

"You will find out what you need to know when the time is right. Give me your phone."

Annja pulled it from her pocket and handed it over. Hamez dropped it on the ground and smashed it underfoot. He waved over two men. One of them forced Annja to her knees and secured her hands behind her back with disposable cuffs.

Annja barely controlled her anxiety. As long as her hands had been unbound, she wasn't helpless. She could have reached for the sword. She knelt quietly beside Smythe.

"Annja?" Fear showed in Smythe's eyes as he looked at her. "Who are these people?"

"I think they work for a man named Habib ibn Thabit."

"But who is he?"

"I don't know." Annja took a deep breath and tried to remain calm.

"What does he want with you? With us?"

"I don't know that, either, but I think it has to do with the scroll Mustafa found." Annja scoured the countryside for MacKenzie and his people, but saw nothing.

"What's the significance of the scroll?"

"I don't know that, either. I only got a piece of it." Annja looked at him. "Have you ever heard of a Muslim historian named Abdelilah Karam?"

"No. Why?"

Annja sighed. "I wish I knew, but that man—dead for hundreds of years—seems to have started all of this."

"But that doesn't make any sense."

"Not yet." Annja studied Hamez, who was talking over a commlink. She couldn't overhear the conversation. "I thought at first they were just here for the rest of the scroll. But they wouldn't want us if that was true."

She wondered what was really at stake. If Thabit was after her for some reason, and MacKenzie was *not* after whatever the scroll represented, that could only mean that MacKenzie—or whoever he was ultimately working for—was after Thabit.

Quite the little triangle you've got yourself involved in, Annja. Things were definitely interesting, but she hadn't given up hope of getting away. She just couldn't do that with all the dig team at risk. Getting away later with Smythe was going to be difficult enough.

26

Several minutes passed and Annja's knees started aching from the strain of kneeling. She was also conscious of the earwig in her ear canal and her connection to MacKenzie's unseen masters. They probably had a GPS lock on the device, as well. She didn't know whether to be relieved or concerned.

The possibility remained that Hamez or his men might find it.

Boots crunched across the dry soil. She looked up and saw Hamez returning, followed by two men. Between them, they forced Mustafa to stumble along. The Bedouin leader's hands were bound behind his back. They threw him on the ground in front of Annja.

Bruised and battered, one eye swollen shut, several teeth missing in front and blood running down his chin, Mustafa still managed to glare at Annja. "I should have killed you the night I saw you."

She had bigger problems than he was currently in position to offer.

Hamez looked at Annja. "This is Mustafa?"

"Yes."

"He killed one of my men while they were trying to take him."

Mustafa spat blood at Hamez's boots. "Put a knife in my hand and give me the chance to kill another."

Hamez ignored him, then produced the scroll. Annja's heart leaped. "Is this the scroll that was found? The one you have been asking about?"

So they were interested in the scroll? Annja filed that away, but she still didn't know where she fit into their scheme. "Yes."

Hamez stared at her, then spoke quickly to one of his men, who took Smythe by the arm, pulled him to his feet and led him a short distance away. Hamez pulled out his knife.

"The man I work for wishes to know what you have learned about the scroll."

Annja hesitated.

"If I get the impression you are lying to me, or holding back, I will have Professor Smythe executed. Do you believe me?"

Annja swallowed. Her mouth was dry. "Yes."

"Then tell me."

"The scroll belonged to Abdelilah Karam, a historian of the caliphate during Muhammad's reign."

Hamez walked away and said something into his commlink. He was too far away for Annja to hear, and she didn't know much of the language, anyway.

Mustafa lay on the ground and cursed his pain and the men who held him captive. He promised them unholy wrath once he was free.

Hamez returned to Annja. Her stomach threatened to roll. She didn't know anything else to tell the man. She hoped it had been enough to keep Smythe alive.

"What is in the scroll?"

Annja returned the man's gaze. "I don't know. The only thing I can tell you is that it belonged to Karam. I've traced down other leads to Fes. There was a professor at the university there who studied Karam. I planned to take the scroll there to see if I could get it translated. Or at least compare it to other examples of his work."

Hamez frowned. "You cannot read the scroll?"

"No." Annja looked at the old paper. "But if you let me examine it, I might be able to learn something."

For a moment, Hamez hesitated. Then he leaned down behind her, thrusting his face into hers. His breath blew warm on her cheek. "If you try to escape, I will have Professor Smythe killed. And I will kill you. Do you understand?"

"Yes."

Hamez leaned in a little more. Annja felt the cold steel press against her flesh. A second later, the plastic cuffs fell off her wrists. Hamez helped her up.

"Remember, if you run, I kill your friend. And you will not get away." Hamez's expression was hard.

Before Annja could respond, Hamez pulled his pistol and shot Mustafa through the head. The Bedouin warlord relaxed back against the ground, his face a mask of surprise.

Annja got the message.

As he holstered his pistol, Hamez looked up. Gazing in the same direction, Annja spotted the two small cargo helicopters speeding toward them. A moment later, the chopping beats of the rotors passed over them.

Hamez's men laid down flares to mark out a landing zone. The helicopters set down easily, the rotor wash whipping up a wave of sand and dust.

Annja wrapped her arm over her nose and mouth to keep from choking, and squinted through the haze. Hamez put an arm on her shoulder and pushed her forward.

"Let's go."

Annja took a final look around the mountain. The fires in the Bedouin camp had died down, and four of the tents had been reduced to faintly glowing embers. Burned bodies lay in all of them, though whether they had been killed by flames or gunfire, she didn't know.

There was no sign of MacKenzie or his men, but they would be out there watching. She wondered if, had she not been wearing the earwig, they would have killed her, or if they would have gambled on her eventually leading them to Habib ibn Thabit.

David Smythe was put on the second helicopter, Annja on the first. As it lifted from the ground, she shook the earwig out of her ear and flicked it through the open cargo bay doors without being noticed, then went to the back of the storage area.

She sat on the floor and leaned her head back. But just to be sure, she reached out and felt the haft of the sword in the otherwhere. It was there, and touching it made her feel better.

"WELL, THAT WAS STUPID, Annja." MacKenzie glared down at the earwig at his feet.

The tiny device resembled a small seashell against the dry ground.

"They found the device?" Sophie sounded calm and distant over the commlink.

MacKenzie knelt and recovered the earwig, closing it in his fist as he lifted his eyes to where the helicopters faded against the stygian horizon. "No. She got rid of it."

"What was she thinking?"

MacKenzie grinned. He knew exactly what Annja Creed had been thinking, and he respected her for it. "That she'd rather deal with one enemy than a pair of them."

"Who does she think is going to help her get out of this?"

"You haven't seen her operate. She's good." MacKenzie put the earwig in his pocket and waved to his remaining people. He'd lost two more men, cutting his force to seven, not counting him and Yahya. "Maybe she doesn't have a taste for blood, but she'll kill to save herself or others. She believes she's going to get herself out of this."

He waved Yahya over and the young man looked up at him expectantly.

"Go through the Bedouin camp. Find whatever arms Mustafa had and see if you can round up some of those horses for pack animals." The horses had scattered as soon as the first attack had started, but some of them hadn't gone far. "Let's salvage as much as we can."

Yahya nodded out at the darkness. "What about them?"

The archaeology team was scattered and in hiding, staying well away from MacKenzie and his team. Evidently they didn't trust anyone.

"Leave them alone. Let them take whatever water and supplies the Bedouins have that we don't need. They've got enough locals there to survive the walk to Marrakech. They aren't our problem."

"I should have shot that woman when I had the chance," Yahya said.

"No." He knew that Yahya hated the way Annja Creed had monopolized his attentions lately. The young man was still intent on learning how to be everything MacKenzie was.

"She is bad luck."

"You picked up too many superstitions from those West Africans you've been hanging around with. That woman isn't bad luck. She's one of the luckiest I've seen. Go get those munitions like I told you."

Yahya frowned, considered a rebuttal if the studious look on his face was any indication, then went without another word.

"What are your plans?" Sophie asked over the commlink. "If you're not going to provide aerial support—"

"I don't want to draw Thabit's attention in any way."

"—then we're going to ride back to Marrakech and see about securing vehicles."

"To go to Fes?"

"She did mention that was where she needed to go next to understand that scroll." MacKenzie craned his neck. "If we ride all night, we should be in Marrakech before daybreak. She's not going to be able to get into that university until it opens."

"Fes is two hundred and fifty miles northeast of Marrakech. By the time you get back to the city, it will be several more hours till you get to Fes."

"Maybe. She might not go there, anyway."

Sophie sighed irritably. "We don't have any other leads."

"Then I'll go to Fes. Even if she gets there ahead of me, she has to find whatever it is she's looking for. That will take time, too."

Sophie was silent for a moment. "Fine. I'm going to see if I can field an asset or two in the city to help out with the surveillance."

That caught MacKenzie's attention. "This op is so big you've got to backstop me?" He couldn't decide if he was more surprised or annoyed.

"No, but the costs are starting to mount. You should have been done with this by now."

MacKenzie couldn't think of anything to say to that. He hefted his rifle and walked over to Mustafa's body. Taking a Mini Maglite from his pocket, he quickly rifled through the dead man's clothing.

Aside from some personal items and paper bills and coins, MacKenzie turned up one more item: a scarred brass key slightly longer than his middle finger and almost as big around as a pencil.

Gripping the key by the barrel, MacKenzie trained the flashlight beam on the end. The writing there had worn down from use, but with a little effort, he could make it out. Arabic. He still couldn't read it.

MacKenzie clasped his fist around the key and smiled. Perhaps Annja Creed and Thabit did not have all the chess pieces in the game.

27

Fes-Saïss Airport
Fes
Kingdom of Morocco

The changing pitch of the helicopter rotors woke Annja from her restless sleep. She lifted her hand to wipe an errant hair from her face only to discover she had been once again hand-cuffed. Thankfully, though, her hands were in front of her, which was a lot more comfortable.

The cargo door was closed, so she had no idea what they were headed into. Around her, many of Thabit's shock troops lay asleep, weapons cradled in their arms.

Hamez sat at the front of the cargo area just behind the cockpit, which was shut off from the rear compartment. He watched her grimly. If he had slept during the trip, it didn't show.

A few minutes later, the helicopter glided in and touched down. A guard got to his feet and rolled the cargo door open.

Annja stared through the open bay at the tarmac around them. The use of the airfield surprised her. She'd been ex-pecting a clandestine location. Instead, she could see a city in the distance.

David Smythe sat beside her. "That's Fes."

Annja nodded.

"Have you ever been here before?"

"No."

"You'll like the city." Smythe caught himself and grinned ruefully as he glanced around the cargo area as their guards prepared to debark. "Under other circumstances. Our present conditions are not conducive to sightseeing." He pointed with his bound hands. "If you look closely, you can see where the old walled city—Fes el Bali—butts up against the newer sections."

The older section looked like a maze crammed roughly into the center of the new buildings. The alabaster stone glowed the orange hue of the morning sun.

Bracing her feet, Annja started to rise. One of the guards reached out, clamped a big hand on top of her head and shoved her back down. She thought about hooking one foot behind his and ramming her other foot into his knee. If the move didn't break the knee, it would at least be excruciating and possibly prove debilitating. Instead, she forced herself to remain in a sitting position.

The guards had changed clothing during the flight and now wore casual businesswear. They carried pistols in shoulder holsters and machine pistols in messenger bags. If an onlooker didn't notice the scars and the cold, impersonal stares, the men could have been mistaken as businessmen.

A few minutes later, three SUVs pulled to a halt on the tarmac. A man with a shopping bag got out of one and approached the helicopter. He handed the bag to Hamez, who quickly glanced inside, then nodded.

Before handing Annja the shopping bag, Hamez took out a pair of pants, a shirt and a lightweight jacket and gave those things to Smythe. Then he addressed her. "Change your clothing." He pointed to a small compartment in the back of the helicopter where a man had just strung a tarp. "You must be presentable." He pulled out a knife and cut the plastic strap that bound her wrists.

Not wanting to start an argument, she took the bag and her backpack to the curtained area. A quick glance told her that there was no way out.

She dropped the shopping bag and delved into her backpack. She had a clean T-shirt inside and she put that on. Using a scrunchy, she put her hair back in a ponytail. Then she stepped back out from behind the curtain.

Smythe stood in the new clothes he'd been given and still managed to look like a recent kidnapping victim. Gaunt and haggard, with half-healed scabs on his face. She had a notion to try her luck getting away. Only she'd never be able to bring Smythe and the scroll with her. For the moment, she was trapped.

Hamez scowled at Annja. "Where are the clothes I gave you?"

"In the bag. I'm not wearing them."

"You don't have a choice."

Annja folded her arms. "I do. I'm exercising it."

"If you do not do as I say, I will kill this man."

Meeting Hamez's level gaze, Annja held steady. "If you want to find out about that scroll, you're not going to do that."

"Do not test me."

Agitation tightened Smythe's face.

"It's not a test. I'm setting some boundaries. You can keep me a prisoner here, but I'm not going to dress up for you."

Hamez looked apoplectic.

"I'll do what I have to in order to keep David alive, but you and I both know you're not going to harm him unless you have to." *Or until you've gotten everything that you want out of us.* "Besides that, he probably knows more about this time period and Abdelilah Karam than I do. What really matters to you?"

Jaw tight, Hamez turned and stepped out of the helicopter. "Bring her and the man. Put them in separate vehicles."

One of the men reached out to grip Annja's upper arm. She trapped his hand, twisted it quickly and pinched a nerve on his little finger. In instant, agonizing pain, the man dropped to his knees. Another man drew his sidearm and leveled it at Annja's head.

Slowly, Annja released the captured hand, trusting that the man wouldn't shoot until he had permission to. Quietly, she stared at him until he reluctantly put his weapon away. She slung her backpack over her shoulder and stepped down from the helicopter toward the SUV Hamez had climbed into.

One of the guards opened the back door and Annja was directed to the last row of seats. Seated with her backpack at her feet, she watched as Smythe was taken to another vehicle.

A few minutes later, they got under way.

Berlin, Germany

"Who is she?"

Startled from his reverie, Garin turned from the rain-streaked window overlooking Potsdamer Platz and the Tiergarten. He'd been contemplating both views and wondering which called out more strongly to him.

When he'd been young and traveling with Roux, Garin had often complained of the hardships of camping out under the stars. Back then he hadn't considered it camping under the stars. He'd thought of it as camping out in the rain, in the snow and with vermin in his blankets. Those had not been good times.

Yet, on occasion, he missed them.

He'd loved the cities, loved the noise and activity of them, loved the way they had changed and grown, collapsed and struggled toward rebirth. And always in the center of his world, Berlin had remained close to his heart. No matter what guise it wore, the city was as close to home as Garin knew these days, and he could never go back to the Berlin he had known all those long years ago.

These days, Berlin seemed too big, a fertile ground for skyscrapers and impossible things he'd never dreamed of. He had known Karl Friedrich Schinkel, the Prussian architect who had first conceived of Potsdam Gate and laid out the streets in the early nineteenth century. Garin, under another name at the time, had been a major investor in the rebuilding of the area.

At that time, the Potsdam Gate had been the edge of the city. The wall surrounding the metropolis had existed to keep out the peasantry.

Looking at the rain clinging to the outside of the penthouse windows, Garin realized that—at times—he missed those simpler days very much. He grinned a little at his reflection, remembering they only seemed simple now. When he'd been fighting for his life and the wealth he desperately wanted to acquire, times had not been so simple.

"Garin?"

Garin spotted Chandra's lovely reflection in the glass. He remembered her name with effort, because she was new and because she had not consumed him. It took a very special woman to do that these days.

She was American, a rhythm-and-blues singer starting to build an audience there and in Europe. He'd met her a few weeks ago and taken up with her shortly thereafter.

She was in her twenties and beautiful, with a milk-chocolate complexion. The Southern croon to her voice was her most intriguing facet. When she'd discovered that he truly hadn't been interested in anything permanent, and that he was wealthy, she'd come after him. He'd allowed her to catch him. But it wouldn't be for long.

"I thought you were asleep."

Chandra sat swaddled in the silk bedclothes. Her chin rested on her bended knee and she studied him with liquid brown eyes. "You didn't answer my question."

"What question?" Naked, Garin walked over to the wet bar in the corner and poured them each a glass of wine.

"Who is she?"

"She?"

She frowned. "Don't play coy with me. I sing sad songs for a living. And I know when a man has another woman on his mind."

Garin took her the glass of wine and sat on the bed. "No one you know." So far his people hadn't been able to trace Annja.

She sipped her wine, and seemed equal parts intrigued and incensed. "If you're going to think about her so much, maybe I should get to know her."

Garin smiled. "No. I don't think that's a good idea."

"Why?" Chandra frowned, obviously taking offense. "Don't think I'm good enough?"

Garin shook his head. "That's not it at all."

"Is she a lover?"

Garin laughed at that. "No."

"I know there are other women."

He didn't bother to deny it. Between Chandra's flourishing career and his business interests, their time together had been limited. And no one these days captured his heart. He had seen too many lovers die in the past, and there had been nothing he could do to prevent those deaths. Or the old age that had preceded them. In that regard, he was absolutely bulletproof. People around him died. Everyone but Roux. The old man was the only constant in Garin's life.

But it was captivating to try to figure out what might become of Annja Creed.

If she lived. His attention flicked back to the woman on the bed and he knew that she was waiting for a response. "She isn't a lover."

Chandra cocked an eyebrow. "Maybe you wish she was."

The thought had crossed Garin's mind. Annja was a most enticing woman, and the sword made her even more intriguing.

But the sword also made her dangerous.

Throughout his long life, Garin had learned to fear very little. He did fear the sword. As long as it had been lost, his youth was assured. But now that Joan's sword had been found, he had found a few gray hairs. Things were changing, and there was no telling how much more they would change.

More than that, now that the sword was made whole again, what would happen to it if something happened to Annja?

Garin smiled. "That woman will never become a lover."

"You're sure."

"I am."

"Do you know women so well?"

"I do." Garin smiled at her playfully. "I knew *we* would become lovers."

Her eyes flashed. "Some women would mistake that confidence as arrogance."

"It is arrogance."

"I know many who don't like arrogant men."

"I know very few. And you happen to like arrogant men."

Laughing, she wrapped her arms around Garin's neck. "I do."

Garin kissed her, but his amorous intentions were blunted when his sat phone rang on the side table. He scooped it up at once, saw that it was coming from the agency he was using to find Annja and answered.

Chandra shot him a petulant grimace.

"Yes?"

"We have news of the Creed woman."

Garin waited.

"She is still in Morocco. Apparently she's been captured by Habib ibn Thabit's men and has landed in Fes."

"Get me transport there." Garin pushed up from the bed and walked to his immense closet.

"Already waiting, sir."

Garin punched off the sat phone as he stepped into the closet. "Feel free to stay as long as you like." He shot Chandra an apologetic smile because he did like her.

She pouted. "Is this about her?"

"It is." Garin stepped into clean underwear and pulled on a pair of pants.

"A lesser woman would be jealous."

"If you were the jealous type, neither of us would be here." Garin reached for a silk shirt.

"Do you know when you'll be back?"

"No."

"Call me when you are?"

Garin crossed the room and kissed her. "I will." But his mind was already filled with arrangements for the Morocco trip.

28

The SUV caravan had to slow as it approached the old city sandwiched in the new. When Fes had been built at the turn of the eighth century, it had been constructed for carts to travel the narrow, twisting streets along the banks of the Fes River.

Annja glanced over her shoulder at the two SUVs that trailed the one she was riding in. She felt certain she could have gotten away. She'd gotten quite inventive since coming into possession of the sword. Leaving Smythe wasn't an option, though.

When she turned back to face forward, she found Hamez scowling at her.

"Do not even think about it."

Annja blinked, wide-eyed innocence. "Think about what?"

Hamez cursed. "You are useful only as long as you are controllable, Creed. Remember that."

"What does your employer want?" With Karam's writing, she had no clue. "It would help if I knew what I was looking for."

Hamez shot her an appraising glance. "What is it you normally look for?"

The question caught Annja by surprise. "Everything. I look for everything."

"Then look for that." Hamez turned back around to face front.

Annja reached into her backpack and took out her journal. Diligently, she went back over her notes. It didn't take her long to realize, again, that she simply didn't have enough information to form a hypothesis.

PARKING HADN'T BEEN a consideration when the University of Al-Karaouine had been built in 859. Judging from Hamez's scowl when they had to leave the SUVs in private parking, he hadn't known about that. He assigned two men to Annja, and two also to Smythe, and made sure they were kept separate. Other guards trailed along on the opposite side of the narrow street, in front and behind. Their coats disguised machine pistols.

Annja approached the university with mixed feelings. Smythe had promised to spend a day with her here.

Muslim and Jewish scholars had flocked to the university when it had opened, followed later by Christian sages, to learn from the documents of students who had gone before them. The university was still considered, by some, to be the oldest continually operating academic school in the world.

The architecture was ancient, all keyhole doorways, towers and peaked roofs. It had begun as a mosque, funded by the daughter of a wealthy merchant. The early days had fostered classes on religious instruction and political discussion, which had been tightly intertwined.

And still were.

As they approached, Hamez spoke rapidly on a sat phone. Nearer the university, he changed directions and headed right, toward one of the buildings away from the main entrance.

Annja regretted that. She'd hoped to see the central hub

of the monastery. She was also pretty sure Hamez wouldn't be able to get her in to see the documents she'd told him she would need to continue her research. She was weighing her chances of calling out for help to the young men who were obviously security guards standing at the door when Hamez and the entourage were waved inside.

Glancing back at Smythe, Annja saw the professor was surprised as she was. She followed Hamez through the beautifully tiled corridor. Few students were up this early in the day. College students were the same around the world.

Their footsteps echoed through the long corridors. Display cases lined the hallway with books, scrolls and other artifacts.

After traveling through a maze of corridors, they arrived at a small library.

"Wait here." Hamez waved his men into place. "And watch her."

Annja stared out over the stacks of books that filled the center of the low-ceilinged room. There were desks with computers on them at the front and back of the room, and a small office equipped with photocopy equipment.

An elderly librarian returned with Hamez. He was thin and elegant, with a neatly trimmed salt-and-pepper beard, sad eyes and an easy smile. "Good morning. I am Professor Mahfoud Daoudi and I will be assisting you. I am told that you wish to see the journals left by Professor Ulker Bozdag."

Hamez looked at Annja.

"Yes." She stepped forward and extended her hand. "I'm Annja Creed."

The professor smiled. "My wife loves your show. She said if she had known history could be so interesting, she would have paid attention to me a long time ago."

In spite of the guards around her, Annja laughed. "I'm flattered."

Daoudi waved that away. "Now, if you'll accompany me,

I'll take you to the Bozdag holdings." Daoudi took off at a spry pace and Annja instinctively fell into step with him.

Hamez caught her by the elbow and held her for just a moment, letting her know that she was at the end of a very short tether. She took a couple quick strides to match Daoudi's pace again.

"Ulker Bozdag isn't a well-known writer." Daoudi counted the aisles as they passed. "Would you mind telling me about your interest in the man?"

"I'm not so much interested in Bozdag as I am his research on Abdelilah Karam. Have you heard of him?"

Daoudi shook his head. "Sadly, I am not a student of Bozdag. I don't know of anyone here who is. Until the call I got last night, I was not really aware that we had anything by him in the collections. As you might imagine, we have numerous holdings."

"I'm sorry about that call last night."

Daoudi shrugged. "A little bit of excitement in an otherwise boring day."

Annja tried to remember the last boring day she'd had but could only remember the last day she hadn't been shot at.

"I was given to understand that this was a favor for one of our benefactors."

Annja would have killed to know which benefactor had called in the favor, but she didn't want to involve the professor in whatever trouble might come from Hamez. The professor stopped and walked down an aisle. Gently, he took books from the shelf and passed them to Annja. She wiped off the dust and looked at the unappetizing covers. Time had yellowed the pages and the books felt fragile.

"Are these first editions?" Annja looked at the sketched image of an androgynous angel with a flourish of peacock feathers spreading as wings. The title was *The Order of the*

Peacock Angel: A Summary of Apocalyptic Warnings That Have Been Ignored. Thankfully, the book was in English.

"Yes, they are." Daoudi cocked his head ruefully. He held three more books in addition to the two Annja had. "I have a small room you can use."

"That would be great." Curiosity overwhelmed Annja's survival instinct for the moment.

"Please follow me." Daoudi led the way and Annja followed him as she leafed through the table of contents of one of the books.

"HOW MUCH LONGER will this take?"

Hamez sat in a straight-backed chair near the door of the small office space Daoudi had guided them to. She and Smythe each sat at one of the two tables and divided the books between them. After his captivity among the Bedouin, Smythe looked like the victim of a car wreck.

Two large picture windows overlooked the main library area. Maps of Fes and Morocco lined the walls under glass covers. The maps were decades old and depicted the various stages of the country's formation and documented the events that had shaped the colorful history.

Annja locked eyes with Hamez. "You're welcome to start reading with us. This is a lot of material to cover, and we don't know what we're looking for."

Hamez didn't say anything.

"If you want to do something productive, you might send out for lunch." Annja returned to the book. "We're going to be here for a while."

Hamez's chair creaked as he got up and walked out. The three guards he'd assigned to watch Annja and Smythe remained in place.

Dawnchaser
Mediterranean Sea

"ANNJA TELLS ME SHE does not know how long this will take."

Habib ibn Thabit stood on the flying deck of his yacht as she sailed through the gray-green waters of the Mediterranean Sea. "What she is looking for has been hidden for a very long time, my friend." The cool breeze washed over him and wrapped him in its salty scent. He had grown up on dry desert, but he had learned to love the sea.

At the other end of the sat phone connection, Hamez hesitated. "She says it would help if she knew what she was looking for."

For a moment, Thabit was tempted to reveal what he knew about his ancestors. The secret had been protected for generations. "Just have her keep searching."

"Every minute we spend here increases our risk of discovery. The people that sent the mercenary—MacKenzie—will still be searching for us. And if they find us, they will find you."

"Would you give me up so easily?"

"No. Of course not."

"It gladdens my heart to hear that." In truth, though, Thabit knew Hamez couldn't give him up. The man didn't know where he was, and Thabit wasn't about to tell him.

Thabit watched an albatross wing by overhead. The ungainly creatures trailed the yacht, hoping for food, because the winds were favorable. Once they shifted, the albatrosses would go.

Hamez was silent, and Thabit knew the man was frustrated because he didn't know the significance of the mission he'd been assigned.

"Have patience with her. Give her more time."

"It has been hours."

"That only means she is hours closer to finding that which we seek." *If it is to be found.* Thabit prayed that it was not. It would be far simpler and more rewarding to discover that Annja Creed couldn't find any trace of Karam's histories. Then Thabit could have Hamez put a bullet through her head and be done with her. "I will reward you handsomely for your efforts when this is done."

"I don't do this for the reward. I do this to strike back at our enemies."

"Then know that this is part of that effort." Thabit broke the connection. He stared out at the sea with his hands behind his back. Someone called his name and he turned to find Rachid standing there with a troubled expression.

"There is an unpleasant development in Fes."

Thabit ignored the foreboding he felt. "What?"

"A covert team is en route to the city. I only just learned of this."

"The Americans?"

Rachid shook his head. "The British. They have an MI-6 strike team within three hours of the city."

"How did they find us?"

"I believe someone within the CIA alerted them. I have only been able to get a little information about the operation. It appears the attack on the Bedouin attracted more attention than we had believed."

Thabit considered the situation. The British wanted him as badly as the Americans, but not so badly as the Israelis. They would continue their search, as well.

"Should we tell Hamez?" Rachid asked delicately.

After a moment longer, Thabit said, "No. The work he is doing there with the American archaeologist is important. If they are not finished in three hours' time, the British close in on them and Hamez will put a bullet through Annja Creed's head."

29

"I think I've found something."

Head aching from lack of sleep and sustained intense reading, and maybe from the dust, as well, Annja pushed up from her seat and joined David Smythe at his table.

Some of Smythe's fatigue disappeared with the excitement of discovery.

Hamez hurried over, too. He had sat quietly for the past two hours, but Annja had sensed his growing tension. He kept his hand on the gun at his hip under the jacket.

Smythe trailed a finger over a page. "Bozdag evidently tracked down another book that had entries regarding Abdelilah Karam."

"Why, if there was so much interest in this guy, have we never heard of him?"

Smythe shook his head. "You know as well as I do that we don't know everything. In some ways, history is like space. We really know very little about it except what's around us. The farther you go—back, in the case of history—the less we know. This is only thirteen hundred years, as opposed to figuring out what happened eleven thousand years ago when Atlantis was reputedly still above the Atlantic."

"If it was the Atlantic."

"Exactly, though I am of the opinion that in our present location, we aren't that far from—"

"*Silence!* You chatter like children." Hamez glared at them. He pointed at the book. "What have you found?"

Smythe looked at Annja and she nodded. "As I was saying, Bozdag was evidently basing some of his research on work another historian had done. This other historian—" he bent closely to the page "—Miskawayh, was writing a history of Adi ibn Musafir al-Umaw." He glanced up. "Do you know who that was?"

"Twelfth-century sheikh of Kurdistan. A descendant of Marwan ibn al-Hakim, the fourth Umayyad caliph. Reappointed as caliph by Muawiya I after Ali removed him."

"Exactly. And you recognize the significance of Muawiya, right?" Smythe was riding the excitement high. Before Annja could answer, he explained. "Muawiya's rule was the first caliphate after Muhammad died. That succession split the Islamic people."

"Muawiya was a usurper, a traitor to the beliefs of our people." Hamez surprised Annja with his vitriolic intensity. "Muawiya seized leadership, but did not have God's ear. Only the true family of Muhammad has that." He stared at the book. "This person you are reading about is a false prophet. What you read there is doubtless lies."

"Lies or not," she said, "do you want us to continue?"

Hamez pursed his lips. "Continue. But you are wading in sacrilege."

"According to this," Smythe said, "al-Umaw was supposed to have a book written by Abdelilah Karam concerning some of the events after Uthman's murder."

"It was *not* murder." Hamez kept his voice tightly controlled. "His death came as a result of true believers trying to bring our people back to God."

Annja faced Hamez. "Maybe it would be better if we did this on our own."

Hamez stood his ground.

Annja reached for her tablet PC, disconnecting it from the wall outlet where she was charging it, and started saving images of the sections concerning Karam.

"Where does the Telek Maus fit into this?" She captured another image.

Smythe turned the page and revealed the black-and-white illustration of an androgynous angel with spreading peacock wings. "Because Sheikh Adi ibn Musafir founded the Telek Maus and was believed to be an incarnation of the peacock angel."

The ink drawing looked a little faded. She leaned down and examined the drawing, finally placing her finger on a line of script. "This looks like an artist's signature."

Smythe picked up the magnifying glass he'd borrowed from Daoudi. "If it is, I can't read it. It's Arabic." He glanced up at Hamez. "Maybe you can."

Carefully, as though this was a trick, Hamez leaned down to read. "Ata ibn Wassaf."

Smythe studied the illustration. "I've never heard of him, but he seems to have collaborated with Bozdag on this book as well as the other one I've been through."

Curious, Annja returned to the three books on her table. "Wassaf illustrated one of these books, which is about Karam and the spread of Islam into Morocco." She looked at Hamez. "We need to speak with Daoudi."

"As it turns out, Ata ibn Wassaf was a popular illustrator for Moroccan books." Daoudi led the way through the stacks. "He worked on a number of projects involving religious studies."

Annja trailed at the scholar's heels. She already had an armload of books.

"According to our files, Wassaf died nine years ago."

"Where?"

"Here in Fes. He only left the country a few times. He studied art at Oxford."

"Do you know when he was there?"

"In the 1960s." When Bozdag was studying at the university. With both of the men being young, from Islamic countries, Annja easily saw how they could have come together.

But what had bound them so tightly?

SEVENTEEN BOOKS LITTERED the two tables in the small office. Annja and Smythe had divvied them up. Wassaf's skill was amazing. He'd illustrated histories, children's stories and maps.

She was going through a child's book about the white horse, al-Buraq. It contained several plates of the prophet and the winged animal. In compliance with Muslim belief, Wassaf had left depictions of Muhammad faceless. In Persian art, the horse was nearly always given a human head and features.

The dedication in the children's book caught Annja's eye. It was written in Arabic as well as English.

To my father, Wassaf ibn Fadlan, who first showed me his angel and taught me to draw.

"WASSAF'S FATHER WAS AN illustrator, too?" Annja had returned to Daoudi's desk with Hamez, her entourage.

Daoudi read something off his computer. "Yes. We have some of his books, as well."

"May we see them?"

"Of course."

After writing the reference number down, Daoudi quickly found the books illustrated by Wassaf ibn Fadlan.

Consumed by curiosity, Annja sat on the floor and leafed through the books as quickly as she could. Wassaf ibn Fadlan hadn't been as popular as his son. There were only three books in the university collection, but one of them was about the peacock angel. The illustration of the figure was much like the one Ata ibn Wassaf had drawn in Bozdag's book, but there were differences.

Smythe peered over Annja's shoulder. "Same source material, don't you think?"

"We can't ignore the possibility."

"What are you talking about?" Hamez snapped.

Annja pointed at the illustration of the angel in the book. "This looks like the same angel that was in the other book."

"They were father and son. Perhaps the father taught the son."

"And perhaps there is a source document."

"You are grasping at straws."

"When artists sketch the statue of David, it tends to look the way Michelangelo sculpted it." Annja stared at the man. "Whoever your boss is, he seems to be pretty concerned about what's going on. Is he the kind of boss that would want every stone overturned or not?"

Hamez grimaced. "What do you need?"

"To know if either of these two artists left any journals or personal information about their work." Annja returned to the desk to find Daoudi once more. "Sorry. Last question, I think."

"Of course." The old librarian still acted friendly, but Annja suspected she was wearing out her welcome.

"What can you tell me about the family of these two artists?"

"I am afraid I probably cannot help you with that." Daoudi

hesitated. "Unless the family contributed the artists' personal things for the collection here." He consulted the computer and smiled. "You are in luck. I have both an address and a telephone number."

"Great."

"May I call for you?" Daoudi reached for the phone. "I cannot just give out that information without permission."

"Of course. Please."

Daoudi called and the mechanical response of a recording picked up after a few rings.

"Yes, this is Professor Daoudi at the university." There was no reason to mention another university. Al-Karaouine was the one any resident of the city would immediately think of. "I would like to speak—" He stopped and grinned at Annja. "Someone is there, after all."

The conversation continued in Darija and in a dialect Annja couldn't follow, but when they'd finished speaking, Daoudi turned to her, beaming.

"It seems that Iskandar ibn Silahdar would be delighted to see you. He is, as my wife is, a fan of your television show."

30

Garin stepped off the private plane and accepted the keys to the Land Rover that a well-dressed young man held out for him.

"Welcome to Fes, Mr. Braden. I hope you enjoy your stay in our city."

"Thank you." Garin unlocked the door and swung inside.

"Your agency said you would not be needing a guide through the city."

Garin started the engine. "I won't. It's not my first time here."

"I see." The young man looked anxious. Probably because he was seeing bonus money driving away.

Dropping the transmission into gear, Garin gunned the engine. His sat phone rang for attention and he pulled it out of his jacket.

"Yes?"

"Annja Creed is leaving the university."

"Why?"

"I do not know, Mr. Braden. You asked us to keep at a discreet distance."

"Is she still with Hamez?"

"Yes. And his men. Quite a few men, it would appear. We should have gotten more men ourselves. It is not too late to add them."

"No." Garin stepped harder on the accelerator. With a larger group, Hamez's team would have a better chance of seeing them. "We stay small. We stay invisible. Until we act."

"Yes, sir."

"Are you prepared?"

"Of course." His hired man gave Garin the address where to meet him. Garin knew where it was. He had, after all, been in Fes many times.

Like this time, he had been here to kill someone.

"WE ARE NOT ALONE." MacKenzie sat inside a small teahouse across from Al-Karaouine. Only a few customers were at the other tables, but business was brisk this morning as many students got their orders to go.

Tracking Annja Creed to the university was a no-brainer. She was an archaeologist searching for missing information. It stood to reason she would turn up there. MacKenzie and the surviving members of his team had only arrived an hour ago, but they hadn't had to look too hard before they'd recognized Hamez's men positioned in a loose perimeter around the school.

Yahya sat on the other side of the table eating his pastries. He'd developed a sweet tooth for the *halwa dyal makina*, chocolate-dipped cookies.

"What do you mean?" Sophie said over the earwig.

"I've just spotted a British team in the area." MacKenzie watched the MI-6 agent he'd recognized from past encounters.

"Who?"

"Rallison." MacKenzie pointed the small camcorder on the table toward the man. A satellite link had been hidden within the camera's housing to transmit images or straight video for short periods of time.

Felix Rallison looked like a rugby player, short and power-fully built, but he was a man who could be easily overlooked in a crowd. He was dark, possibly biracial, with cropped hair and a short, full beard. A scar bisected his left eyebrow and trailed down his cheek.

"We see him. Impressive scar."

MacKenzie grinned. "I gave it to him."

"He will know you if he sees you."

"Yeah. I nearly took his eye, and he almost cost me a kidney. He's a dangerous guy."

Yahya lifted a hand, made a pistol and pulled the trigger. He blew imaginary smoke from the imaginary barrel. "Every man dies. You taught me that."

"Not being able to hide in plain sight is a problem for you." Sophie sounded distracted.

"The flip side is that I recognized Rallison and I know the Brits are here. We could have walked in blind to whatever's coming." MacKenzie sipped his tea. "By the way, what is coming? Why are the Brits here?"

"They want your real target as much as we do."

MacKenzie watched Rallison sitting next to a building as if he were only taking advantage of the shade there. A careful scan of the surrounding neighborhood told MacKenzie that MI-6 had at least seven agents working the scene, and more would doubtlessly be posted around the university campus.

"Rallison and his people have the numbers to make a snatch. Or we could throw in with them."

"This is one the boys at MI-6 won't want to share. That's not acceptable."

MacKenzie patted his pocket. "We still have the key."

"But we don't know how the key fits into this. Or even if it does. And that could be something we want to keep off the table."

"No luck with the key, then?"

"Not yet. We're still searching."

Across the street, Rallison's head came up. It was just

enough to tip MacKenzie off. Tracking Rallison's line of sight, MacKenzie spotted Annja Creed walking out of the university surrounded by Thabit's men.

MacKenzie stood and felt the weight of his pistol resting comfortably on his hip under his jacket. "I've got to move."

"Understood. Be advised that our technological presence there is limited."

That was because the city wasn't filled with cameras the way so many metropolitan areas were these days. MacKenzie didn't worry about that. Africa had been a theater of operations for him for some time. He knew how to handle third-world situations with limited intel. Rallison, as far as MacKenzie knew, was used to working with high-tech backup. He'd be out of his element.

That proved true almost immediately when Rallison and his people dropped into close cover on Creed. It wouldn't take long for Hamez to spot the tails and take action.

MacKenzie planned to be in position to capitalize on that mistake.

ONLY BLOCKS FROM THE university, Garin swept the street corners at the irregular intersection and spotted the slim-built young Moroccan standing at the corner just short of the confluence of streets. He carried a duffel bag.

It wasn't who he'd been expecting.

Signaling at the last minute, Garin cut off a taxi jockeying for position, receiving an instant blare of honking reproach. Garin unlocked the door and the young man got in. As soon as the door closed, Garin got under way again.

The young man pulled on his seat belt and sat quietly. He was in his early twenties, hard bodied, with muscular, calloused hands. His face was slightly rounded, his beard cut short and his eyes almost dark enough to look black. He wore jeans and an *X-Men* T-shirt, allowing him to be mistaken for a local or a tourist.

"Did you get everything?"

In answer, the guy unzipped the duffel bag and revealed the gleaming, oily black surfaces of the weapons inside. There was a small selection of pistols and three assault rifles with the butts telescoped in to shrink their size.

"Which would you prefer?"

"Something big." Garin navigated around vendors and pedestrians as he rolled through the streets. The GPS held him on course to the university.

"Desert Eagle .50 caliber. Hard to acquire. But for you, the very best." He took the huge pistol out and offered the weapon to Garin.

"Loaded?"

"Of course."

Garin took the pistol and shoved it under his thigh. He placed the extra magazines for the weapon in his pockets. "What's your name?"

"Qurtubi."

Garin watched how efficiently the young man readied the weapons while keeping them all out of sight of the street traffic. "That's not your name."

"It is."

"That was the name of the man I used to work with. The one who agreed to meet me here."

The young man smiled. "Qurtubi was not my father's name, either, Mr. Braden."

"Family business?"

"Yes."

"Then I hope you're as good as your father."

"I will never be as good as my father, but it will take the most discerning eye to see that difference." Qurtubi stared through the windshield. "And the four of us are going to have to be very good."

"Why?"

"Your target has picked up two other teams that are pursuing her."

"Do you know who they are?"

"One team belongs to the CIA, as you suggested. The other is British. They have received information from local assets who owe my family favors."

Garin continued driving, thinking furiously.

"Our goal here is to save the woman?" Qurtubi asked as calmly as though they were discussing the weather.

"Yes."

"And the others?"

"If they get in the way, we kill them." Garin looked at the other man. "Is that amenable?"

"Of course." Qurtubi glanced at Garin curiously. "Did you take your father's name, as well, Mr. Braden?"

"Why do you ask?"

"Because my father spoke as if he expected me to be meeting with a much...more distinguished man."

"You mean an *older* man." Garin laughed.

"Yes."

"I did take my father's name." That was the easiest explanation.

"Then I hope you are as good as my father said your father was."

"Not quite." Garin glanced at his comrade in arms. "But most people wouldn't be able to tell the difference."

IN THE BACK OF THE SUV again, Annja flipped through the images she'd stored on her tablet PC. Once more, she and Smythe had been split up. Frustrated, she returned the device to her backpack and relaxed into the seat, determined to get some rest before things got busy again. Hamez wouldn't kill them yet, and she was curious about the mystery of Abdelilah Karam.

She had almost dropped off to sleep despite the vehicle's careering through the narrow streets when it came to an abrupt stop. She blinked her eyes open and rubbed them with her palms.

The SUV caravan had pulled to a stop in a narrow alley. Doorways opened into courtyards off the alley on either side. But the doors were all closed. The few pedestrians quickly gave ground to the large vehicles.

With the SUV parked against the wall on her side, Annja couldn't open the door. She slid across the seat and got out on the other side. Fatigue made her feet feel heavy. She automatically reached for her backpack and shrugged into it, resenting the weight.

One of the doorways on her left opened and an Arabic man in his early thirties peered out at her. "Miss Annja Creed?"

Annja put on a smile. If the meeting went well, no one would get hurt. She didn't want this family injured—or worse—on her account. "I am. Mr. Silahdar?"

"Please. Call me Iskandar. I feel as though I know you."

Annja walked toward him and Hamez matched her step for step. David Smythe and two other guards followed. Seeing all the people converging on him, Hamez and his guards looking so somber, Iskandar drew back.

"It's okay." Annja tried a smile and wished that it didn't feel so false. "They're with me."

Skepticism lifted Iskandar's eyebrows. "*These* are your friends?"

Yeah, I wouldn't believe it, either. Annja kept smiling. "More like, they're…associates." That was the smallest lie she could tell, and it was huge.

"All right." Reluctantly, Iskandar pulled the door open.

"I really was not expecting so many people. The man at the university implied that you might be the only one to come calling."

Feeling guilty at bringing trouble to the man's doorstep, Annja stepped into the small courtyard. Flowers, fruit trees and, in the center, a small fountain, which filled the courtyard with the sound of running water.

Iskandar looked nervously at Hamez and the other two men. "The man at the library—"

"Professor Daoudi, yes."

"—he said you were interested in documents my family might have retained from my grandfather and great-grandfather."

"Yes. I know that the university has some of their materials, but I was hoping there might be more."

Iskandar ran a nervous hand through his black hair. "You are putting together a museum show?"

"Not exactly."

"Then what are you doing with these materials?"

"Research for a project." Annja felt Hamez tensing beside her.

"What project?"

Annja didn't blame the man for asking questions. She would have been asking questions, too. But Hamez didn't care for the delay. His voice was sharp when he spoke. "Do you have materials such as Miss Creed suggests?"

Iskandar hesitated again, then nodded. Maybe he truly wanted to help Annja, or maybe he was afraid of Hamez and his thugs.

"There are some materials that my family has been holding on to. You are fortunate to have come here. My two older brothers—"

Hamez strode forward and took Iskandar by one arm. "Let us go get those materials. Time is an issue."

Iskandar had to skip to keep up. "Of course. No problem."

Annja started to follow.

Hamez fixed her with his gaze. "Stay there." His eyes flicked to the two guards. "Make sure she does."

Annja folded her arms. *These guys are* so *not my friends.*

31

In a few minutes, Iskandar and Hamez returned. Iskandar carried a large box and looked apologetic as he sat everything in front of Annja. She hunkered down with him and began to go through books and journals.

Iskandar hesitated, then said in a low voice, "I thought you would have better-mannered associates."

"I apologize for that. You got me on a bad day."

The journals and moleskine notebooks were filled with illustrations and sketches of works in progress at the time, or of places the two artists had visited. But there was also a bundle of letters tied to an old book. The letters had been addressed to Wassaf ibn Fadlan, the older artist. Most of them dated back to the 1920s.

"My father thought they belonged in a museum, but my mother—she was the daughter of Ata ibn Wassaf—insisted they were family possessions and should be honored."

Some of Iskandar's fear had subsided as his interest in Annja increased.

Hamez nudged the box with the toe of his shoe. "So a cardboard box was the best you could do for these honorable things?"

Iskandar's face flushed with color. "I got these two years ago. After my mother died. I did not know what to do with them. My brothers did not want them."

Annja flipped through the book that had been tied to the letters. "They're in good shape."

"I did not ask for this." He looked pointedly over his shoulder at Hamez. "I did not ask for any of this."

"Have you studied these?" Annja's heart sped up a little when she saw the title page of the journal. The peacock angel soared over a desert landscape where a woman sat on a camel and faced an army of swordsmen.

"Yes. Many times." Iskandar sidled around to Annja as Hamez peered over their shoulders. "My mother was my great-grandfather's favorite. She loved to draw and to paint. While he was alive, he taught her. She always said this was my great-grandfather's *special* book."

"What made it special?" Annja turned the page and found another drawing of the woman on the camel, this one much closer and more detailed.

"My great-grandfather was a man of peace. He believed in the future of Islam, and that we needed to all once more learn to live in peace." Iskandar pointed to the page. "This drawing is of the war that split the Muslim people."

"The Battle of the Camel."

"Yes." Iskandar nodded enthusiastically.

"But what is the peacock angel doing there?"

"My great-grandfather told my mother that out of this battle came the knowledge of the peacock angel."

"Adi ibn Musafir al-Umawi was the founder of the peacock angel."

Iskandar looked at her in surprise. "Not many people know that history."

"I've been learning a lot about it lately."

"I do not know much about it myself."

"It is godless blasphemy." Hamez frowned in disgust. "A celebration of Shaytan. Those people are wrongly turned."

Annja didn't comment. She continued leafing through

the pages. Several contained head-and-shoulder sketches of major players in the struggle to inherit Muhammad's mantle. She had Iskandar translate, quickly learning to recognize the names of Aisha, Muhammad's young widow; Ali ibn Abi Talib, the prophet's cousin and son-in-law; and Uthman ibn Affan, the third caliph, who was assassinated by rebels supporting Ali's claims to be the next caliph.

A few more pages into the journal, Annja found a page with an old man's face and a familiar name—even in Arabic—under it. This sketch showed the man in his older years, with a long beard, hollow, haunted eyes and thin shoulders.

Annja pointed at the sketch. "Do you know him?"

Iskandar leaned in and read. "Abdelilah Karam? Mother said this man was a historian, and that he was the man who knew the secret."

Annja's heartbeat picked up. "What secret?"

Iskandar shrugged. "She said my great-grandfather hoped to tell the story of the battle for caliph, that he might be able to bring the Muslim people together once more." He wiggled his finger over the pages. "Keep going. There are other sketches."

Annja saw several images depicting armed men climbing over a courtyard wall. Once they were in the courtyard, they advanced on the main house. Over the next few pages, more violence ensued, some of it very graphic.

"This is my great-grandfather's interpretation of the assassination of Uthman, the third caliph." Iskandar smiled. "It is a very horrible thing, is it not?"

"Yes."

"But my great-grandfather was a brilliant artist. These are just thumbnails—sketches. It would have been wonderful to see these fully realized."

"Yes." Annja turned more pages and discovered yet another assassination.

The sketch showed a regal figure kneeling in prayer with

an armed man poised to strike him with a sword from behind. In the next sketch, he was pierced with the sword, but in the one after that, he was still fighting. At the end of the sequence, guards had the assassin in custody while the praying man lay upon the ground.

Annja felt the power of the art. "This is the assassination of Ali?"

"Yes." Iskandar's voice was somber. "The assassin was Abd-al-Rahman ibn Muljam, a Kharijite seeking revenge for some fight."

"The Battle of Siffin."

"Perhaps. My mother said during that battle Ali declared a truce but the Kharijites did not agree."

"The Kharijites believed God would declare the victor, and Ali had turned away from the will of God. That was why they later assassinated him after he became caliph."

Hamez shifted behind them, obviously ready to go. "They—and all their descendants—should have been executed and their blood spilled on the ground."

"Not exactly something Judge Judy would agree with." Arabic script flowed across the next few pages, leading finally to a section written in Kufic, the same language used in the scroll. "Do you know what this says?"

"The Arabic part, of course. It is about this man Karam. As I said, he was a historian." Iskandar reached for the book. "It says Karam was driven from his homeland. He spent time among the Yazidi people in Sinjar."

Iskandar shrugged and added, "To get peace after all the bloodshed he had seen. It also mentions that he brought his histories with him, and that there were people pursuing him to destroy those books."

"Why?"

"Because of this secret. Whatever it was."

Annja pointed to the section in Kufic. "Do you understand any of this?"

"No. My mother said she could not translate it."

"Did your great-grandfather translate this?"

"I don't know. Possibly. My mother said he was very good with languages."

"Is there any chance a translation exists within this material?"

"If it is there, I have not ever seen it."

"How closely have you been through these things?"

Iskandar smiled wryly. "I am a carpenter. If you want a house built or reconstruction done, I can do those things."

"Would it be possible for me to borrow these? I promise to get them back to you."

Iskandar hesitated. "My mother wanted me to care for them."

Hamez snorted derisively. "That is not much care." He looked at Annja. "Do you need these books?"

"I can take images of them if he wants to keep the physical copies."

"We do not have time for that." Hamez nodded to one of the guards. "Take the box."

The man bent and lifted the box.

"Wait! They do not belong to you!" Iskandar stood and started after the guard.

With blinding speed, Hamez whirled and slammed his left palm against Iskandar's chest as he slid a leg behind the younger man. Iskandar hit the ground and groaned in pain. Hamez drew his pistol in his right hand and pointed it at the man's head.

Annja stepped forward and hammered Hamez's arms to the side with her forearm. The pistol's detonation sounded incredibly loud in the courtyard.

Hamez spun on Annja. Rage tightened his features into a hard mask.

Annja kept herself from pulling the sword. David Smythe was in enemy hands, and her chances against Hamez with a gun weren't good. She raised her hands.

"You don't have to kill him."

Hamez's eyes narrowed to slits. "You do not tell me whom I may kill and whom I may not."

Annja kept her mouth shut and her hands in the air. She had done all she could do. Chest heaving in fright, the young man stayed put.

Hamez lowered his pistol and nodded toward the courtyard entrance. "Go."

Annja walked toward the doorway, listening for the gunshot that she feared might come. If Hamez did kill Iskandar, she was going to go for the sword and kill him. Her throat was dry, but they walked out into the alleyway without incident. She didn't let out a breath until the courtyard door closed behind her.

One of the guards opened the SUV door and she slid in, trapped into place by the guard who had opened the door while the second man put the box in the back. Hamez had just slid into the driver's seat and was starting to move into the passenger seat when the man standing beside the open door sagged. His head rained down in pieces around him.

32

"Sniper," Qurtubi said in a hushed, urgent tone.

Garin had trailed the SUV caravan easily because it stood out in the neighborhood, and he'd chosen to watch them from an alley two blocks away.

"He has to be on a rooftop." Garin flipped up the sun visor and stared, trying to figure out where he would be if he were the one sniping.

"There." Qurtubi pointed at one of the buildings ahead of them. Three stories tall, it loomed over the caravan. A muzzle barrel barely broke the line of the roof's edge.

"Good eyes. CIA or MI-6?" Garin engaged the transmission.

"Low-velocity rounds to keep them subsonic, as well as a silencer." Qurtubi picked up one of the Belgian-made FN FAL assault rifles he'd brought. "My guess would be the British."

"Mine, too."

The man in the back of the SUV tried to clamber out but a bullet to the back of his head dropped him.

"Can you distract the sniper?"

Qurtubi opened his door, threw out a leg to brace himself as he sighted with the rifle, then fired two quick shots. Both bullets chipped the roof's edge just below the rifle barrel, which disappeared almost instantly. Satisfied with his marksmanship, Qurtubi slid back into the Land Rover.

"I do not think I was seen."

Garin watched the alley and spotted Annja climbing over the seats in the SUV. Freedom was just a few seconds away.

"STOP HER!" HAMEZ YELLED from the front seat as he shifted the SUV into gear. "Do not let her escape!"

Annja didn't intend to escape, not with David Smythe being a hostage. She wanted to tell Hamez that, but there wasn't time. The rear compartment was open and she was afraid they'd lose the box of books and journals.

As she lunged over the seat, trying not to look at the dead man sprawled halfway inside the vehicle, the other guard roped an arm around her thighs and held on. She could only just reach out and touch the side of the box as the guard started hauling her back in. She curled her fingers over the bloodstained side and pulled, rocking with the motion of Hamez steering down the alley. The dead man fell out in their wake, quickly run over by the SUV following them.

A half-dozen rounds cored through the top of the SUV, blasting the windows to pieces. At least one shard hit the guard hanging on to Annja and he slid back, his breath rasping in his throat.

Hamez applied the horn vigorously, honking at the other SUV in front of him to drive faster. He spoke venomously in Arabic, too fast for Annja to understand more than a few frenzied commands to go faster.

Clutching the box of books with both hands, Annja lifted it over the seats and dropped it into the floorboard. The guard beside her clawed at her shoulder. She turned, prepared to deck him.

He lay back in the seat, one hand pressed hard against his neck. Blood streamed from under his hand. "Help…help me."

Annja turned to Hamez and started to ask where the first-aid kit was. Maybe she was among enemies, but she couldn't just sit by and watch a man die like that.

Before she could ask, though, the SUV in front of them accelerated out of the alley onto the narrow street, then brake lights flared as the driver tried to bring his vehicle to a halt. Several gunmen on the other side of the street opened fire. Bullets hammered the lead SUV, shattering glass.

They've got us blocked at both ends. But who are they? Hamez didn't hesitate, pulling hard to the left. She ducked behind the seat, at first thinking Hamez was going to get their vehicle stuck behind the other as metal crunched, but then the SUV shouldered the other one forward and into the gunmen on the other side of the street.

Once the first SUV was almost across the street, Hamez yanked on the wheel again, ripping free of the other vehicle in a long, strident scream of tortured metal. The SUV jerked and stuttered, but it kept going forward, rocked loose from the other vehicle.

Tossed in the backseat, trying to stay low, Annja spotted the first-aid kit secured up under the middle-row seat. She reached under, pulled it out and took out the biggest bandage she could find. She had to stop the blood.

Out of the corner of her eye, Annja spotted a truck pulling into position to cut them off ahead. Hamez pulled hard to the right, skidding almost out of control as the tires failed to keep a grip on the street. The shrill of tires and the burning stink of rubber invaded the SUV.

Gunmen filled the alley Hamez had chosen. They opened fire at once and the window became a blurred network of bullet perforations. Hamez roared through them—*over* at least one of them—and kept going. The SUV swung wildly, kissing both sides of the narrow alley with a brief crunching sound. The open compartment hatch bobbed up and down, coming close to shutting but not quite catching.

Controlling her panic, Annja turned to the wounded man, who stared at her in fright.

"It's going to be all right." She tugged at his hand covering his wound. "Let me see."

Finally, the wounded man removed his hand. Immediately, blood pumped from the tear across the side of his neck. Before Annja could place the bandage, not even certain if she did it would do any good, the blood stopped pumping. The man let out a final breath, relaxing in death.

Annja looked behind her and saw that the first SUV, the one transporting David Smythe, sat still as armed men surrounded it. One of the doors was opened and Smythe was yanked out, still alive and apparently unharmed.

The dead man toppled over onto Annja when Hamez took a sharp corner and bumped the rear quarter panel into a stone wall. The car's fender and bumper tore away. Annja stared back at it, barely seeing it through the dust they'd raised.

Hamez laid on the horn, his attention divided between the street ahead and the alleys on either side. The steering wheel and the gearshift kept both his hands busy. Their eyes met in the rearview mirror.

"If you jump, you will injure yourself, Miss Creed." Hamez jerked the wheel to avoid a head-on collision with a cart filled with produce. He didn't quite avoid the cart, though, and ended up scattering vegetables and fruit all along their back trail. "If the fall does not kill you, I will."

If she didn't break her neck by jumping out, she'd be able to get up and disappear before Hamez could stop the vehicle. There was a good chance of escape.

She gazed longingly at the books. Hamez had left the scroll on the helicopter, as well. All of those things would be lost, and she might never know the end of the story. She reached for the seat belt to buckle herself in.

Before she succeeded, a truck shot out in front of the SUV to block the street.

Hamez cursed the other vehicle and whoever was driving it. He pulled hard on the wheel and downshifted. Bullets beat a rapid tattoo on the side of the SUV, but neither she nor Hamez were hit. They headed down a new alley, but the truck roared after them in quick pursuit.

Gunners leaned from the passenger's side and rear driver's side windows. Their weapons chattered, but the numerous potholes and Hamez's weaving made them hard to hit.

Ducking, Annja scooped up the pistol the dead man had been carrying. She leaned back over the seats, took aim at the truck's tires because she didn't know who was following them, got the timing of both vehicles and squeezed off some rounds.

She fired seventeen times as quickly as she was able, aware of the bullets slapping into the SUV and exploding through the seats. She didn't know how many of the bullets found a home in the truck's driver's-side tire, but enough of them had to deflate it. In seconds the metal rim chewed the tire to pieces and bit into the alley, throwing the steering off. The truck swung into the wall and settled like an arthritic dog on the bare rim.

Annja pressed the magazine release and dropped the empty clip, then leaned down to start going through the dead man's clothing for a spare.

"Stop."

Not believing what she was hearing, Annja looked up to see Hamez pointing his gun at her. "What are you doing?" she snapped.

"Throw the pistol out the window."

"You've got to be kidding me. I just saved us. If I hadn't shot that tire out, those guys were going to fill us full of holes."

"Yes. You are a fine shot. That makes me even more nervous about you carrying a weapon." Hamez jerked his gun, struggling to keep an eye on the road and on Annja. "Throw it out. Do it now."

Annja could wrest the gun from Hamez. He was distracted by his driving. That would give her a split second to work. But even if she got the weapon, he could still wreck the SUV. The books could get damaged or the vehicle could catch fire and everything would burn.

She threw the pistol out the window and watched as it bounced off the stone wall and into the street.

"Good. Now buckle yourself in." Hamez watched her till she did as he ordered. "Sit still. If we get very lucky, we might arrive at the airport in one piece."

"That helicopter isn't going to be able to get us far enough away. It doesn't have range." Anyone who had the resources to field a team like the one pursuing them would have air support. She didn't know whether it was better to remain Hamez's hostage or hope for capture. The new arrivals seemed pretty bloodthirsty.

"Then it is a good thing we have something more than a helicopter awaiting us." With the street open in front of them again, Hamez stepped on the accelerator and shifted gears.

"Do you see them?" Garin drove too fast for the street conditions, barely maintaining control of the Land Rover. He plowed through a clothing display set outside a small shop, narrowly avoided a donkey, and watched as pedestrians dove into alleys and shops to get out of his way.

"They are over there. To the right." Qurtubi sounded excited and held on to his assault rifle.

"Can you see the woman?"

Qurtubi leaned in the seat and peered through the occasional alleyway that was straight enough to permit a view of the parallel street. "Yes, yes, I see her. She is fine."

Garin risked a glance at the GPS screen but the streets were a confused maze of interconnecting lines. He glanced back at the road just in time to yank the Land Rover away from a building. He lost the side mirror in a shower of glass and twisted metal.

Qurtubi never flinched. Evidently the son was a chip off the old man. Garin grinned. He'd always liked Qurtubi. The original. And he had a growing fondness for this version, as well.

The young warrior pointed ahead. "There. Three blocks, maybe four. That street they are on will intersect with this one. If you hurry, we can beat them there."

Garin stepped harder on the accelerator. The Land Rover's engine whined louder, but the vehicle picked up speed at once. Just before he reached the intersection, a midsize sedan braked to a stop and men with assault rifles started to get out. Evidently one of the other teams was well-versed in geography, too.

"Shoot them."

Obeying instantly, one of the things Garin had always respected about the first Qurtubi, the second Qurtubi leaned out the window and opened fire. Bullets stitched the sedan's side and the men retreated back into the vehicle.

Out of the corner of his eye, Garin spotted the SUV that Annja was traveling in only half a block away. The sedan was blocking the intersection and two other vehicles were trailing the SUV. If Annja were stopped, there was no doubt that she would be killed by the CIA or MI-6. He saw the gunners inside the sedan preparing to disembark.

Garin braced himself and drove straight for the sedan. "Hold on." He lay on the horn.

33

As soon as the Land Rover's front end smashed into the sedan, the air bag ballooned out of the steering column and slammed into Garin. At the same time, his seat belt bit into his chest like a vise. Air emptied out of his lungs in a rush, stifled for a moment when he face-planted into the air bag.

The impact nearly knocked him out and the steering column collapsed under him. The windshield fractured and dribbled in chunks into his lap and around his feet. Blurred images of the sedan, the street and the surrounding shops pinwheeled through his head, but he felt certain the Land Rover was driving the other vehicle ahead of it. The smell of gunpowder from the air bag stung one of his nostrils. The other was filled with blood.

Dazed, Garin reached for the gun still trapped under his thigh. The Land Rover ground to a stop. Shifting the Desert Eagle to his left hand, Garin put the transmission into Reverse and tried to back away. The engine was no longer responding. A quick glance at the tachometer confirmed it was dead. He hadn't been able to hear the silence because he was still partially deafened from the crash.

His first thought was for himself, but he knew from five hundred years of battle that he was whole enough to walk away. His second thought was for Annja. He looked over his shoulder, but all he saw were the two vehicles that had been following her across the debris-strewn intersection.

INCREDULOUS, ANNJA TURNED in the seat and glanced back at the intersection where the Land Rover had seemed to appear out of nowhere and knock the sedan into the next alley. Hamez had never let off the accelerator, had been closing on the sedan like some kamikaze pilot. She'd taken a firm grip on the seat belt and braced herself against the seat in front of her.

Some of the vehicle parts from the collision bounced across the windshield and she'd thought it would cave in. Miraculously, the glass had collapsed in on the passenger's side, but it had held. Wind whipped through the bullet holes and the spaces left from the windshield pulling away. She didn't know what the driver of the Land Rover had been thinking.

The two vehicles roaring in pursuit made her forget the Land Rover, though. They were hard to see through the dust, but they were there.

"We've got two vehicles following us."

"I see that." Hamez flicked his gaze to her in the rearview mirror, adjusting the angle to pull her into view.

"Who are they?"

"I do not know." Hamez pulled hard on the steering wheel again, careened sideways into a shop front and left a collapsed awning and several boxes of broken pottery scattered across the street. Luckily, no one was harmed because they'd all retreated into the nearest buildings or alleys.

The lead pursuit vehicle came screeching around the corner and fishtailed as the driver overcorrected. He slammed into the building, as well, skidded across the pottery shards before gaining traction, then once more picked up the chase.

One more turn and they were on the main road headed back to the airport. Hamez accelerated and whipped the SUV back and forth across the road to prevent the other vehicles from overtaking them. The SUV swayed precariously, nearly slipping out of control again and again.

Bullets ripped into the back of the SUV and Annja threw herself down in the seat. In the next moment, Hamez hit the brakes, fishtailing wildly, but holding the road. The closest pursuit vehicle tried to shut down, tires shrieking as they fought for traction, but slammed into the SUV.

The impact tore the rear door away and lifted the SUV's back wheels off the ground. When the wheels touched the road again, the SUV sped up and left the trailing vehicle slewed sideways in the road. On the other side of the broken window, men fought the deployed air bags. Fluids leaked from the front of the vehicle and steam billowed from under the hood.

The second vehicle following them, an SUV similar to the one Hamez drove, evidently avoided collision for the most part. The dents and scrapes down the right side of the other vehicle showed that it hadn't entirely escaped damage. Inside the SUV, men jockeyed to bring their weapons to bear as they shot past.

The SUV shivered with the effort of allowing Hamez to catch up to the other vehicle. Before the driver or the armed passengers could react, Hamez pulled up so that the SUV's front end was even with the other car's rear bumper. Then he banged into the other SUV and gunned the accelerator.

Caught on the SUV's front end, the other vehicle lost traction and swung sideways, coming around in front of them, and flipped over sideways.

As soon as the other vehicle started to overturn, Hamez pulled to the left, tapped the brake just enough to sever contact, then accelerated around the out-of-control vehicle. Annja watched the other SUV come to a rest at the side of the road.

No one climbed out.

TWO AIRPORT SECURITY CARS sat on the other side of the red-and-white-striped crossbars. Annja thought Hamez might surrender then, but he hunkered down behind the steering wheel, fought the uncertain steering and barreled through.

The airport security guards fired a few token shots, some of which hit the SUV, but none that stopped the vehicle. The SUV shattered the crossbar and shivered through the two security cars like a halfback blasting through a defensive line.

Smoking and sputtering, the SUV continued across the tarmac. Hamez talked hurriedly on a sat phone and then spotted the plane he was looking for, hung up the phone and drove straight for it.

The small jet sat near the runway. Four men in suits stood at the bottom of the open fuselage door. As Hamez stopped in front of them, they pulled out machine pistols and took up defensive positions around the SUV.

"Out!" Hamez pointed toward the jet. "Get on! Quickly!"

Annja grabbed her backpack and struggled to force the dented door. She finally got it open with a loud screech. She turned back to the box of books from Iskandar ibn Silahdar, but Hamez already had gotten them and was handing them to one of the guards.

The guard sprinted toward the jet. Fleetingly, Annja thought of trying to escape during the confusion, feeling that she had a better than even chance of making it. But she had to know what all the destruction had been for. She wanted to know what secrets Abdelilah Karam's manuscript held.

Your curiosity is going to get you killed one of these days.

Hitching her backpack over her shoulder, Annja ran after the guard up the steps and ducked into the jet.

"QURTUBI." GARIN LOOKED at the younger man in the passenger seat. He sat supported by the air bag. "Qurtubi."

"Yes. I am still with you, my friend." Qurtubi forced himself to sit up straighter. Instinctively, he pulled his assault rifle up to the ready position. Blood leaked from a cut over his left eye and dripped onto his cheek, running into his beard. He looked around and got his bearing, finally settling on Garin. "That was a desperate thing to do. The woman is worth it?"

"I don't know." Garin took a fresh grip on his pistol and turned his attention to the door. "This is *not* my fight. Sometimes she makes me crazy."

Qurtubi chuckled and wiped blood from his eye. "That is the way it is with women. My father taught me this."

Despite the tension of the situation and the police sirens closing in on them, Garin laughed. "This one is different. I just don't know how different yet." He put his shoulder into the door and hit it hard. With a shriek, the door popped off its hinges and fell to the ground.

He already knew the Land Rover was a loss. The vehicle wasn't registered in his name, so it didn't matter. And the man who had met him at the airport wouldn't give him up, either. Even if his name was somehow connected to the incident, Garin had a host of international lawyers just waiting to take care of situations like this.

With the Desert Eagle in his hand, Garin strode to the other vehicle. Through the cracked windshield, Garin saw that the man in the passenger seat was dead, crumpled by the door when it had given way. The man sitting behind him was in the same shape.

The three other men were at the very least unconscious. He didn't recognize any of them. He looked over at Qurtubi, who had followed him around the car.

"Do you know these men?"

Qurtubi shook his head. "Not by name, but they are with the British intelligence team that landed in Fes a short time ago."

"What were they doing here?"

"They showed interest in Annja Creed."

But what was Annja doing snooping around Fes? What could she possibly be looking for that would draw so much attention? Frustrated, he worked his jaw, tender to the touch.

The sirens closed in on their position.

Qurtubi looked at Garin. "If we stay, there will be entirely too many questions."

Garin agreed and followed Qurtubi toward the nearest alley. As he walked, he tried to figure out his next move. Annja was still in enemy hands. That wasn't acceptable. But chasing after her was going to be dangerous.

"SIT DOWN. STRAP IN." Hamez roughly guided Annja into one of the large seats inside the jet's passenger area and took another on the other side of the cabin.

She dropped her backpack into the seat next to her, strapped it in, then fastened her own seat belt. Across from her, Hamez flicked an intercom control on the panel in front of him as he pulled his belt into place.

"Get us airborne. Now."

The two security men sat with three others behind Annja and Hamez.

Turning to the window beside her, Annja gazed out at the tarmac. The view was limited, but the airport security were en route. The jet's engines thundered and shook, and the aircraft lumbered forward awkwardly. Then the jet vaulted into the air.

Bullets slapped against the fuselage, but none seemed to penetrate the jet. The only way they would know if there was any real damage was if the jet reached an altitude that required it to be pressurized. Then she spotted the larger passenger jet ahead of them, directly in their path. She forced herself to take a slow, deep breath and couldn't keep from arching her back in an effort to get over the other jet.

For a moment it looked as if the smaller jet was going to end up scrapped against the larger one, but then the smaller one gained enough altitude. Anxiously, Annja watched as they flew over the jet. The tires had to be within inches of touching the other aircraft. Imminent destruction seemed to waver around them and the cabin filled with the thunderous roar of the larger jet's engines. It seemed as if the jet's proximity, or the thrust of the other jet's engines, was going to suck them in and expel them like they'd been through a Cuisinart. Or at least throw off their trajectory.

In the end, neither of those things happened.

Hearing Hamez speaking rapidly in his native tongue, Annja turned to face him. He gradually stopped talking over the sat phone and started listening. Even over the roar of the jet engines, Annja heard the male voice at the other end yelling, and she recognized some of the curse words.

Evidently the boss wasn't happy with how things were turning out.

Finally, Hamez shut the phone off and returned it to his pocket. He held his pistol in his right fist.

"Care to share?" Annja said.

Hamez gave her a dead-eyed stare. "Your fate is being decided."

"Decided how?" Annja couldn't help asking even though she was fairly certain she knew.

"Getting to you has proven too much trouble. We do not know why so many intelligence agencies are involved in this matter."

Annja pushed aside her fear. She wasn't dead yet, and she'd been in worse circumstances. Just not lately. She forced herself to be calm. "Since we're having to wait, maybe I could look in the box. See what we've gone to all this trouble for."

Hamez regarded her and nodded.

Now that the jet had leveled off, Annja unbuckled her seat

belt and retrieved the box. Hamez's guards kept close watch over her. She didn't think that any of them would want to risk shooting her, but men like that wouldn't hesitate to kill with their bare hands, and they probably carried knives.

If the situation devolved to a physical confrontation, the jet's size limited how many of them could come at her at one time. And they wouldn't expect the sword.

The trick was to figure a way out of this by her wits. The only way to do that would be to discover what information Thabit was after and how to get it.

Then her life would be in jeopardy again. It was a catch-22, but she would think of something. If Iskandar's ancestor's books actually had any real information that related to what Thabit was searching for.

Annja dug into the materials, separating what she could read from what she couldn't. Thankfully, some of the journals were in Spanish, photocopies of work prepared by Philip Gardiner, the English historian who had been aboard one of the ships in the Spanish Armada when it had gone down in 1588.

34

Curtain Bar
K Street
Washington, D.C.

Anxious but hopeful, Brawley Hendricks walked down the stairs that led to the underground control center beneath the bar. Two guards, one of them a man he had seen before, followed him down. The one in the lead waved a card in front of the lock.

"Ma'am, your appointment is here." The lead guard stood in the way and didn't permit Hendricks to pass.

In the shadowy back section of the room, Sophie sat at her appointed place. The light from the large screens lifted her features from the darkness. She waved for Hendricks to join her.

Stepping past the man, Hendricks shot a glance at the wallscreens. One showed a small jet flying over a body of water. The other rolled footage captured by video cameras and cell phones of a battle that had taken place in the streets of Fes.

At Langley, news was already circulating about an ex-CIA agent who had turned up dead in a battle with men who were believed to be British intelligence. No one there knew what was going on yet. Hendricks's gut roiled. He was afraid the events he'd put into motion were about to spill back onto him. He reminded himself of Paul Gentry's murder at Thabit's hands. Whatever price he had to pay was worth it as long as Thabit went down.

"That's the plane that took off from Fes?" Hendricks stood in front of Sophie.

"Take a seat, Brawley."

He sat.

"Yes, that is the plane."

"And Annja Creed is aboard?"

"We believe so." Sophie steepled her fingers and stared at her personal computer screen. "She got on at the airport. That's been verified. However, Hamez or his men could have jettisoned her from the aircraft. Our initial surveillance of the jet was limited. Things…could have happened."

Hendricks felt bad about that. His primary concern, though, remained Thabit. "Do you know where they're heading?"

"No."

Hendricks just stared at the craft. "Where are they?"

"Somewhere over the Atlantic Ocean."

"How long have they been in flight?"

Sophie checked. "An hour and forty minutes."

"How much fuel does that type of aircraft hold?"

"Five to six hours' flight time."

Hendricks thought furiously, cycling through the various factors. "How much does one of those go for? Ten? Twelve million?"

"Seventeen million, conservatively."

Concentrating on the wallscreens at the other end of the room, Hendricks sat up straighter and felt a little more hopeful. "Thabit wouldn't throw away that much money to lay down a false trail."

"No. Which means that whatever he's after is worth a lot."

Sophie studied Hendricks. "And you maintain that you know nothing about what that is?"

Hendricks looked at her. "Sophie, I swear to you, if I knew I'd tell you. It would put us one step closer to nailing that man."

Sophie held his gaze for a moment, then nodded.

"Have you been able to track ownership of the jet?" Hendricks hoped that Thabit had left himself exposed. If Thabit was willing to risk the jet, maybe he'd left a trail.

"To a shell company in the Caymans, yes. Getting through those layers is going to be next to impossible if it's done right. We'll know soon enough. I've got some of my best asset recovery people on it. But if the CIA hasn't been able to track any of Thabit's finances, I wouldn't hold out any hope."

"What about MacKenzie?"

"He's still operational. He's lost half his team. I'm trying to rectify that." Sophie continued shifting through images on the computer screens. "Right now I'm working on getting him out of Morocco."

"You're sure what Thabit is looking for isn't there?"

"Aren't you?"

Hendricks sighed. "I don't know."

She nodded. "I don't think it is. Thabit's people have made a proper mess of things there. If whatever they wanted was still in-country, they would have stayed. Especially with someone as high profile as Annja Creed."

Hendricks relaxed a little.

"Creed remains our hole card, Brawley." Sophie's voice was smooth and unemotional. "If she's still on that jet, if she's still alive and as long as Habib ibn Thabit has need of her, then we have a chance at finding your quarry. Just as you had known from the start of this."

"I'd hoped we'd get her cleared of this situation before she stepped into the lion's den."

"Thabit would have taken Creed, anyway. We just made that particular enterprise more risky and forced him to reveal himself. Otherwise, he could have ordered her killed at any time. As it stands now, we're probably the only chance that woman has of getting out of her present predicament alive. When we do, she should thank us."

Fes el Bali
Kingdom of Morocco

GARIN SAT DRINKING KRUG champagne in the back of the luxury vehicle parked beside the tarmac at the airport. Although the police and military still covered the area, no one bothered him. All bribes were in the proper hands.

Qurtubi sat at Garin's side, quiet and resolute in a business suit that fit him well. He looked like an up-and-coming young executive. He had agreed to stay on with Garin to see the current mission through till its end. Garin had other troops standing by.

On Garin's knee, the sat phone rang. He touched the speaker phone function. "Inga."

"Mr. Braden, I have your party on the line." His young assistant's voice was cultured and feminine. "Please hold on while I connect you."

"Thank you."

"Of course, sir. Have a good day."

A moment later, the connection buzzed, and a rough, querulous voice came on the line, speaking French. "Too busy to call me yourself, Garin? Don't expect me to be impressed when you trot out the underlings."

"Hello, Roux. No insult was intended. I had other things that needed arranging. My attention was diverted and I knew it would take time to chase you down through the contact numbers I have for you."

Garin truly didn't know where his relationship with Roux fell most days. Somewhere between friend and enemy, he supposed, and both of them were at fault for that. On good days, they tolerated each other because no one else on the planet shared the experiences they'd had. On days like this, when Annja Creed's life might hang in the balance, they worked together.

Usually.

"What is this about?"

"Annja is in danger." Garin paused, knowing the old man had feelings for Annja that he'd never really felt for Garin. Roux had demonstrated paternal care for her.

What Garin felt for the young woman would in no way be confused with brotherly, but there was an odd, discomforting kinship. Joan's sword bound the three of them in so many ways. Or, perhaps, it trapped them. Even after all the years he'd spent alive, it was hard to say.

Roux became instantly more attentive and less defensive. "What's going on?"

Garin laid out the events that had brought him to Morocco, and what had happened afterward.

"You lost her?" Roux's accusation was sharp.

"I kept her from being killed. Earlier, there was a chance for her to escape. Annja chose to remain with her captors."

"Why?"

Garin smiled. "Seriously? I don't think you and I have much room to question her thinking. I remember plenty of times when you led us into the eye of the storm while searching for one artifact or another. Safety wasn't exactly your primary concern." He watched the police and military milling around the tarmac as crews put everything back in place. "I think Annja is more like you in that regard than you believe."

Roux ignored that. "Do you know what she's looking for?"

"No, but whatever it is, Thabit is looking for it, as well.

And for him to have this much interest, it's something he knew about before Annja and the British archaeological group found that scroll out in the Atlas Mountains."

"Agreed." Roux was silent for a moment. "You say the CIA is tracking Thabit's people?"

"They were. So was MI-6."

"They're not looking for the same thing Annja is."

"No. They're looking for Thabit."

"And they think Annja is leverage to get them Thabit."

"Or whatever she's looking for."

"We need to find her."

"I'm open to suggestion. That's one of the reasons I called you."

Roux cursed. "How much do you know about Thabit? Can you find him?"

"The American and British intelligence agencies don't know where he is. I don't have their resources."

"No, but you do work with some of the same criminal agencies Thabit undoubtedly works with. Can you get access through those people?"

"If I could have, I already would have. Hamez, the man Thabit sent here, was the only lead I had."

"All right. Then if we can't track Thabit, we track Annja."

"How?"

"She uses internet sites to research different projects. If she's doing more of the same for Thabit—and I see no other reason for the man to want her working for him—doubtless she'll use some of those same sites."

Garin growled. "It will only work if she accesses those sites."

"If she brings her computer online, many of those sites come on in the background. They're automatic."

"I thought you didn't pay attention to technology."

"I don't, but I've heard her talk about it enough when I've

been with her. She depends on those sites. Once she accesses them, I will find her."

"What if she doesn't?"

"Then she's lost to us," Roux said without hesitation. "She'll be on her own."

Qurtubi touched Garin's shoulder and pointed to the other end of the field, then held up the binoculars he'd been using.

"Hold on, Roux." Garin took the proffered binoculars and trained them on the figures at the other end of the tarmac. He recognized the black man as one of the men who had been following Annja. His intelligence people had identified him as MacKenzie.

MacKenzie stood near the private runway, obviously awaiting transportation just as Garin was. The CIA agent was still in the game.

Garin handed the binoculars back to Qurtubi, then opened the backseat to reach into the rear compartment for the equipment bag the young man had arranged for. He took out a GPS transponder and handed it to Qurtubi.

"Think you can arrange to put this with MacKenzie's people?"

Qurtubi smiled. "Of course." He opened the car door and got out, striding swiftly across the tarmac and disappearing into the crowd of workers and onlookers.

Garin returned his attention to the phone. "You follow Annja. I'm going to track one of the men following her."

"What if he has lost her?"

"If we're headed in the same direction, we know that isn't true. I'll be in touch." Garin punched the phone off and forced himself to relax. If he could have, he'd have taken MacKenzie down here, but with all the police and military around that wasn't possible.

But soon Garin would find the man and hold him accountable. And if Annja was hurt, MacKenzie would die even more painfully.

Dawnchaser
Mediterranean Sea

THABIT LOOKED OUT OVER the sea as the yacht sailed through the rolling water. His body shifted unconsciously with the rise and fall of the waves. His anger rose as he listened to the man at the other end of the phone connection.

"Habib, I am your friend. You know that I am your friend." Rasool Bahanor sounded almost desperate. He'd been with Thabit the longest, spending years working with him so that Thabit could rise to the top of their organization. They had attended school together, and they had made their first kills at the same time. "I have been your friend nearly all of our lives."

"Then be my friend now."

"I am trying."

"You make this sound like a hard thing to do."

"Many of the others we work with are upset by your recent actions. You manage monies they depend on. They feel that when you risk yourself, you also risk their investments."

"What recent actions?" Thabit resented that so many people were focused on him now. It wasn't just the intelligence people around the world. Many of them were also fellow believers that no longer believed in him as they had. He would not tolerate their interference or their lack of faith.

"Ambushing the CIA in Algeria."

"We live and breathe so that we might strike our enemies, Rasool."

"I have not forgotten. Neither have they. But I also know

that we must be clever about everything we do. Especially you."

"Dying in battle against the Americans is a good thing. A blessed opportunity that should not be missed."

"I understand this, but you are not a man who should fall into enemy hands."

"You think I would willingly go into the hands of my enemies?" Thabit's voice shook with rage. "When I die, trust that I will take my enemies with me."

"No. *No*. That is not what I said. Not what I meant." Bahanor sighed so uncomfortably that Thabit almost felt sorry for the man.

"That is what you said."

"I misspoke."

"Then what did you mean to say?"

"Only that the Americans and the British are actively looking for you now, my friend. This is the time you should be wary. You know so many of our secrets and our plans. If we have a weakness, it is you."

"I am our *strength!*" Thabit roared over the ocean as a wave smacked against the bow. "Without me, many in our organization would be working in pitiful independent efforts, only awaiting an executioner's bullet. I have saved many from dying wastefully. I have made our battles count and increased our successes. And we are poised to make war against the West even more magnificently. *I* am the reason for that."

"I understand that, but many of the others do not. They have seen how you are chasing the American archaeologist, and they want to know your interest in her."

"That is my business." Thabit forced himself to speak calmly. "And I am no longer chasing her. I have her now."

"That is good. Very good." Bahanor sounded excited. "Then, whatever business it is that you have with her, get it over with quickly and kill her. Your continued safety is all they are concerned about."

"Let them know that the matter will soon be finished." Thabit broke the connection and looked into the sky. Somewhere out there, Annja Creed flew in a private jet that he owned. It would be easier to have Hamez kill her and throw her out of the aircraft.

He couldn't do that. The secrets that had been put into that scroll all those years ago were closer to spilling out than ever before.

They had to disappear.

Forever.

35

Annja leafed through the books they had taken from Iskandar ibn Salihdar, upset that she couldn't read the Kufic script that covered many of the pages. She was missing a lot.

But a story was beginning to take shape. Philip Gardiner's notes were mixed in with work from the original authors. Whichever ancestor of Iskandar's had compiled the materials had been meticulous, and a historian.

Annja wrote notes in her journal in longhand, jotting down anchoring points that would only make sense to her. Several times, she looked up and found Hamez peering over her shoulder. She hadn't gotten over her paranoid tendency of looking for a knife in his hand each time.

"Have you found something?" Hamez stood behind her again.

Annja answered without looking at the man. She tracked his shadow on the floor and on the wall. If he moved, she would see it and take action. "It would help if I knew what I was looking for."

"I was told you would know it when you saw it."

"There's a lot here to find. You're talking about thirteen-hundred-plus years of history, and a lot of moving parts."

"Tell me what you think you know."

Annja looked at Hamez then. "Do you even have any background on this? Do you know who Abdelilah Karam was?"

"Pretend that I do not."

Grimacing, Annja knew that wasn't something that needed pretending. Habib ibn Thabit had not told him about Karam. She gave Hamez a small smile. "Could be dangerous for you to know. Just Karam's name could be more than your boss wants you to know."

"This is your life we are concerned with. Tell me about Abdelilah Karam and the scroll that was found." Hamez acted as if he didn't care.

So far, the jet hadn't changed course and had maintained a heading out to the Mediterranean Sea. Annja figured that was a bad sign. She also knew that the jet couldn't keep on the heading forever. It had to land sometime. She was grimly aware that the flight didn't have to land with her aboard. She wasn't going without a fight.

"Abdelilah Karam was a historian that had first been appointed to that position as a boy by Muhammad."

That interested Hamez immediately. "The prophet chose this man?"

"From everything I've been able to find out."

"To do what?"

Annja frowned. "Karam recorded events. Primarily the history of the first four caliphs before the Umayyads took over the succession."

"After they killed Ali. The succession rightly belonged to Ali and those of the blood of Muhammad."

She sidestepped. "Karam remained in the courts, recording history until after Ali was assassinated."

"By Kharijite dogs."

"Some time after that, Karam fled Damascus, where

Muawiya moved the caliphate after being appointed as leader of the faithful."

"Muawiya robbed Ali's son Hasan of the right to lead our people. Undoubtedly Karam was a true supporter of Ali and Muhammad's family. He feared for his life because they knew where his heart lay."

"According to these documents, Karam ended up in Mosul, where he continued his work."

"Recording the histories of the caliphs?" Hamez sat up straighter in his seat and didn't pay as much attention to the pistol in his hand.

"If we believe these notes, then yes."

Hamez glanced at the papers. "Who wrote these notes?"

Annja spread her hands across them. "Several people. Other historians who were around at that time believed Karam left a great body of work in Mosul."

The idea was exciting and intriguing to Annja. The Muslim faith had been splintered for centuries, constantly at war within itself.

Hamez's eyes glittered. "Then these works, if they are found, could potentially unite the Muslim faith with the truth of what Muhammad wanted for his people."

Annja didn't bother to point out that another document relating what took place during those turbulent times wouldn't much affect the Muslim belief. They had centuries of infighting behind them. Any new document would be more fuel to the fire.

She was more eager to find a new firsthand account of the events during the formation of the early caliphate. That would keep historians busy for years.

"Do you know where Karam left his work?"

"No. What kind of papers or artifacts does your employer have?"

Hamez's eyes darkened with suspicion. "I know of no papers or artifacts."

"Then what focused Thabit's attention on this scroll?"

Hamez drew back and idly lifted the pistol. "Be careful, woman."

Annja met Hamez's gaze full measure. "Thabit—and you—stepped into my world. I didn't step into yours."

For a quiet moment, Hamez regarded her with cold fury. "You presume too much. You are not worth as much as you believe."

"I'm here. On this jet. I've come this far with searching out whatever your master wants. If he thinks he could do any better than I have, he'd have already told you to get rid of me. I mean, there's a big sea out there. You could have already done it."

Hamez tensed and his nostrils flared. Her hand behind her back, Annja reached for the sword and felt the leather-wrapped hilt under her fingers.

She raised her voice. "Thabit needs me right now. It doesn't matter how much you don't like it. He needs me, and I need to see what he's holding. MacKenzie is probably tracking this flight. We're running out of time."

Not bothering to reply, Hamez got up and returned to his own seat. He picked up the sat phone, spoke briefly in his native tongue, then hung up and called someone on the intercom.

A few minutes later, the pilot made a course correction, veering sharply and climbing to a higher altitude.

When did you get so brave? She had no answer. She knew having the sword hadn't given her the stubbornness she had. The nuns hadn't been able to break her of it in the orphanage. But having the sword certainly put an edge on her need to use it.

31,500 feet
Over the Mediterranean Sea

MACKENZIE TURNED THE heavy brass key in his fingers as
Sophie spoke into his ear over the satlink. He sat in the back
of the cargo plane the woman had arranged as transport out
of Fes. The cargo plane wasn't capable of the same speed as
the jet carrying Annja Creed, but their destinations—for the
moment—were different places. MacKenzie was still working that out for himself, wondering if the woman and his target were slipping through his fingers.

"We've had the writing on the key analyzed. It's not Arabic, as you believed."

That surprised MacKenzie. "Then what is it?"

"Kurdish."

MacKenzie closed his fist over the key and glanced at the
laptop computer also connected to Sophie's transmission. The
image there showed a magnified view of the key. MacKenzie
had sent an image once he'd boarded the plane a few hours
ago. "Kurdish."

"Yes. My expert tells me it's an old form used by the Yezidi
people."

"What do the Kurds have to do with this?"

"We don't know yet. Maybe the key has nothing to do with
what Thabit is after."

"It has to. It was with the scroll."

"That doesn't mean they came together. A lot of things
could have happened to those remains Creed and her associates found out in those mountains."

"Then why am I headed to Mosul?"

"Because that's where the largest percentage of Kurds live
these days. And because there is a tie there to the peacock
angel you discovered with Creed."

MacKenzie had sent her images of those manuscripts, as well. "What tie?"

"Sheikh Adi ibn Musafir was the man believed to be the first incarnation of the Melek Taus, the peacock angel. His tomb lies north of Mosul, in the Hakkari Mountains. As it turns out, Musafir was also a descendant of the Umayyad caliph Marwan ibn al-Hakim. Abdelilah Karam would have known Marwan."

Shifting on the bags of grain that filled a lot of the cargo space, MacKenzie tried in vain to find a comfortable resting spot. "Creed was puzzled over the link between the Melek Taus and Karam. She said four hundred years passed between the two periods."

"Yes, and we're chasing after a scroll that was buried on a mountainside over a thousand years ago because Habib ibn Thabit wants it." Sophie's tone carried mild rebuke. "Just so we can get a shot at a terrorist leader right now. I don't claim to understand these things. I just deal with them. You should be dealing with them, too."

"Fine." MacKenzie tucked the key into his shirt pocket and stared up into the darkness of the cargo area's upper reaches. "What do you want me to do in Mosul?"

"Put boots on the ground. I'll have another retrieval team there waiting for you. If we're right about this, Annja Creed will be there soon enough."

"What if you're wrong?"

"Then we do what we always do. We adjust."

MacKenzie took a breath and stared at the image of the key. The light reflected in Yahya's dark eyes. "Do we know what the key unlocks?"

"No. Wait for Creed in Mosul. When she shows up, take her and find out what she's uncovered."

MacKenzie cursed silently. The instructions were simple.

Executing them had been anything but. "Are the Brits still along for the party?"

"They can track that jet as easily as we can. Once it touches down, our coverage becomes spotty. That's why we want you in Mosul. Let's get a step ahead of Thabit if we can."

MacKenzie broke the connection and leaned back.

Yahya grinned at him in the darkness. "You know what being ahead of Thabit means, don't you?"

"Yeah." MacKenzie's mood soured. "The man has a gun at our backs." He blew out an angry breath. "We get down there, we have to look out for each other."

Yahya nodded. "Sure. Like always."

36

Marsala
Province of Trapani
Sicily, Italy

When Hamez opened the door of the luxury car waiting for them at the Palermo Airport, Annja stepped out into the warm salty breeze blowing in from the Mediterranean Sea. She settled her backpack over her shoulder. The afternoon sun slanted in from over the whitecapped waves.

One of Hamez's men brought the box of journals. Together, they walked toward a small coffee shop set back from the port. Annja refrained from asking questions. She knew Hamez wouldn't answer. He hadn't talked to her during the past several hours of crisscrossing the island to throw off potential tails.

The coffee shop was low-end touristy. Fishing nets filled with plastic sea life hung from the ceiling and slow fans stirred the air, serving only to push the aroma of fresh-made coffee onto the boardwalk.

Habib ibn Thabit sat alone at one of the tables. He looked overdressed for the surroundings, a businessman who had ended up in the wrong meeting place. Several of the men scattered around the room watched Annja, as well, and she knew that Thabit owned them all.

Thabit smiled when she approached his table. He stood up like a gentleman and waved her to a seat on the inside of the booth.

"Miss Creed." Thabit's smile never touched his eyes. A mask that he wore among polite company.

"Mr.—"

He held up his hand and quieted her immediately. "I would rather my name not be mentioned, if you please."

"Fine."

"My associate has informed me that you have made some inroads to my quest."

"We've been lucky."

"Lucky?" Thabit frowned and looked at Hamez.

"I didn't know what you were looking for. Even now, I can only guess."

"And what is it you guess?"

"The discovery of Abdelilah Karam's body so far from home started all of this, so I'm guessing that it has something to do with his work as a historian of the succession following Muhammad."

Thabit's expression never changed.

Annja leaned back in the booth. "If that's not the answer, then I'm ready to order the daily special with a cup of highly caffeinated coffee, because I've been up for most of the night shuttling between airports and cars, and call it a day."

"You have a cavalier attitude for someone in your position."

"My position." Annja stared at Thabit. "You've got the CIA and MI-6 chasing you. You're one of the most wanted men in the world at the moment."

"Thank you." Thabit adjusted his tie.

"If I stand up and start yelling your name, it'll be a footrace for you to get out of Sicily before someone puts you down."

"Perhaps. But first, all of these people will die." Thabit

nodded at her. "And you will die, of course. I will kill you my-self. And the footrace? You would be a fool to wager against me. I can get out of this country anytime I wish. Just as eas-ily as I got in." He paused. "Do you wish to yell?"

Annja waited a beat just to be difficult. "No. But if you expect me to find what you're looking for, I need to know what it is."

Thabit sat quietly for a moment. "You were close when you thought it was Karam's scrolls."

Annja's heart sped up. So the scrolls did exist. She checked herself. Thirteen hundred years had passed since they'd been written. At one time, those scrolls had existed.

Thabit reached inside his jacket and took out a flat metal box not much larger than a cigarette case. "My family has been looking for Karam's books since the man went missing."

"Missing?"

Thabit shrugged. "Karam bolted from the country ahead of an assassin. One of my ancestors almost caught up with Karam in Morocco, but he disappeared."

"He was killed. I saw the body. Someone crushed his skull." Annja could still see the broken bone.

"My ancestor would have killed Karam if he was able, but that did not happen. Otherwise, those scrolls would not still be hidden."

Annja filed that away. That was a mystery that might not be resolved. More than likely, the old historian and his party were ambushed by bandits who had taken horses and provi-sions and left the gold because it might have marked them as thieves. Or maybe the gold had been buried nearby to prevent such a theft. Or it had been sewn into Karam's gar-ments for emergencies and left loose when that clothing had rotted away.

"The trail turned cold." Thabit tapped the metal case, then pushed it across the table. "Except for this."

Gently, senses tingling, Annja lifted the lid off and found a folded piece of vellum inside. It felt soft and pliant in her fingers as she unfolded and spread it over the tabletop.

She knew at once it was a map. She recognized Abdelilah Karam's signature across the bottom. The writing was in Kufic.

"What does this say?"

"'The way to knowledge is paved in gold.'"

"Karam had a treasure?"

Thabit shook his head. "He was a poor man, only privileged in the caliphs' courts."

The symbol of the peacock angel stood out on the thin skin.

Annja studied the ink for a moment and knew that it wasn't the same quality. The image of the peacock angel was slightly faded.

She looked up at Thabit. "This is not part of the original document."

"We believe it was added in Mosul, during the reign of Adi ibn Musafir. A sign of ownership, perhaps."

"If you have a map, why haven't you been able to find Karam's scrolls?"

"Because no one knew what area to use that map on."

"There's only one place you can find the Melek Taus."

"That is not precisely true."

"Only one birthplace of the religion," Annja amended.

"My ancestors searched across Mosul. Nothing."

"Where did they get this?"

"From a tomb robber in Mosul a thousand years ago. It has been in my family ever since."

Staring at the vellum, Annja tried to make sense of it. Points were marked on the map, as well as symbols that looked like Arabic letters. Those had half circles traced around them in very light ink. The marks were exactly uniform, each having small imperfections, but they were all about the size of—

Annja took a deep breath as the pieces fell together in her head. She looked at Hamez. "When you took the scroll from Mustafa, he also had coins. Did you get those?"

"Yes." Hamez scowled at her.

"Do you have them?"

Hamez reached into his jacket and took out a small manila envelope.

Once she had the envelope, Annja dumped the heavy gold coins into her palm. "I thought it was unusual that a man like Karam would be traveling with gold coins. He would have been playing the part of a pauper, a poor merchant hoping to improve his fortune. Flashing gold coins would have ruined his chances of that and made him a target for bandits or even thieves within the group he traveled with. He wouldn't have traveled alone. But he had these coins. And they were freshly struck, no signs of usage." Annja ran her fingers across the coins and felt small ridges across the raised surfaces. The last time she'd seen them, it had been night and she hadn't had time to examine them.

Working carefully, Annja put the coins on the vellum, matching the Arabic letters marked in the half circles to letters on the coins. While doing that, she discovered that the coins also fit together with small ridges on the edges, forming an interlocking puzzle.

Thabit stared at her.

"This is why Karam was carrying the coins." Annja fit the last one into place. "They're the map."

Thabit studied them. "I see no map."

Annja reached into her backpack and took a sheet of paper from her journal. She laid the paper over the coins, then delicately rubbed graphite over the surfaces.

Slowly, the unmistakable image of a path lifted from the other designs stamped on the coins. The map Karam had been carrying on him when he'd been killed.

"He must have been headed to Tetuan. That city was old back when Karam was alive, and he could have lived there in peace among the Berbers. With his skills as a writer, he could have even lived out his days in comfort as a scribe for traders." Annja thought of the skeleton they had taken from the ground. "Only that didn't happen." She couldn't take her eyes off the coins. "Karam lived through some of the most pivotal events in all of Islam. He knew he was leaving behind a legacy in historical documentation, and he intended to preserve it and wanted it found. Those coins were the key to that legacy."

Carefully, Thabit picked up the coins and put them in the metal case. "You have done very well, Miss Creed. I am impressed." He laced his fingers. "Now, I want you to tell me *where* in Mosul those scrolls are."

Excited, but still aware of the grave danger she was in, Annja reached into her backpack. Hamez trapped her hand.

"I'm getting my computer." Annja stared at the man. "If you want me to find that location on that map, I'm going to need access to the websites I set up for researching these documents. Otherwise, I'm going to have to start all over again."

Thabit nodded and Hamez took his hand away. "Remember. We are watching everything you do," Thabit said quietly.

"Go ahead. But I bet you get bored. Poring over maps isn't for the faint of heart." Placing her computer on the table, Annja powered up and set to work.

37

Mosul
Ninawa Governorate
Republic of Iraq

Wearing khaki pants, a loose-fitting shirt and a keffiyeh, Garin had no trouble passing among the people who continued to struggle for survival in Iraq's war-torn city. It broke Garin's heart to see the city in such disarray. Mosul had never been one of his favorite places to do business, but he hated to see so much loss.

Broken people squatted around small fires in the shattered buildings. The smell of cooking fish and spices trickled through the gentle breeze that floated in from the Tigris River. Small fishing boats still trolled the water on both sides of the slow-moving current of greenish-brown water.

The river split Sunni and Shiite Muslims displaced during the war, as well as Assyrians, Kurds, Turkmen and others. Too far away from the river, on the wrong side of the bank, violence would break out between the groups and bodies would hit the ground. But here on the river, the violence seemed more contained. The river was life to everyone who lived on it, and the people here respected that.

The Iraqi military still maintained tenuous order in the city. Garin had passed a few outposts filled with armed, nervous men. Despite the downfall of Saddam Hussein and the efforts of the Americans, peace had not returned to the country.

Garin doubted the city would ever know prosperity or harmony again.

As he passed a narrow alleyway flanked by buildings reduced to rubble, a shadow separated and came toward him. Garin closed his hand around the pistol in his pocket. Before he could pull it out, a sharp blade rested at his throat.

"Too slow, *mon ami*," a rough voice whispered in Garin's ear. "If I wished, you would now be dead."

"So would you, old man." Garin made his point by pressing the tip of the Spyderco tactical fighting knife through his attacker's shirt and coat. "With my dying breath."

"*Touché.*" The old man sounded delighted. "You have learned a lot."

"And if you had any sense, you would have tried to kill me without engaging me."

"That would draw the attention of the local militia. Something neither of us can afford. Also, your bodyguard would have killed me."

"You're lucky he didn't."

"Nonsense. I knew he was there. He wouldn't shoot me." Roux stepped back, removing his knife from Garin's throat.

Roux looked like a man in his sixties, but he moved with a young man's speed and strength. Under the hood of his ratty coat and keffiyeh, his gray hair brushed his shoulders. His blue eyes glowed in the darkness. Like Garin, he'd dressed in clothing that fit the neighborhood.

"You couldn't know he wouldn't shoot you." Garin returned his weapons to their hiding places. Qurtubi must not have been as good as his father if he let Roux get so close.

"Of course I did." Roux turned and lifted his voice. "Qurtubi, come on out."

The young man, dressed as they were, emerged from the shadows with a sheepish grin on his face.

Garin frowned. "You were supposed to keep me safe."

"I did. Roux gave me his word he would not hurt you."

Garin looked at the old man. "You know Qurtubi?"

Roux embraced the younger man. "I've known several generations of Qurtubis. All fine men." Qurtubi didn't appear at all disconcerted by Roux's seeming ability *not* to age. "You couldn't do any better for personal protection out here."

"Except, it seems, when it comes to safeguarding myself against you."

Roux strolled toward the river. Since electricity was being rationed, the full dark of evening was settling over the city.

"I'm the exception, Garin. I'm always the exception."

Reluctantly, Garin fell in behind the old man the way he'd done for so long so very many years ago. Sometimes it felt as if they'd never put their past relationship behind them, and at other times it seemed as if their relationship would never be the same again.

Their bond was…complicated…even without the sword and Annja Creed.

"I take it since you're here, Annja is here."

"Not yet." Roux waved to a passing fisherman who poled his boat over to the bank. "But she will be soon. Her research has pointed to this place. Well, not exactly to Mosul, but to the mountains north of the city. She and her captors are coming. You and I will deal with them there."

"The mountains? What's in the mountains?"

"A hiding place, for starters. Perhaps some very old scrolls that, for some reason, have some bearing on the events that have placed her in danger." Roux took a few coins from his pockets and gave them to the fisherman.

The fisherman smiled and thanked Roux in his tongue,

then he handed over a stringer of fish. Qurtubi took the fish and appraised them.

They started back into the wreckage of the city, toward the fires where survivors had gathered.

"Why did you buy fish?" Garin followed the old man, hating the feeling he always got around Roux. That he was losing control.

"I'm hungry and we're going to eat them."

Qurtubi nodded happily. "Roux is a very good cook."

Garin stumbled over a loose rock but recovered quickly. Even after all these years, the old man could still surprise him. Garin couldn't help wondering what Roux had done that would require the help of Qurtubi. Especially this Qurtubi whom Garin hadn't met until yesterday.

"Garin, would you collect some firewood?" Roux didn't even bother to look back.

Cursing, Garin started looking for someone to buy firewood from. There were vendors among the scavengers. He wasn't going to search for firewood in the gathering darkness. As he walked, he tried to figure out exactly how Roux had taken control of Garin's expedition to save Annja.

On the other hand, he had to admit that he felt better with Roux running the show. It was like old times.

Qodshanes Plateau
Hakkari Mountains
Republic of Iraq

THE CARGO PLANE HUGGED the nap of the earth as it raced across the Hakkari Mountains hours before dawn. Seated in the back, outfitted with a parachute, Annja waited tensely, wondering if she had put herself in too deep this time, thinking maybe she had and hoping she'd get to see what Abdelilah Karam had hidden that Habib ibn Thabit wanted so badly.

Thabit had brought thirty men, enough to keep her from seeing what he was chasing if he so chose.

Try to kill me. I'm not going to let that happen. She wrapped her arms around the parachute secured to her chest and felt the extra weight of the primary chute on her shoulders. Her backpack was tied to her with a leash and was stored in a protective case that would shield it from the jump.

She felt well rested. Even with all the resources he had at his fingertips, it had taken Thabit almost two days to put together transportation to Syria, then the flight to Mosul. Annja had spent the time researching and shoring up strength. Her "host" had made certain she was guarded, but he had also seen to it that she was left alone.

The plane powered down.

A moment later, Hamez walked through the cargo area and kicked the feet of the sleeping men, snarling at them. Immediately, they gathered their gear and readied themselves. Hamez stopped in front of her.

"It is time." Hamez bristled with weapons—an assault rifle, two pistols and at least four knives that Annja could see. He wore camouflage military gear and heavy combat boots. A ballistic helmet dangled from the fingers of his left hand.

Annja got to her feet without a word.

"If you try to get away on the ground, I will personally track you down and kill you."

Annja pulled her hair back into a ponytail, then slid on a pair of protective goggles. She reached down for the case containing her backpack.

Obviously not pleased at her lack of response, Hamez growled and moved on, checking his men with the authority of a drill instructor.

Thabit stood at the back of the group. Like the others, he was dressed in camo, but his outfit looked new.

Hamez gave an order, then one of the men cranked open

the side door. Cold wind rushed into the plane. One by one, the men attached static lines to the overhead cable and jumped through the door.

Annja followed them out of the plane. She plummeted in freefall for only a moment, then the chute popped open overhead, blossoming into a wide black rectangle that blotted out the stars. She dropped the protective case containing her backpack and used the steering line toggles to stay with the group as they fell.

Curtain Bar
K Street, Washington, D.C.

"WE'VE FOUND THEM."

Brawley Hendricks shifted from lethargy to operational mode. He'd spent the past two days with Sophie in the underground control room, hoping desperately to pick up Annja Creed's trail again.

Once the jet had touched down in Sicily, Sophie's people had lost Creed. The GPS locator MacKenzie had planted on Hamez's people had gotten discovered or was lost. Hendricks had expected to lose the group and he'd tried to be prepared for it, but accepting that the trail had gone cold was hard. But they'd found her again—in Syria of all places—when a Russian journalist covering the Syrian unrest had recognized Annja Creed and tweeted about her.

Tweets and blogs had become some of the best spy networks in the world. Managing all the information required a lot of data miners, though. Thankfully, Creed was a major draw for the tech crowd. When she was visible, she was highly visible.

Once Sophie had locked on to the information, she'd used her local contacts in Syria—and she was more heavily invested in that uncertain arena than Hendricks had been aware of—and ferreted out Thabit. They hadn't been able to muster a team inside Syria, but they had MacKenzie in the air.

All they'd needed to know was where Thabit planned to deploy.

And now they had that.

With rising anticipation, Hendricks watched the satellite view of the parachutes spilling from the cargo plane Sophie's intelligence team had locked on that had flown from Turkey into Afghanistan. He turned to Sophie.

"How far out is MacKenzie?"

"Twenty minutes." Sophie patted his hand. "We're almost there, Brawley. Just sit tight. These people know what they're doing."

Hendricks rolled his head in an effort to loosen the tension in his shoulders and neck. It didn't help.

38

Qodshanes Plateau
Hakkari Mountains
Republic of Iraq

"The bogey just deployed parachutes."

Seated in the back of the Hummer, Garin Braden watched the computer screen connected to the sat-relay originating from his DragonTech Security offices in Germany. He'd gotten the equipment and the security personnel from ongoing operations in Iraq. DragonTech was one of the private security teams the Iraq government maintained after the U.S. troops had started leaving.

All the unrest in the world had given Garin new inroads to several streams of revenue, some of them legal and some of them not. DragonTech was a growing—and profitable—concern. The security agency was one of the crown jewels in Braden Enterprises International.

Roux watched the images on the computer with great interest. Instead of looking ridiculous in the Kevlar armor as Garin had expected, the old man looked like a soldier—despite the overgrown hair and beard. He wore his weapons with grim authority.

Only the ancient French saber scabbarded over his right shoulder seemed out of place. Roux had insisted on carrying the blade, though. Garin didn't begrudge him that. He carried one himself—a katana that was perfectly suited for close work.

Old habits died hard. Garin loved and appreciated firearms, but his first weapon had been the blade, and Roux had trained him.

Roux pointed at the plane. "You're sure this is the one?"

"Yes."

Roux sat back and stroked his beard thoughtfully. "Then it appears they have reached their goal. How far away are they?"

"Minutes." Garin patted the driver's helmet. "Let's roll."

The Hummer jumped forward, following one of the trade trails that cut through the Hakkari Mountains.

ONCE ANNJA WAS ON THE GROUND, landing between three guards assigned to watch her, she unstrapped the parachute and dumped the secondary one. Then she fished her backpack from the protective case, checked her electronics and repacked them. She pulled the backpack into place.

The parachutes were gathered and quickly buried under brush and rocks.

Thabit walked over to Annja. "Which way to the cave?"

Annja took out her GPS compass and the map she'd drawn as much to scale as she could from the topographical references inscribed on the gold coins. They'd landed on the north side of the mountains and had to backtrack to the south.

Annja pointed. "That way." She folded the map and put the GPS compass away.

"How far?"

"A mile. Maybe. Depends on how close the map was."

Thabit nodded to Hamez, who gave the order to move out.

The soldiers fell into a point-and-wings formation that was textbook military, and were flanked by a rear guard.

As it turned out, the cave wasn't a mile away. It was only a half mile and they reached it in seven minutes by traveling up into the mountains. The landmarks Karam had provided—a cleft in the mountains, a rocky outcropping and a spire that had crumbled with age and taken a couple minutes to confirm—were mostly intact.

In the center of it all was a jumble of rock that had slid down onto the boulder that was supposed to cover the cave entrance.

Thabit surveyed the landslide. "Are you certain this is the place?"

Annja pointed out the landmarks again. "This is the only place it could be." She scowled at the landslide. "But it's going to take earth-moving equipment to dig it out."

"Or explosives." Hamez stood at Thabit's side. "I have men who can remove the debris."

An image of fire running down the throat of the cave filled Annja's mind. "You can't do that. If the cave is shallow, everything that Karam left behind could be destroyed."

Thabit didn't hesitate. He nodded. "Blow it up."

Hamez turned sharply on his heel and called out to his troops. Three men stepped forward and started rummaging in their kits.

Annja stared at Thabit, understanding the man's motivations then. "You're not here to *find* what Karam left. You want it to stay lost."

Thabit shook his head. "No, I do not want it to stay lost. I want it obliterated."

"You can't do that. You don't realize how much history could be in those scrolls."

"Too much." Thabit walked away from her.

Annja started to follow him, but the three guards trapped her in place. Helplessly, she watched as Hamez's demolitions team set the charges. They were good at what they did and finished in minutes.

Then they blew the charges and rock and earth flew into the sky. Hunkered behind a boulder, Annja groaned. She'd thought Thabit had been looking for a treasure, something to prove his case as a Shiite as to the true succession of Islam. She couldn't imagine anyone wanting something so historically significant destroyed.

Gradually, the smoke and dust settled. Little by little, the cave mouth that had been hidden by the boulder came into view.

The chase wasn't over yet. She stood and shoved through her guards. Since she wasn't headed for Thabit and they were no doubt interested in the results of the explosion, they let her walk.

Hamez studied the cave with distaste. "We can set bigger charges, bring down the mountain."

"No," Thabit said. "What we're looking for could be deep inside the cave. We must make sure it's gone. Once and for all." He spat a curse. "Get your men together. We go inside." He turned to Annja. "It appears I still have need of your expertise."

Annja didn't respond. One of the men shoved her from behind and she fell into step, following Thabit and Hamez into the cave.

In the passenger seat of the Jeep, MacKenzie watched the cloud of dust and smoke drift across the northern horizon. He clicked the headset that linked him to Sophie. "What happened?"

"Thabit's people just blew up a section of the landscape. From what we can see, they've uncovered a cave."

"You got a history of the area?"

"There are a lot of caves in those mountains. Wars have

been fought there for centuries, from ancient times to World War I, and even present day. There are trade routes all over those mountains, too. People would have stopped in caves to rest for the night or for protection. We have no information about this cave."

MacKenzie took a deep breath. "Evidently Creed does. You've got to be wondering what Thabit is looking for."

"It doesn't matter. Your job is to get Thabit—alive if you can—and bring him back."

"Understood." MacKenzie braced himself for the rough ride and looked at the Jeep's driver. "Faster. That's our mark."

The man nodded and the Jeep picked up speed, bouncing across the rough landscape.

MacKenzie fingered the brass key in his shirt pocket. Maybe they still had a wild card to play.

As they stepped into the mouth of the cave, Annja reached into her backpack and took out a flashlight. Hamez and Thabit did the same, as did their men.

Dust and debris littered the opening, and the air was thick with dust. Annja pulled a kerchief over her mouth and nose to filter out particulates. The men followed her lead. The kerchief helped somewhat with the air, but grit stung her eyes.

She shined her flashlight over the cave's interior, hoping for some kind of instruction or markings that would cement her belief that this was the cave Abdelilah Karam had mapped on the coins.

The cave walls remained stubbornly blank. Drawn by the dark pool at the end of her flashlight beam, she started forward. Small rocks crunched under her boots as she followed the light into the unknown.

Excited voices rang out behind Annja. Thinking she had

missed something, she glanced back, realizing immediately that the men were pointing down the incline at the long dust cloud trailing close to the ground.

Someone had followed them.

While Hamez and Thabit's attention was on the approaching vehicles, and her guards were distracted, Annja plunged into the darkness.

"MR. BRADEN, YOU'RE NOT the only interested parties arriving at ground zero."

Garin swiveled his attention from the front windshield to the computer screen. The sat-relay jumped occasionally, but it was still locked in. A line of vehicles sped toward the area where smoke from an explosion still drifted through the air.

"Do you know who they are?"

"Negative, sir. We haven't managed to get a visual on them yet."

"It must be this other man you mentioned. MacKenzie," Roux said quietly. "The CIA operative."

"That means he's got an intel support team somewhere." Garin watched the screen grimly. "Can you get me an ETA on this group?"

"They'll arrive on-site in two minutes."

"How far out are we?"

"Four minutes."

Garin smiled and reached for the rifle Qurtubi held for him.

The young warrior smiled back. "It sounds like things will be interesting upon our arrival."

"Just don't get yourself killed."

"Of course."

"And if it comes down to protecting Roux or me, which will it be?"

Qurtubi only smiled.

ANGRY SHOUTS ECHOING in her wake, Annja ran through the darkness. She reached a curve in the passageway just as bullets sparked off the wall in front of her.

She stayed low and ran. A stone chip stung her neck and she felt blood run down into the hollow of her throat. Despite the fact that it was impossible to hold the flashlight steady and run at the same time, she lengthened her stride.

The ground tilted downward at a steep slope that she didn't see until it was too late. Her foot hit the stone floor wrong, twisted beneath her and gave way. Instinctively, she reached out with her hands to break her fall but caught herself and kept her arms folded and loose, up in front of her to protect her face. When she hit, she went limp, felt the air go out of her, but started pushing herself back up at once as the flashlight shot out of her hand and skittered down the passageway. The light spun crazily, briefly illuminating different sections of the walls, floor and ceiling, all of them showing tool marks from where someone had carved the passageway.

Annja stooped to pick up the flashlight and started running again just as lights crept into the tunnel behind her. Excited cries rang out.

Ahead of Annja, the tunnel split into three branches. She had only an instant to decide, and picked the one on the right. She caught herself with her left hand just before she plowed into the wall, shoved off and got up to speed again.

Shots blasted into the wall behind her and ricochets whined like angry bees as they filled the air. Someone cried out in pain and she thought she heard the sound of a falling body. She leveled the flashlight and kept running.

39

"Keep going! Run them over!" Even as Garin gave orders to the driver, he leaned out the window and trained his assault rifle on one of the vehicles carrying the CIA operatives toward the cave.

The driver put his foot down on the accelerator and jockeyed the vehicle across the uneven landscape. A couple of times the Hummer went airborne for short flights.

Garin took up trigger slack and fired at the other vehicle from thirty yards away. He aimed two three-round bursts at the tires.

Out of control, the Jeep veered toward them.

"Hold on!" The Hummer driver geared down to grab traction and cut the steering wheel hard to the left. Their bumpers crossed for just an instant, then the Hummer's heavier weight and momentum brushed the out-of-control Jeep aside with a quick shiver. The Jeep rolled over onto its side and fell apart, throwing passengers in all directions.

"Don't stop until you reach the cave!" Garin yelled.

Some of Thabit's Shiite warriors had remained behind while the rest of the group poured down the cave entrance. Garin swept his gaze over the assembled troop but didn't see Annja among them.

One of the CIA Jeeps was closing on the cave and was

going to reach the destination well ahead of the Hummer. In frustration, Garin leaned out the window again and started firing.

LESS THAN A HUNDRED YARDS from the cave, the driver of MacKenzie's Jeep took a bullet through the head that painted the windshield with blood. The dead man slumped and the Jeep started to veer.

Cursing, MacKenzie shoved the dead man aside, grabbed the steering wheel from the passenger seat and shoved his foot on the accelerator. He drove right into the teeth of the waiting Shiite warriors as their bullets hammered the front of the Jeep. Thabit's men scattered an instant before the Jeep smashed into the cave mouth and lodged, stuck on both sides.

Bruised and breathless from the impact, MacKenzie drew his leg back and kicked out the windshield in a spray of safety glass. He released the seat belt, then crawled through the window onto the vehicle's hood. Turning back, he pulled the rifle to his shoulder and fired at the Shiite warriors converging on the cave mouth.

Yahya scrambled out of the wedged Jeep, as well, and added his firepower to MacKenzie's. The young man ducked behind the vehicle and slid a fresh magazine into his weapon. "We are likely dead men now that we are trapped in here."

MacKenzie slipped around the side of the Jeep and grabbed a flashlight from the emergency kit under the seat. Bullets ricocheted from the Jeep's body. Beyond the opening, the mountainside had become a battleground steeped in blood.

"We're not trapped yet." MacKenzie switched on the flashlight and tracked it down the passageway. "Places like this, there are usually more than one way out. A rat never builds itself a nest with only one door. And we're better off in here than out there. Those people are going to die. Not you and me." He slapped the young man's shoulder. "C'mon. Get moving. Let's find Thabit or Creed. Either one of them and we'll be holding cards everybody else has to count."

He started down the passage, with the echoes of the gunfire ahead and behind in the enclosed space around him.

GARIN FOUGHT THE CENTRIFUGAL force of the Hummer slewing around as the driver came to a jerking stop not far from the Jeep jutting partially out of the cave mouth. The vehicle slid into two of the Shiite warriors and knocked them backward.

Stepping out of the Hummer, Garin took quick aim with his rifle and put rounds into both men. He spared only a quick glance at the vehicles engaged in battle out in front of the cave, then turned his attention to the wedged Jeep. Slinging his rifle, he hauled himself over the jammed vehicle and clambered into the cave.

Breathing hard, staying low, Roux and Qurtubi ran at his heels. Garin plucked a flashlight out of his combat vest and turned it on. The stink of gunsmoke filled his nostrils but there were no bodies in the passageway.

Yet.

ANNJA PASSED INTO THE LARGE room before she knew she was there. She came to a stop when she spotted the dark pool in front of her and realized the sound of running water was echoing in a much larger space than her running steps had been.

She was breathing fast but easily. Currents in the water showed that it was fed by an underwater tributary, probably a spring. From bank to the back wall of the cave, the pool was about fifty feet across and sixty feet wide, nearly the width of the cavern. As she flicked her light around, blind white fish nearly the length of her arm surfaced and disappeared just as quickly.

If the fish were here, there might be an underground opening to the tributary. But that could run underground for a few yards or a few miles.

She pointed the flashlight beam around the cavern, searching desperately for another passageway. The running footsteps behind her were closing fast.

The cavern was easily eighty feet wide and a hundred feet long. Although the light was uncertain, Annja felt that the cavern was thirty or forty feet deep. On both side of the doorway, steps led up to loft areas where small caves had been cut out of the solid walls.

Sometime in the past, the cavern had been used as a hideout for large groups. Broken spears, arrows and bows littered the floor, along with ashes from cook fires.

The cavern itself was a great find. In years past, the Assyrians, the Kurds, the Persians and the Ottomans had all lived and warred in the area. So much unrecorded history lay around her.

Except you've got gunmen closing in. Annja turned to the left and fled up the stone steps carved out of the wall.

At the top of the steps, she slid out of her backpack and shoved it into a niche behind a ragged outcrop. Then she turned off her flashlight and crept back to the ledge fifteen feet above the bottom. She reached into the otherwhere and took hold of the sword, then pulled it into the cavern with her. In the absolute stygian darkness, she lay in wait.

Less than a minute later, flashlight beams intruded into the area. Six armed men spread out around Hamez and Thabit. Hamez gave orders to his men. They blanketed the room with their flashlights, shining the beams into every crook and crevice.

Annja ducked back from the ledge as one of the beams passed over her position. Then she peered back down.

At another command from Hamez, the warriors ignited flares. The red glow and twisting smoke filled the enclosure.

The men spread out, obviously searching for another passage-way, then quickly reached the conclusion that one didn't exist.

Hamez glared around the room again. "Miss Creed, come out now. If you do, things will go much easier for you."

Annja sincerely doubted that. The only chance she had was to get past Thabit and his men and escape into the mountains.

One of the men standing near the far wall called excitedly to Thabit. For a moment, all the attention in the room shifted in that direction. Annja measured the steps to the entrance and thought she'd have a chance to get away if she moved quickly.

Then she noticed what Thabit and his men had found: an Arabic symbol of the House of Muhammad carved into the wall. She froze where she was and waited.

Thabit immediately turned from the marking on the wall and walked back to the wall beneath the ledge where Annja lay. He spoke with rising excitement, then began marking off a distance from the wall where the steps were cut. Four steps over, he stopped and faced the wall.

Obviously he didn't tell you everything he'd deciphered from that map. With breathless anticipation, Annja watched as two of Thabit's men took out trenching tools and checked along the wall.

A moment later, the men wedged the trenching tools into the rock and pulled out thick slabs that had been mortared into place. Leaning out over the ledge, Annja spotted a smooth stone face inset with a keyhole.

She thought at first Thabit was going to produce the key, but he didn't. Instead, he stepped back into the dying glow of the flares. Then she thought Thabit was going to have his men force the door. The keyhole was there for a reason. If he forced the door whatever was inside might be destroyed. Not that he cared.

Then one of the men slapped a chunk of plastic explosive to the stone door and inserted an electronic detonator. He retreated as Annja tried frantically to figure out what to do to save Abdelilah Karam's papers.

In the next instant, a gunshot split the relative silence inside the cavern. The muzzle flash briefly illuminated Rafe MacKenzie in the doorway. Then he was firing again.

40

Acting quickly, Annja dropped over the ledge, grabbed the plastic explosive from the wall and heaved it toward the pool. Then she vaulted onto the steps as Thabit spotted her and started yelling. Out of the corner of her eye, she saw the plastic explosive drop into the pool.

Then the explosive detonated, filling the cavern with light and thunder and water. A deluge flooded over Annja as she rolled over onto the steps, and bullets chopped a ragged line against the stone wall where she'd been standing.

She stayed in a crouch as she ran up the steps. The blast had knocked Thabit, Hamez and the Shiite warriors off their feet, but they recovered quickly. Two of them pounded after Annja while the others returned MacKenzie's fire.

Ears ringing with the explosion, all the gunshots and frantic shouts now muted, Annja reached the top of the steps and crouched. The flares had burned out and the only light in the cavern was created by the muzzle flashes. The effect was like strobe lights in the darkness. Slices and flashes of images loomed suddenly out of the dark and made everyone look as if they were moving in stop-motion.

When the first man reached the top of the steps, Annja slashed with the sword and knocked his rifle aside. A line of rapid-fire bullets slapped into the far wall, throwing off showers of sparks. Annja pivoted on her left leg and drove her right boot into the man's face. He crumpled at once and she moved forward to meet the next man, giving no quarter.

She used the sword to catch the man's rifle barrel on the cross hilt and force it up. The rifle fired repeatedly till Annja reached out with her other hand, caught the front of the man's uniform and heaved him over the side. She vaguely heard him scream before he hit the ground. In the reflected glow of the shots, she saw him lying silent and still on the stone floor.

MacKenzie and Yahya dashed into the cavern even though Thabit and most of his men still fought. On their footsteps, more Shiite warriors filed into the room. MacKenzie led his protégé up the steps on the other side of the room, but the young man quickly went down under a hail of gunfire. He lay there, crying out for MacKenzie, who reached back and pulled him onto the ledge with him.

The newly arrived Shiites tried to rush up the steps. MacKenzie opened fire from a prone position and chopped three of them down before they reached the top. The others scattered back into the darkness.

Annja sank into the shadows, too, marking positions in her mind and trying to come up with a plan. The entrance was a deadly no-man's-land, a kill box for anyone who tried to leave that way.

A flare arced out from the ledge and delivered blinding light as it plummeted to the center of the cavern.

"Thabit!" MacKenzie's harsh voice rang out and penetrated the dense cotton in Annja's ears.

Thabit answered from somewhere in the darkness. "What do you want?"

"I see you found your little treasure box over there." MacKenzie's tone mocked the Shiite leader. "The way I hear it, a lot of those little hidey-holes are set up with traps. i've got the key that goes to it. Maybe you want to negotiate."

Oh, man. Everybody was holding out on me. Annja remained flat against the wall.

"There is one problem." Thabit was on the run and Annja barely tracked his movement through the darkness. "I do not want anything from that vault. So we have nothing to negotiate." The warriors around him opened fire.

Bullets chipped stone along the ledge where MacKenzie lay in hiding and ricocheted from the ceiling and walls. Yahya yelled again in pain. MacKenzie was pinned down, unable to return fire.

Hamez led a small group of Shiites up the steps toward MacKenzie's position.

Unable to watch the American be executed, Annja sprang forward. Thabit's entourage caught sight of her and brought their rifles around. Annja ran her sword through one man's chest, then grabbed him by the shirt collar and held him as a shield. She let go of the sword and it faded away at once as she caught the man's rifle before it could hit the ground.

Sweeping it up, Annja held the trigger down and emptied the magazine into the three men in front of her. She threw the weapon away and pulled the sword to her again, shoving the dead man aside and stepping through the strobing muzzle flashes toward Thabit.

Thabit turned and fired at her almost point-blank. Reacting instinctively, knowing she couldn't get out of the way, Annja flipped the sword so the flat of the blade came between her and Thabit. The bullet slammed into the sword and stopped. The vibration shivered through Annja's arms as she took another step before he could fire again and delivered a roundhouse kick that caught him in the face.

Hamez lifted his rifle and aimed at Annja as she threw herself forward. The sword vanished again and she rolled forward as Hamez's rounds cut the air where she'd been standing. She caught herself, rolled to the side and kicked the legs out from under the final guard who was standing almost on top of her. He fell heavily. She grabbed the back of his head and hammered his face into the stone floor.

Then she rolled away again as Hamez fired another burst that struck the man she'd knocked unconscious. She came to a crouching position behind Thabit and encircled the man's neck with her arm as he tried to get to his feet. She came up with him, and the sword was again in her hand.

Together, she and Thabit faced Hamez and the remaining Shiite warriors.

Annja lifted her voice. "Put down your weapons or I'm going to kill him." She held the sword at his throat.

"I do not believe you can kill a helpless man, Miss Creed." Hamez strode forward, locked behind the sights of his rifle.

The pool was behind her, leaving her nowhere to retreat to.

"I will, however, have no problem at all killing you." Hamez froze, and a sick expression stretched across his face. Slowly, he looked down and saw edged steel protruding from his chest. Blood trickled out of the corner of his mouth, then he sagged to the ground as his rifle clattered beside him.

Garin Braden stood silent and grim above the dead man. Behind him, Annja spotted Roux and another man. They each held a sword.

"Hello, Annja." Garin cleaned his weapon on the dead man's shirt. "I trust you are well."

"I am."

Roux came forward and inspected her in the glow of the dying flare in the center of the cavern. "You didn't really think this through, did you?"

Annja grinned at the old man. "I don't know what you're talking about. I had them right where I wanted them."

"Poppycock. You and your curiosity." Roux stood there with blood dripping from his sword. "So what is it that brought you all this way?"

"I don't know. Yet." Annja nodded toward the locked vault. "I haven't gotten to open it."

"I believe there was some mention of a key." Roux looked up at MacKenzie on the ledge. "Don't make me come up there and get it."

"I don't know who you are, but I've got your skinny butt covered. I'll ventilate you before you can blink an eye."

Roux smiled. "We've got Qurtubi."

For the first time, Annja realized the young man behind Garin and Roux was no longer there. In the next instant, she saw someone's arm as the rifle was plucked from MacKenzie's hands. MacKenzie rolled over onto his back.

Then something metallic winked as it spun through the air toward Annja. She released the sword back to the otherwhere and caught the brass key.

Garin pointed his sword at Thabit. "Down on your knees."

Reluctantly, Thabit dropped and Garin secured the man's hands and feet with zip ties. Qurtubi, the young man, brought MacKenzie down the steps similarly secured.

Roux walked with Annja to the vault and she placed the brass key into the keyhole and turned. The locking mechanism ratcheted, then she caught hold of the heavy door and swung it outward.

Inside the vaulted room lay several dusty scrolls. The sight took Annja's breath away. She carefully opened one and saw Abdelilah's signature on the page. Then she rolled the scroll back up.

She turned to Habib ibn Thabit. "Why did you want to destroy these?"

He refused to answer.

Annja grinned. "Don't answer. It doesn't matter. I'll have them translated. I'll have the answers soon enough."

Roux cleared his throat. "Actually, I read Kufic." He pulled at his beard. "And I have to admit to being a trifle curious myself now."

epilogue

Istanbul
Republic of Turkey

Annja found Roux where he'd promised to meet her, which was somewhat surprising because he didn't always do what he said he would. She took a seat at a table in the small outdoor café on a terrace of the Kanyon shopping mall overlooking Buyukdere Avenue. She'd stepped inside to answer a phone call from David Smythe, letting the archaeologist know she would be returning to the dig site in the Atlas Mountains soon.

Roux, in tourist-gray pants and a vibrant Hawaiian shirt and Panama boater with sunglasses, glanced up at her and smiled. "Your phone call went well, I assume?"

Annja nodded. "David said they were able to recover most of the site. The well diggers had hung on to Abdelilah Karam's remains, so the excavation can continue—more or less. Since the real story is the recovery of Karam's scrolls and all the history those will reveal, the authentication of the site is not going to be questioned. David is excited to get his hands on those scrolls."

"You've sent them to him?"

"By courier. It was his dig, after all. I was just along for the ride."

"So you'll be splitting the fame and fortune of your find."

Annja shrugged. "I found something incredible. I don't do this for the adulation of the masses."

"Of course not." Roux scowled. "You have that reprehensible television program for that."

Annja grinned. "You're still peeved about the flash-mob autograph session at the hotel this morning."

"It interrupted breakfast."

"Those are my fans."

"Ptui. Give me anonymity any day."

"Wearing that shirt?"

"It's a perfectly lovely shirt. I've had a few people ask me if I was Tom Selleck."

"Aside from that, did you ever find out why Thabit wanted to destroy the scrolls?" Annja had spent the past two days photocopying the scrolls while Roux read them.

"I did. Last night after you'd gone to sleep."

"You could have mentioned that this morning."

"You didn't ask."

"This is me asking now."

Roux flagged down a server and ordered another round of drinks. "As it turns out, an ancestor of Thabit's was one of the men who was supposed to assassinate Uthman ibn Affan."

"The third caliph."

"Yes. Thabit's ancestor went to Abdelilah Karam and tried to warn the caliph about the assassination attempt. The ancestor felt like the murder would only further split the Muslim people."

"Which it did."

"Yes. The ancestor told Karam this in confidence, but it was recorded and evidently the man knew this. One of his sons, who also knew what his father had done because the man confessed on his deathbed, decided to destroy the records. He was the one who chased Karam from the caliphate."

"Thabit's lineage could be traced back that far."

Roux nodded. "That was how he was able to influence so many Shiite supporters to his cause. He hadn't counted on it ultimately providing his downfall."

"Would that really matter these days?"

Roux grimaced. "The Middle East has been at war with itself since Muhammad's death, Annja. Everything that happened then matters. They're probably fortunate they don't know more."

Annja sipped her drink. "Except Karam's scrolls may bring even more things to light."

"Perhaps. But people need to make their peace with the past." Roux sighed. "Though that is often more difficult than it should be."

Garin approached, dressed in a fine suit and seemingly content with his life in general. "Well, well, how go the history lessons?"

"Do you really want to hear about it?" Annja asked.

Taking a seat at the table, Garin shook his head. "Not really, no. By the way, you never thanked me for saving your life, Annja."

"Really?" Annja arched an eyebrow. "The way I hear it, you just ransomed Habib ibn Thabit to the United States government."

"It wasn't ransom. It was a bounty. Quite impressive, actually."

"So maybe you owe *me* a thank-you."

Roux lifted a hand casually. "Or, at the very least, a finder's fee."

"Nonsense. I did all the heavy lifting on this. It was my security team, after all. How about if I take you to lunch?"

Annja laughed. "You'll take *us* to lunch."

Roux finished his drink. "And it had better be a big lunch."

* * * * *